Desires Uncovered

Ardor Creek, Book 3

By

AYLA ASHER

Contents

*For every Teresa out there who deserves her
very own happy ending...*

A Note from the Author

♥

W ell, Dear Reader, here we are again! As previously stated, I decided to tackle some heavier issues in this series. Why? Well, first of all, it's fun to write about things you don't often see in romance novels. Secondly, I really enjoy writing about atypical romance main characters.

When I wrote Hearts Reclaimed, the image of Scott's therapist, Dr. Teresa Roe, formed in my head along with her backstory. As someone who is child-free by choice and single in my mid-forties, I thought it would be refreshing to write about forty-somethings finding love. As you already know, older characters are a staple of many of my books. (And, honestly, are forty-somethings really "old?" Come on!)

I racked my brain to remember if I'd ever read about a female main character in her forties who can't have biological children finding her HEA. I'm sure there are stories out there but I couldn't think of one. So, you know what? I decided to write one! I mean, don't women who fall under those parameters deserve their happy ending too? I sure think they do! And not a happy ending where *she suddenly becomes pregnant in the last chapter!* No, she deserves a man who chooses her and loves her exactly the way she is.

This is the story you'll find in this book with Teresa and Mark. They work hard to find their HEA but eventually get there. Teresa's journey with infertility is discussed openly, as well as Mark's sister's domestic abuse by her husband, so please take that into consideration before reading.

Here's hoping you enjoy Teresa and Mark's story as much as I enjoyed writing it. Our forty-seven-year-old female protagonist wins the day, and it was such a pleasure to write. Happy reading!

Chapter 1

♥

Dr. Teresa Roe sat at the bar of the newly built hotel in Battle Falls, Pennsylvania. She loved the town, which resided in rural Pennsylvania between Ardor Creek and Nestwood Township. In her youth, Teresa enjoyed living in Philadelphia with its fast pace and deep-seated culture and history. Once she'd received her various degrees and practiced psychology in the city for several years, she felt an urge to slow down. Not too much, but enough that she could begin to focus on other things. Most importantly, she wanted to have a family.

She'd settled in the small town about a half-hour drive north of Scranton over ten years ago. Armed with her experience and the confidence she'd always possessed, she opened her therapy practice and never looked back. Teresa immensely enjoyed helping people in upper Lackawanna County and had built a thriving career.

Her social life on the other hand? Well, it had crashed and burned so many times, she wondered if she'd somehow pissed off the universe. Whatever bad karma she'd built up in previous lifetimes must've been intense because she'd tumbled down the chasm of being extremely unlucky in love and, unfortunately, hadn't been able to figure out how to return to the light.

It wasn't for lack of trying. At this point, she'd most likely dated every man within a fifty-mile radius.

"Like it did you any good," she mumbled, looking over the bar menu.

"Sorry, sweetie, I missed that," the chipper bartender said, white teeth flashing under her green eyes. "What can I get for you?"

"Oh, I was just talking to myself," Teresa said, waving her hand. "How's the cabernet? And, by that, I mean, how long has it been open?"

The bartender laughed and turned to squint at the half-full bottle sitting on the liquor shelf. "Probably a week, and that's being conservative. I'll open a new one for you if you want a glass."

"I'd love that. Thank you. Sorry to be a pest."

"I get it," she said, holding up her hands. "My name's Sara and I can put it on your room if you like."

"Oh, yes, that would be great. I'm in two twenty-five."

Sara nodded and trailed away as Teresa suppressed a sigh. If someone had asked her years ago whether she'd be sitting in a staid hotel bar about to embark on what was a new—and quite daunting—experience, she would've laughed. Never in a million years could she have dreamed she'd end up using a hook-up app. Life, it seemed, had other plans.

She'd tried the dating apps. The ones where men took you to dinner and you tried to get to know them on a personal level. She'd never enjoyed the experiences and had certainly never clicked with any of the men once they met in person. Several had seemed angry they paid for dinner and she didn't sleep with them in return. Is this what it had come to? One dinner and you were expected to give up the cookie?

"No fucking way," she uttered, smiling at Sara as she delivered the wine.

"Just you tonight?" Sara asked.

Biting her lip, Teresa shook her head. "I'm meeting someone."

"First date?"

"Um, not really. First...uh, encounter, I guess you could say. We'll see how it goes."

"Well, I wish you luck. I'll let you know if I'm getting any creepy vibes. You pick up on this stuff when you're a bartender."

Chuckling, Teresa nodded. "Thanks. I need all the help I can get."

Settling in with her wine, Teresa checked in with her body. The nerves were present, but not overwhelming. As a therapist, she'd done a lot of self-reflection on the decision she'd ultimately made and understood how to process it. She was comfortable in her sexuality and felt it imperative she still explored that part of herself, even though it was now strictly for pleasure.

Lowering her hand to her abdomen, she caressed the part of herself that was broken and beyond repair. For someone who'd wanted children, the loss was devastating. Feeling the tears well, she let them fester for a moment because suppressing emotion wasn't healthy. But wallowing in it wouldn't change anything and it was important she learn to live with her body's limitations. To focus with gratitude on everything she had instead of the one crushing deficiency. Years of social work had shown her that life came with harrowing challenges in all shapes and forms. This was her challenge and she was determined to forge ahead with strength and positivity.

A brisk wind blew in from the sliding doors several feet away at the hotel entrance. Gazing over, Teresa saw a tall man enter and run his fingers through thick, wavy brown hair, dislodging several snowflakes. Glancing up, his eyes locked with hers and he flashed a gorgeous grin.

Teresa's heart slammed in her chest as the strikingly handsome man approached. After removing his scarf, he extended his hand. "Rachel?"

Smiling, she shook, internally laughing at the fake name she'd set up on the app's profile. "Yes. You must be Michael?"

"That's me," he said, nodding toward the seat beside her. "Mind if I slide in?"

"Not at all."

"What can I get you, sir?" Sara asked, appearing behind the bar.

"I'm having a freshly opened cabernet if you like," Teresa said, pointing to her glass.

"Hmmm..." he said, picking up the laminated bar menu. "I think I'm in the mood for a beer. I'll have a Heineken."

"Sure thing," Sara said, reaching into the nearby cooler and returning with the chilled bottle. Popping off the cap, she set it on the coaster. "If you all need anything just holler. I'm doing my chemistry homework at the other end of the bar."

Once they were alone, Teresa lifted her glass. "To new experiences."

Chuckling, he clinked his bottle against her wine. "So I guess this is your first time meeting someone from Pure."

Wrinkling her nose, she nodded and took a sip. "I tried dating apps and the experiences were major failures. Finally, I decided a hook-up app was what I needed and Pure seemed like the easiest one to navigate."

"It's pretty easy."

"I'm guessing this isn't your first time?" she asked, arching a brow.

"I've met a few women through the app before, although not for a while now. Life has been busy. But I experienced a pretty awesome wedding over Thanksgiving dinner a few weeks ago and it made me long for some companionship, I guess."

"I love weddings," she said wistfully. "Was it someone in your family?"

He shook his head. "Two friends I've known since elementary school. They've been in love forever but it never worked out. Somehow, after decades, they finally figured it out. It was really nice to see."

"How romantic. They finally got their happy ending."

"Yep." Deep brown eyes roved over her. "Sorry to hear the dating apps didn't work out. I never tried any of those. There aren't enough hours in the day to date and have a career—in my life, at least. I don't know how people do it."

Teresa chewed her lip, dying to ask what he did for a living but knowing anything personal was off-limits. "Me neither. Seems tough. But if you want something badly enough, I guess you find a way."

"Guess so." Lifting the bottle to his lips, Teresa noticed the tanned skin of his forearm under a smattering of tiny brown hairs. Swallowing thickly, she imagined his long fingers trailing over her breasts. She hadn't had sex in almost four years, which was understandable with everything she'd been through with her infertility treatments. God, but she was ready to feel alive. To remind herself that even though some parts were broken, she was still a full-fledged woman, capable of experiencing desire and pleasure.

"Rachel?" he asked, waving his hand. "Did I lose you?"

"Oh, uh..." she gulped her wine. "Sorry. I...well, this is weird and I'm probably not supposed to bust this out since we just met, but my name's not Rachel."

His lips curved. "No?"

"It's Teresa," she said, shrugging. "I figured Rachel was a nice name and I didn't want to use my real one on the app."

"I completely understand. I'm actually Mark, not Michael. Although, they aren't really that different," he said, rubbing his chin. "My mom did always say I wasn't very creative."

Laughing, she tilted her head. "Well, that's not a very nice thing to say."

"Oh, I have other talents, don't worry. I'm kind of cerebral and numerically minded. My sister got all the creative genes. I accepted that years ago."

"At least you know your strengths," she said, lifting her glass. "Nothing wrong with that."

"To knowing our strengths," he said, clinking his bottle against her glass.

They shared a nice moment, quiet surrounding them as they settled into what would happen once their drinks were finished.

Clearing her throat, she said, "Well, I'm glad you didn't send me a, um, picture of your...well, you know. I thought that was standard practice nowadays."

"Yeah, maybe I'm just old—I turned forty two weeks ago—but sending a dick pic isn't high on my list. Plus, I don't want any pictures of my goods out there. It wouldn't bode well for my professional persona."

"I get that. I feel the same way. I'm in my forties too so I guess we missed the generation that shares that stuff freely."

His eyes shifted over her, and Teresa could tell he was trying to discern her age.

"You listed your age as forty-five on Pure," he said, eyes narrowing. "Is that fake too?"

"Depends," she said, shrugging. "Do I look forty-five?"

He squinted one eye. "You look around my age, I guess. I'm pretty bad with guessing ages. Regardless, you're very attractive, Teresa."

A flush rushed over her cheeks at the compliment. In truth, she was forty-six but felt that listing herself as one year younger wouldn't hurt anyone. Desire simmered in Mark's eyes as he continued to give her that lazy smile.

"Well, I'm in my mid-forties, but thank you. My parents are both from Barcelona and I inherited their olive skin. Neither of them has noticeable wrinkles and they're in their eighties so I hope I inherited their anti-aging genes."

"Barcelona is beautiful," he said, leaning back in the seat and sipping his beer. "I went there for a law conference—," he abruptly stopped speaking and flattened his lips. After a moment, he continued. "I went there for a *work* conference a few years ago and loved it."

"Not a lawyer," she teased, holding up her finger. "Got it."

"Man, I'm bad at this." He rubbed his forehead, giving a sheepish grin. "I'm kind of an open book so it's hard not to divulge things about myself. I need to learn to be more discerning."

"It's tough, especially knowing what we came here to do."

His gaze raked over her. "Are you nervous?"

Biting her lip, she shook her head. "No. Well, maybe a little bit. I haven't been with anyone in a long time. I think I'm excited more than anything."

Sliding his hand over hers as it rested on her thigh, he laced their fingers. "I'm excited too. It's always a bit weird, I guess, to be with a stranger but this is intimacy in the modern age, right?"

"Right," she said, squeezing. "I also brought my most recent test results as we discussed over the chat. I was sure you'd run for the hills when I suggested we share them."

"Why?" His eyebrows drew together and he looked genuinely perplexed. "I thought it was refreshing. In this day and age, what other way is there to truly know? Mine are on my phone and I'll pull them up for you when we get to the room."

"Okay. I got a King room on the second floor."

"I'll give you cash to cover my half. Or, if this works out, maybe I can just get the room next time we meet."

Her breath fluttered at his words. "So, you're looking for more than a one-time thing?"

"If we're compatible, yes. Finding someone as gorgeous as you who wants a no-strings-attached affair is pretty fortuitous. If we enjoy it, why waste time looking for someone else? I'm under the impression we both joined Pure because we don't want to date and our lives are too busy for a relationship. Am I correct in that assumption?"

Teresa nodded, although her reasons were a bit more multi-faceted. Dating when you had no chance of bearing a child was tough, especially in your forties when many men still had hopes of having children. Combine that with the fact that Teresa had made a commitment to focus on herself and her emotional recovery for a while, and there was no space for a relationship.

"That's pretty much where I'm at."

"I'm glad we're on the same page," he said, squeezing her hand before reaching for his wallet. "Want another glass of wine?"

"Oh, no," she said, taking the last sip and pushing the glass across the bar. "Sara's going to put it on my room." Lifting her hand, she waved to the bartender who slid the check across the bar.

"I would've paid," Mark said.

"Next time," Teresa said, smiling as she signed the check. Closing the holder, she lifted her brows. "Well, might as well get to it. Although, now, I think I am nervous."

Smiling, he cupped her cheek, the skin of his palm sending tingles through her body. "Don't be. I'll take care of you."

Inhaling a ragged breath, she nuzzled his hand. "Can't wait."

Chugging the last of his beer, he set the bottle on the bar and stood. "Come on, sweetheart." Extending his hand, he waited.

Filled with anticipation and pulsing desire, she took his hand and followed him to the elevator.

Chapter 2

Mark entered the hotel room behind Teresa, his hand on the small of her back as the door clicked behind them. As his eyes adjusted to the dim light from the lamp on the bedside table, he gazed at the woman before him.

Long, curly dark hair fell below her shoulder blades to rest above the luscious curves of her hips and ass, accentuated by her tight black knee-length skirt. Shapely calves extended into black high heels, and he damn near felt his mouth water. She was absolutely stunning.

After setting her bag on the table, she turned to face him and lifted her hands to the top button of her shirt, which barely showcased the cleavage from her ample breasts. Mark had skewed toward dating less curvaceous women in his past, and he suddenly wondered why. Teresa had a voluptuous hourglass figure reminiscent of the pin-up girls Mark's grandfather used to wax poetic about from his era, and she was breathtaking. Aching to run his hands over every curve, he stepped closer.

"Should I take this off?" she asked, her voice raspy as her fingers toyed with the button.

"Yes," he whispered, struggling to control his breathing. "Slowly. I want you to bare every inch of skin to me along the way."

Smoldering hazel eyes locked with his as she unclasped the button, tugging the shirt slightly to bare the mounds of her breasts above the cups of her black bra. "Like this?"

"Yes," he almost growled, lust vibrating through his tall frame. He was six-four and figured her to be somewhere around five-eight, although she'd be shorter once she removed those sexy-as-sin heels. Loving how he towered over her, he stepped closer, shortening the distance between them. Lifting his hand, he ran his finger over the swell of her breast, blood rushing to his dick when she whimpered.

"Are they sensitive?"

"My breasts?"

He nodded, tracing his finger along the lacy edge of her bra.

"Yes," she said, unclasping another button. "My nipples are very sensitive."

"Let me see." Pulling out the chair, he turned it to face her and sat. "Take off your shirt, sweetheart."

She freed the last of the buttons and dragged the blouse from her body, the fabric trailing to the floor. Placing his palms on her stomach, she gasped before he glided them up to cup her breasts. Sliding his finger inside one of the silky cups, he tugged it down, baring her nipple.

The nub was darker than her olive skin, the contrast of her areola against the paler flesh making his cock twitch inside his dress pants. Leaning closer, he licked his lips before blowing on her nipple.

Her heavy breaths rushed above as the sensitive bud tightened before his eyes. "So pretty," he whispered, expelling another puff of air against her nipple.

"*Please*," she mewled, sliding her hands over his shoulders.

"You can use my name, hon," he said, gently nudging her nipple with his nose. "We already blew that rule."

Laughing, she slid her fingers up his neck and threaded them through his thick hair. Gazing down at him, she whispered, "Please, Mark."

Eyes locked with hers, he closed his lips over her nipple, loving how her fingers tightened against his scalp. Rolling the bud around his tongue, he sucked her deep while skimming his hands up her thighs.

"No hose?" he murmured, placing a soft kiss against her nipple as he toyed with her lacy underwear.

"They're so restrictive, I usually go without unless it's below zero. You men have no idea."

Chuckling, he kissed a trail to her other breast. "How do you know I've never worn hose?"

Her melodious laugh surrounded him. "Just guessing, but you do you. No judgement here."

Grinning, he reached behind and unclasped her bra, tossing it to the ground before she slid her fingers back in his hair. Sucking her nipple into his mouth, he rubbed his finger over her silky panties, releasing a deep exhale as he caressed the damp material.

"Can I touch you here?" He wiggled his finger against her opening through the fabric.

"Yes."

Unable to look away from her gorgeous eyes, he flicked her nipple with his tongue as he glided his finger beneath the damp silk. "There you are," he whispered, circling her opening before slowly urging his finger inside. "So tight and wet. I like feeling you around me."

"It's been a while," she breathed, her hips jutting into his hand in a motion so erotic, he struggled to breathe. "I wasn't sure things still functioned down there."

Laughing, he nuzzled her breast, thrilled at her sense of humor in what could've been an uncomfortable situation. After all, making love to a complete stranger wasn't something one did every day. Mark had met a few other women from Pure over the past few years but they all paled in comparison to the woman before him. Dying to please her, he tugged her panties aside and inserted a second finger.

"Let me get you off right here while you're still wearing those sexy heels," he said, pumping his hand. Touching his thumb to her slick folds, he urged them apart and searched for her clit.

"Oh, god," she moaned, head falling back as her fingers held their death grip in his hair. "Rub it hard and I'll come..."

Increasing the pressure, he circled the pad of his thumb over the sensitive nub as he worked his fingers inside her. Drenched with her honey, he reveled in her body's response to his ministrations. Sucking her breast between his lips, he pulled on her nipple, intent on sending her over the edge.

"*Mark...*"

"Come, sweetheart," he commanded against her breast, his hands working in furious motions against her. Grasping her nipple with his teeth, he gently tugged.

"Mmm...do that again."

Feeling his lips curve at her directiveness, he complied, biting the taut nub before lathering it with his tongue. Her body vibrated under his touch, the tiny convulsions causing his muscles to tighten. Imagining how good it would feel when he was inside her sweet warmth, he groaned.

"So close..." she whimpered. "It feels so good."

His fingers jutted deep into her wet core, covered with her essence as her tiny mewls drove him insane. Working his tongue against her nipple, he felt her body snap and she collapsed against him.

"Can't...stand...*fuck*..."

Mark supported her, burying his face between her breasts as her body quivered around him. Murmuring sweet words against her smooth skin, he held her, humbled at her trust, vowing to ensure she experienced ultimate pleasure.

"My knees are wobbly," she said, sagging against him. "Help."

Chuckling, he slid his arm behind her knees and lifted her. Carrying her to the bed, he said, "Hold on, hon."

She encircled his neck as he pulled down the covers with his free arm. Laying her atop the white fitted sheet, he gazed down as she panted below. Thick curls spread over the pillow, stark against the snowy fabric. Staring at him with droopy eyes, she smiled, her thick lips causing him to ache with wanting. What would they feel like around his cock?

"Let's get this skirt off," he said, reaching underneath her hips and unzipping it before sliding it off her body. "I guess I have to take off the shoes too. Damn."

Biting her lip, she shrugged. "I don't care if you leave them on. Up to you."

He slipped off her underwear as he debated. "Let's leave them on. Holy shit, you look so sexy right now."

She rubbed one leg against the other and Mark almost felt his tongue spool out of his mouth. Lying there, naked and sated, she looked like a satiated goddess. Unable to look away, he removed his clothes and reached into his wallet for a condom.

"I can show you the results," she said, gesturing weakly toward her bag.

"That's okay. We'll do that next time." Rolling on the condom, he crawled between her legs. "I need to be inside you...if you're ready."

"Ready," she whispered, threading her fingers through his hair.

"I like that," he said, nudging his head against her hands. "You can pull if you want. Just don't take out any chunks."

Laughing, she shook her head on the pillow. "I'll be gentle."

Encircling the base of his cock, he aligned it with her opening, hissing at the contact. Balancing on his forearm, he grazed the fingers of his free hand over her cheek, his thumb coming to rest atop her lips. Urging them apart, he slipped his thumb inside her mouth as he gently pushed the head of his shaft inside her body.

She closed her lips around his thumb, enveloping it in her wet mouth as she sucked. The sight of her full lips working back and forth over his skin was so erotic, he damn near lost control. Increasing the pace of his hips, he thrust into her fully, groaning as her inner walls surrounded him.

Drawing back, he held her gaze as he surged again, gauging her reaction. Her hips began to move in tandem with his and she moaned around his thumb. Lost to desire, he began fucking her in earnest, his breath labored as he worked into her tight channel.

"Do you want me to rub your clit while I fuck you?" he gritted.

The little temptress bit his thumb, driving him insane with lust as he growled.

"There's a spot," she said, shaking her head on the pillow. "Go deep and you'll find it."

Sliding his hand behind her knee, he lifted her leg high. Working his body against hers, he changed the angle, circling his hips as he strove to make her scream.

She gasped, eyes widening as she nodded. "There! Yes! Don't stop."

Gripping her leg, he fisted her hair atop the pillow as sounds of wet flesh grinding together reverberated off the walls. Feeling his balls tighten, he clenched his teeth, determined to hold off the orgasm until she exploded around him.

"So good..." she chortled, head tossed back as a vein pulsed in her neck. "I feel you everywhere."

Groaning, he buried his face in her neck, drawing the tender skin between his lips as he gyrated against her. Gently biting the throbbing vein, he felt the release surge in his shaft. "Can't hold it, honey...*fuck!*"

The orgasm blinded him, causing darkness to spread behind his lids as immense pleasure flooded his frame. Losing control, he gave in to the sensation, muscles quivering as his body shuddered against hers. Thick jets of release pulsed into the condom as she purred in his ear, the walls of her core pulsing around his cock.

"Please tell me you're coming," he gritted into her neck, wondering how he was even speaking.

"Yessss..." she hissed, gripping his scalp. "*Mmm...*"

They relaxed into each other, bodies throbbing as dying spasms of pleasure jolted throughout. The velvet folds of her taut channel milked him, tugging the last drops of release from his vibrating frame.

Melting into her, he nuzzled her neck, unsure he'd ever regain the ability to move. Sweat beaded down his face, landing against her silken skin. Extending his tongue, he tasted her, reveling in the salty essence.

"You smell so good," he murmured.

She snickered. "It's Ariana Grande's perfume. Bought it at Macy's last month. I'm not sure any self-respecting middle-aged woman should be wearing an infamously younger pop star's perfume but it smells so damn good."

"You're not middle-aged," he said, grinning. "You're just an experienced young person."

Throwing back her head, she laughed. "Okay, sure. Whatever you say. You could tell me the sky was purple right now and I wouldn't care. Damn, that felt good."

"For me too," he said, squeezing her. Needing to remove the condom, he sighed, longing to remain in the intimate embrace. "Let me get rid of the condom and I'll be right back."

Sliding out, his limp cock mourned the loss of her sweet warmth. Disposing the condom, he strode back toward the bed and lay beside her, resting his head on his hand as his elbow dug into the pillow. She toed off the heels, each making a clunking sound as they hit the carpet.

"Thanks for indulging my fantasy with the heels," he said, grinning. "That felt amazing." Placing his palm between her breasts, he slowly trailed it to her abdomen. Her skin quivered underneath, sending renewed sparks of desire through his still-recovering frame.

"You found the spot," she said, her smile gorgeous as she relaxed against the pillow. "Nice job."

Studying her, he caressed her stomach with his thumb. "Let's do it again in a few days."

"Okay," she said, nodding. "I'm down. If you're comfortable with me emailing you, I can just send you my results that way."

"That works and I'll send mine back. I like the thought of feeling you around me without a condom."

"Me too." She waggled her brows.

Chuckling, he slowly dragged his hand up her abdomen, between her breasts, and over her neck before resting his thumb on her lower lip. Stroking it, he licked his lips, contemplating.

"What is it?"

His eyebrows drew together. "I just realized I never kissed you. We made love but didn't kiss."

Her tongue darted out, swiping against his thumb as she moistened her lips. "Do you want to kiss me?"

"Yes," he almost whispered, his tone raspy. "So fucking much."

Gliding her arm around his neck, she pulled him closer. "Then kiss me, Mark."

Murmuring her name, he pressed his lips against hers, groaning when her tongue darted through them. Slithering his tongue over hers, he drifted over her body, plundering her mouth as she draped a leg over the back of his thigh. Wrapped up in her, Mark felt a sense of true contentment. Never had he dreamed he would find someone so sexy and funny on a hook-up app. Thanking his lucky stars, he eventually drew back to reverently gaze at her while he stroked her hair.

"Can you meet twice a week?"

Smiling, she nodded. "Mondays and Thursdays are best because my office hours start later on Tuesdays and Fridays."

"Mondays and Thursdays," he said, tilting his head. "Done."

"If we're not going to use protection, I just need you to tell me if you're with someone else. You're free to do so, obviously, but I'd want to use condoms again until you're tested."

"Honestly?" he asked, scrunching his features, "Finding you was pretty fortuitous and I'm happy to keep this monogamous for now.

I work a lot and scheduling sexy nights with you is exactly what I need in my busy life."

"That works for me. If anything changes, just let me know."

"You'll do the same?"

"Yes, but I have no desire to be with anyone else right now either. You're pretty hot and you found the spot, so I can live with a two-day-per-week arrangement."

Breathing a laugh, he kissed the tip of her nose. "Done. I think this might be the best *arrangement* I've ever procured."

"Me too," she said, grinning as she ran her hand over his jaw. "I'm not sure how soon you need to leave but we could go again if you have time. I have the room for the night."

"I'd love that but I do need a bit of recovery time. Middle age is creeping up on me too. When I was in my twenties things reset like magic," he said, snapping his fingers. "Now, I need to let him rest for a bit," he said, gesturing with his head toward the juncture of his thighs. "Wish it wasn't so but I promise, once he recovers, I'm going to make your toes curl, sweetheart."

"Can't wait," she said, chucking her brows. "In the meantime, want to watch The Bachelorette?"

He grimaced. "Seriously?"

"I know it sounds ridiculous but, I swear, it's so entertaining. It's also a really good case study on current dating practices for my clients—" Her eyes widened. "Um, for my *friends*, I meant to say."

He squinted one eye closed. "Clients, hmm? That makes you a...dog trainer!"

Snickering, she nodded. "You got it. How'd you guess?"

"I used my non-lawyer skills of deduction. I'm definitely not a lawyer, by the way."

"Noted." She made an X over her heart.

Sliding to lay against her side, he pulled her against his body and reached for the remote. "Okay, let's see this show I'm ninety-nine percent sure I'm going to hate."

"Don't knock it 'til you try it," she said, gliding her leg over his thighs as she snuggled against him. "You might become addicted."

"Not likely," he said, flipping through the channels until he landed on the right one. Holding her close, he settled in to watch the silly show, willing to endure it in exchange for the joy of holding her luscious body against his. Placing a kiss on her soft hair, he stroked the curls as she rested her head against his chest. Lost in her scent, he shot a silent prayer of gratitude to the universe, excited to see where this new experience would lead.

Chapter 3

♥

Three Months Later

Teresa rushed into the hotel, frazzled as she shook the rain from her hair. Craning her neck, she spotted Mark at the bar and headed over.

"I'm so sorry I'm late," she said, removing her jacket and spreading it over the back of the bar seat before sliding into it. "I had a client who needed to be admitted to the hospital and it was...well, it was a rough day."

"That's okay," he said, leaning forward and placing a chaste kiss on her forehead. "I understand how unruly untrained dogs can be."

"Right," she said, grinning as she picked up the bar menu. "Because I'm a dog trainer."

"Obviously. Someone with my non-lawyer skills would never have deduced you're a therapist. Never even occurred to me."

Laughing, she shrugged. "It's been a few months now. Although we agreed not to get too personal, I think I'm fine with you knowing I'm a therapist."

"Well, I'm honored," he said, saluting her with his beer.

"I don't know why I even look at this thing," she said, setting down the menu. "I'm obviously having cabernet."

"Just opened a new bottle for you," Sara chimed behind the bar. Trailing over, she poured a glass and flashed a cheeky grin. "Cabernet and Heineken every Monday and Thursday night. I'm all over it."

"Yikes," Teresa said, taking a sip. "Does that mean we're old and predictable?"

He squinted. "Maybe. Sara's in college. What do you think, Sara? Are we ancient?"

"No way. You guys are awesome. My favorite patrons, for sure. And I'm pretty sure Teresa is wearing Ariana Grande's perfume which is super rad."

"I actually am," she said with a nod. "Thank you, Sara. I feel redeemed."

"You're welcome. Just wave me over if you need anything."

Settling in, Teresa assessed her handsome companion. His lips formed a soft, almost sad, smile and she tilted her head. "Something's up. Is everything okay?"

Sighing, he grasped her hand and laced their fingers before settling them on his thigh. "I don't know how to tell you this so I guess I should just say it."

Her heart fell to her knees. "You met someone else."

"What? No. Definitely not. But, unfortunately, I don't have great news." He inhaled deeply before slowly exhaling. "I need to take a break from our arrangement."

Stiffening, she tried to pull her hand away. "Was it something I did? I swear, I tried to keep it casual. I don't really have the headspace for anything serious right now. I hope I didn't make it weird."

"It's not you, Teresa," he said, retaining his grasp and pulling her hand closer. "I think you're amazing. Honestly, if I had any sort of space in my life for a relationship, I'd love to date you. Unfortunately, I don't, and my life is about to become even more insane."

"Are you going off to war or something?"

Laughing, he shook his head as he gazed at her with mirth. "You're so damn funny. I love that about you."

Her chest tightened at the sweet words. "But...?"

"I filed paperwork today to cement my run for Lackawanna County D.A."

Feeling her eyes widen, she straightened in her chair. "Even though you're not a lawyer?"

"Well, I guess the cat's out of the bag on that one. My face will be all over campaign ads and internet articles so you would've known anyway."

"Mark, that's amazing," she said, squeezing his hand. "I'm so happy for you. Have you always wanted to be in politics?"

"I like helping people and doing it within the parameters of my law license is a bonus. My friend, Chad, is the mayor of Ardor Creek and he's a better schmoozer than me, but I'm definitely the superior debater."

"That'll come in handy."

"Sure will," he said, taking a sip of his beer. "The guy I'm running against—the current D.A.—is an ass and plays dirty politics. I'm ready but my campaign manager says I need to live the life of a boy scout for the next several months so I don't give him any compromising fodder to use against me."

"So, you can't meet your lover from a hook-up app at a clandestine hotel," she said as her lips formed an understanding smile.

"Unfortunately not. It's such a bummer because these nights with you are the highlight of my week, Teresa. I hope you know how much I cherish the time we spend together."

"I know," she whispered, feeling tears well in her eyes. "I feel the same way."

"The election is in November and after things die down, we can resume then if you haven't found someone else. Until then, I just can't chance it. Getting photographed with you would incite all sorts of questions. I already have a strike against me since single men don't poll well with married middle-aged men. I can't be seen as a player or man-about-town or whatever people will make up in their minds."

"I get it," she said, already anticipating how deep the loss of the treasured nights with him would cut. "I hate it but I get it. I'm so thrilled for you and would love to help your campaign in any way I can."

"Thank you. For now, I'm finishing up the planning phase of the campaign but I'll let you know. Unless you've got a million dollars to donate. That would help immensely," he suggested, winking.

"I wish. I'm pretty deep in debt at the moment and am determined to pay it off and buy a house one day, but I'll scrounge up a few bucks to throw your way."

His brows drew together. "I'm sorry to hear that. Debt sucks. It took me years to pay off my law school debt but I eventually began making enough money that I paid it off."

"Yeah," she said, waving her hand. "Not quite sure why I told you that since we're not supposed to get personal. Sorry."

"I don't mind getting personal," he said, leaning back in his chair. "In fact, now that I'm not going to see you every week, I find myself wanting to ask you a thousand personal questions. We know each other so well in some ways and not at all in others."

"The perils of a casual fling," she said, lifting a shoulder.

"Indeed." Brown eyes darted between hers. "Is the debt from school? I assume you have a multitude of degrees if you're a therapist."

"I'm actually a doctor," she said, balancing her chin on her hand as her elbow rested on the bar. "Well, Ph.D., not M.D., but you get the gist."

"No way. Psychologist?"

"Yep. And a licensed social worker and a licensed marriage and family therapist."

"Wow," he said, blowing a breath through puffed cheeks. "I thought I was a brainiac but you've got me beat. *Doctor*."

Chuckling, she said in a sultry voice, "Don't forget it, buddy. I'm kind of a big deal."

"Okay, Ron Burgundy," he teased. "Man, that's hot. I'm really impressed."

"Thanks." She sipped her wine. "To answer your question, the debt isn't from school. I actually made enough to pay off that debt. But I spent the last few years going through IVF and fertility treatments and racked up about eighty thousand in debt."

"Good lord, that's expensive. I didn't realize you were trying to have a baby."

"I was," she said, pulling her hand away and absently tracing her finger over the bar. "I picked out a sperm donor and went through three cycles. They didn't work and all my embryos are gone now."

"Oh, sweetheart," he said, leaning forward and cupping her cheek. "I'm so sorry. That must've been devastating."

"It was. Once things settled down, I decided I deserved some sexy times and wanted to experience some pleasure after all that emotional pain. So, I joined Pure and found you. It was exactly what I needed and I'm so grateful we connected."

"Me too, Teresa," he said, tracing his thumb over her cheek. "I'm just so damn sorry you had to go through that."

"Thanks. I don't dwell on it but it did set me back from buying a home. I still rent but will hopefully be able to own one day."

"I agree that building equity is better than paying rent. I own a townhome in Ardor Creek and love the development. My buddy Scott was the lead contractor on the project and the homes are modern and very sleek. Perfect for my bachelor life, I guess."

"Sounds nice," she said, grinning.

"It is," he said with a nod. "Man, I'm so sorry, Teresa. I still hold out hope of having kids one day but need to find time to date which seems impossible."

"Relationships require work to succeed. I see evidence of that every day in my practice."

"Definitely. My parents have been married for over forty years and they make it look so easy. They're still in love after all that time."

"How romantic," she said wistfully. "And you mentioned you have a sister, right?"

"Justine. She's five years younger and an exceptional painter and sculptor. She definitely got the creative genes. She's married with a little girl but her marriage isn't so great, unfortunately. Her husband's a dick and I'm pretty sure he's rough with them."

"Oh, Mark, that's terrible. Is she open to leaving him?"

He shook his head. "No, although I haven't given up on trying to convince her. It's such a toxic relationship and I do my best to check on Avery—that's her daughter. I wish I could do more but she won't go on record against him so my hands are tied."

"Maybe that's why you want to help other people? Because you can't help Justine."

His lips curved. "Am I being analyzed? How much will this session cost me?"

"Consider it a freebie," she said, grinning. "But I'm so sorry to hear that. If Justine ever wants to speak to a therapist, please give her my number. I would meet with her for free."

"Thank you. That's incredibly generous." Sliding his hand over hers, he gazed so deeply into her eyes, Teresa felt it in her soul. "I thought about asking you to make this more serious. To just say 'fuck it' and give dating a try. But the more I thought about it, the more I realized it would be a terrible idea. First of all, I'm not sure you'd even want to date me."

"I might consider it," she teased.

"Thanks." He gave a playful eye roll. "But you deserve more than I can give, Teresa. I'm going to be swamped with the campaign, and I won't have time to dedicate to a relationship. Also, I'm not sure I'm ready yet. It's not that I'm enamored with being a bachelor but I do crave independence and enjoy my life."

"Being single has a lot of benefits. I enjoy being solo too. There's something so empowering about controlling your own destiny."

"So true. And if I ever do get the urge to settle down, I don't want to form a relationship during a campaign. The process is grueling and I think we'd be doomed from the start."

"Well, no one would accuse you of being a ball of sunshine there, Mr. D.A."

Laughing, he shook his head. "Nope. That sounds pretty pessimistic. Sorry."

"It's okay." She squeezed his hand and laced their fingers. "I get it. I'm not ready either and I have no desire to be plastered across campaign ads as the candidate's girlfriend. But it's encouraging you at least thought about making this more serious. It means you enjoy our time together."

"So much." He tucked a curl behind her ear, his features laced with sorrow. "Like I said, it's not forever. If we're still single in December, let's revisit this."

"Okay," she whispered as her eyes stung with tears. "In the meantime, should we screw our brains out one more time so we remember?"

A sexy growl formed deep in his throat. "Hell yes." Standing, he extended his hand. "Sara," he called, "put it on my room. Thanks."

"You got it," Sara called from the corner of the bar, giving a salute.

Grasping tightly, Teresa followed the man who held a special place in her heart, determined to enjoy their final night together.

The next morning, Teresa sat at her kitchen table, drinking coffee as she recalled the previous evening. There had been something urgent in Mark's tender caresses and she'd felt it too.

Finding someone you were so sexually compatible with, who could also make you laugh, wasn't easy and she mourned the loss. Still, as she'd indicated to Mark, she wasn't fully healed from the emotional distress of her infertility treatments and didn't feel it fair to saddle him with that. Add in the fact he'd mentioned several times over their affair he wanted to have kids one day, and that pretty much closed the door for anything serious between them.

The thought didn't sit well in her gut and Teresa mulled the sentiment as she sipped. Had she developed feelings for her no-strings-attached lover even though the emotions were strictly off-limits? Feeling something flare deep within, she realized she had formed an emotional attachment to him, although it was simmering instead of blazing. Perhaps not full-blown love, but an acknowledgment he was special and their time together meant something.

Sighing, she glanced at her phone and noted it was time to shower. Her office hours began at eleven and her first client was always early. Standing, she shuffled to the shower, determined to begin the day and remain thankful for the months she'd spent with her handsome companion.

The week chugged along, slow and measured, and by Thursday, Teresa felt an aching sadness at the thought of not seeing Mark that evening. They'd always met on Mondays and Thursdays, falling into a comfortable pattern: drinks with Sara at the bar before heading to the room and making love. Then, they would snuggle and watch TV for a bit before loving each other once more. Whoever purchased the room would stay behind, letting the other one leave first and they would exchange one last passionate kiss at the hotel room door.

Lifting her fingers to her lips, Teresa caressed them, yearning for Mark's kiss. Conjuring energy from deep within, she sent it to the universe, hoping it helped his campaign. He was a good man and she hoped he won. She intrinsically knew he would be an excellent public servant.

Perhaps, after his win, they could eventually resume their passionate nights together. For, if there was one thing Teresa appreciated, it was honesty and she wouldn't lie to herself about her feelings for Mark. The thought of rejoining Pure and finding someone else held no interest. She'd found a sexy, thoughtful lover and, even though she'd vowed to stay unattached, feelings had taken hold anyway.

"It is what it is, Teresa," she said, stirring the soup she was heating as she stood over her kitchen stove. "This is the first Thursday you haven't seen him in months. It's okay to miss him."

Alone, with only her words to comfort her, she accepted them and eventually sat down to enjoy the hearty soup.

Chapter 4

T he week was busy for Mark as well and by Friday, all he wanted was to collapse in his bed and sleep from sunset to sunrise. Unfortunately, his phone rang when he walked through the door around seven o'clock on Friday evening. Glancing at the screen, he noticed the Caller ID.

"Hey, Evan," he said to his campaign manager. "I'm all about dedicating time to this campaign but figured you'd let me have Friday nights to myself."

"Sorry, Mark, but this is serious."

Bristling at his tone, Mark settled on the couch in the dim living room. Putting Evan on speaker, he clicked on the lamp. "What's going on?"

"Are you sitting down?"

"Yeah," Mark said, feeling his eyebrows draw together.

"I'm going to ask you a question and I want an honest answer."

"Okay..."

"Did you meet someone on a hook-up app called Pure?"

Straightening, Mark nodded. "Yes. I'm pretty sure that's not illegal."

"It's not, obviously, but it is pretty fucking shocking to a certain demographic. Namely, the middle-aged and senior voters whom you desperately need to have a shot at winning."

Rubbing his forehead, Mark scowled. "I met someone on the app months ago before I decided to run. We were actually quite compatible and were monogamous until I ended it earlier this week."

"Goddammit, Mark!"

"What?" he yelled, standing and gesturing with his hand. "I can't have an open, casual relationship in the twenty-first century? That's ridiculous."

"Older voters want married candidates, Mark. I tried to tell you this. If you're not married, we can deal, but you can't skew towards player or man-whore. It destroys your credibility."

"That's absurd."

"I don't make the rules. Apparently, there are pictures of you two together after your trysts. They're damning."

"Pictures?" Teresa's stunning face flashed through his brain and he remembered her statement about not wanting to be the public image of the candidate's girlfriend. Concern filtered through him at the ramifications her involvement could have for her privacy and career. "What pictures? We were in a hotel room the entire time."

"Apparently, James Chisolm's campaign sent someone to snap pictures the last night you were together. Did you see her on Monday?"

"Yes," he said, crumpling to the couch. "It was our last night together. Chisolm is such a dick. I can't believe he'd send someone to spy on me the day I filed the paperwork. I thought I had a few days before the dirty tactics started."

"You knew running against him was going to be a slog. He's corrupt and determined to win at all costs. I thought you were smarter than this, Mark."

"Hey," he said, feeling the anger surface. "I'm not going to sit here and let you shame me for having a perfectly legitimate sexual relationship with a beautiful, intelligent woman. Fuck the voters and fuck whatever anyone else thinks. Have you seen the pictures? I don't care about me but I'm worried about Teresa. She has a career and values her privacy."

"The Scranton Times-Tribune has already published them online and you can bet they'll be the lead print story tomorrow. I understand you're pissed, Mark, but taking it out on me is futile. I'm just relaying how they're going to play this. They're going to paint you as someone who's not serious and only cares about getting laid. I'm not saying it's fair or true, but politics rarely are. Especially with someone as dirty as Chisolm."

"Fuck," Mark whispered, frustrated and annoyed. He'd hoped to have at least a few weeks of clean campaigning before it turned nasty. Accepting that wasn't in the cards, he shook his head. "Send me everything that's online. I need to call Teresa and warn her."

"I will. I'm also going to put together some polls to see how we can address this. If we don't handle it quickly, it might derail your campaign before it begins."

"Fine. I guess this is what it means to be a politician in this day and age. Polls and misconceptions. Chad tried to warn me but I forged ahead."

Evan huffed a frustrated breath. "You're one of the good guys, Mark. I'm sorry this is happening. I know you're running to create positive change. Unfortunately, the bad guys are better at playing dirty. We always knew this was a possibility."

"We did. Send me the links and call me back when you have the poll results."

"Will do."

The phone clicked off and Mark threw his head back on the couch, harshly rubbing his hands over his face. "Damn it!" His phone began to ding and he opened the texts from Evan, following the links to the news articles.

They all had various headlines like, "**D.A. Candidate Prefers Casual Hook-Ups to Monogamy**" and "**Chisolm Challenger Focused More on Sex than Campaign**." Groaning, he tamped down the urge to throw his phone against the wall. The headlines were false but who could possibly know that?

Mark and Teresa had been monogamous, choosing to exchange test results and have a forthright, exclusive affair. In fact, his relationship with Teresa had fostered more authentic communication than several married couples he knew. It had been freeing and comfortable, and he truly enjoyed their time together.

Knowing he had to warn her, he searched for her name in his phone and dialed.

"Hi," she said, her voice a bit warbled and shaky.

"Hey," he said, aching to comfort her. "I guess you saw."

"Yes. My brother has a Google alert on everyone in our family. I never understood the need for it but it came in pretty handy tonight."

"I'm so sorry, Teresa," he said, voice laced with remorse. "You don't deserve this and I'm going to fix it."

"I don't know how you can. I'm mentioned in every article and they have pictures of us, Mark."

"I know," he said, putting her on speaker and scrolling through the pictures in one of the articles. "There's one of me kissing you as we stood in the doorway of our room and another one of us sitting at the bar. I didn't even contemplate someone would be following us around. I should've been better prepared."

"They have details from other times besides Monday. They knew we met on Pure, how often we met, and a ton of other specifics. The only conclusion I can come up with is that Sara passed along the information."

Mark scowled. "She's such a sweet kid," he said, shaking his head. "There has to be another explanation."

"I can't think of one. Perhaps we should confront her."

"Yes. I'll drive there tonight and ask her. Damn it, Teresa. I wish you didn't have to be involved in this."

"One of the articles wrote something quite nasty about how I must use sex therapy in my practice. I don't but it's actually a legitimate form of therapy for many people. It's disgusting how they attempted to portray it as something dirty or shameful. I don't want any part of this. I'm a very private person, Mark."

"I know," he whispered, furious. "I'm going to fix this, Teresa. I don't care about me but I'm going to try like hell to squash any damage to your practice or reputation."

"I appreciate the sentiment. It will most likely have ramifications for my therapy practice but I'll try to stay positive."

"Let me speak to Sara. I'll report back once I do. My campaign manager is going to call me early tomorrow morning and we'll come up with a plan. I swear, sweetheart, I'll do my best."

A soft sigh carried over the phone and he yearned to hold her. Closing his eyes, he remembered the feel of her soft curls against his chest when he would stroke them after they made love. They'd only ended their affair days ago but he missed her, as he'd known he would. She was remarkable and such a bright light in his quiet, solo life. Well, quiet before he'd decided to run for D.A. and royally screwed them both. Uttering a frustrated groan, he lifted the phone to his ear.

"I'll call you in the morning. I won't rest until I figure this out."

"Talk to you then," she said softly.

"Talk to you then. Good night, hon."

Clicking off the phone, he stood, ready to face Sara and figure out what the hell happened.

Less than fifteen minutes later, Mark stormed through the hotel sliding doors, his gaze landing on Sara as she served a couple at the bar. When her eyes met his, her smile fell and he strode over to wait for her at the empty side of the bar.

"Let me know if you need anything else, Mr. and Mrs. Sterling," she said. Tentatively approaching, she pursed her lips. "Hi, Mark."

"Hi, Mark?" he said, flailing his hands. "How could you Sara?"

"It's my ex," she said, remorse strewn over her features as her eyes filled with tears. "I swear, I didn't tell the P.I. anything."

"A private investigator approached you?" Mark asked, sliding into the bar seat.

"Yes," she said, appearing visibly stressed. "On Tuesday while I was working. I told him to fuck off, obviously, but Dan came in and had a drink at the bar. The P.I. must've been waiting for him outside when he left. I told Dan about you and Teresa because you were so cute. It was awesome you met on Pure and had this super-modern relationship. I never dreamed he'd tell the investigator. He told me this morning and I broke up with him, Mark. I swear. I'm furious."

Exhaling a breath through puffed cheeks, Mark scrubbed his face with his hand. "I assume you told Dan everything? What we did for a living? How often we met? Every detail."

"Yes," she whispered, swiping away a tear. "I'm so sorry. I've been with Dan since high school. I just never thought he'd do something stupid like this for money. The P.I. gave him two hundred dollars. It's despicable." Burying her face in her hands, her shoulders shook as she began to cry.

"It's okay," he said, reaching across the bar and rubbing her arm. "I understand, Sara. I'm not upset."

"You're not?" she asked, peeking at him with wet eyes.

"Not at you. It's perfectly natural to tell your boyfriend these things. I'm certainly pissed at him but I have bigger fish to fry at the moment."

"The articles said such terrible things about Teresa," she said, lips quivering as she tried to control her tears. "The slut-shaming was awful. It's so misrepresentative of how awesome you two are. I'm happy to go on the record and tell the real story."

Burrowing into the chair, Mark wondered if that would even help at this point. "I appreciate it, Sara, and I'll let you know. I think the damage might have been done but we'll see." Grasping her hand, he squeezed. "You don't need to cry, especially while you're working. I know how hard you work to pay for school and I don't want to ruin your shift."

"Thank you," she said softly. "I'm never going to speak to Dan again. Please let me know how I can fix this."

"Did Dan mention the pictures?"

"Yes," she said, biting her lip. "The P.I. surreptitiously snapped them of you on Monday night. The pictures combined with everything I'd told Dan was passed on to the reporters by the P.I."

"I'm wondering if I can make a connection between my opponent and the P.I.," Mark mulled, rubbing his chin.

"The investigator's name is Aaron Robinson if that helps."

"It does, thanks. I'm going to head home and figure out how to handle this but I might reach out if I have any other questions."

"Let me put my number in your phone," she said, extending her hand. After moving her thumbs across the keypad, she handed it back to him. "I put it in and texted myself so I have yours. Please, Mark, I want to help in any way I can. You can call me anytime. You and Teresa were always so nice to me, and really great tippers, and you don't deserve this."

"Thanks." Standing, he stuffed his phone in his back pocket. "I'll be in touch. For now, don't waste your time focusing on it. We'll figure it out."

Tilting his head, he pivoted and exited the hotel, furious he'd underestimated James Chisolm. It was a disastrous mistake and one he would never make again. More determined than ever to beat him—and to repair the damage to Teresa's reputation—he dedicated his fastidious mind to accomplishing those goals.

Chapter 5

On Saturday morning, Teresa threw her thick hair in a bun and waited for the fall-out. After reading several articles on her nefarious sexual practices, she'd barely been able to sleep. Standing in her small bathroom, she scrunched her nose at the reflection, wondering if the tiny wrinkles beside her eyes had deepened during the sleepless night. Pushing the skin with her fingers, she glanced down when her phone lit up.

"Hi, Mark," she said, noting it was barely seven a.m. "You're up early for a Saturday."

"Couldn't sleep. I'm guessing you couldn't either."

"Not really," she said, still pressing the skin around her eye. "Your text last night indicated you spoke to Sara."

He confirmed, updating her on his conversation and Dan's encounter with the private investigator.

"Well, at least she found out he was a dick before they got married. Another divorce averted in Battle Falls."

"Your first thought would be of Sara," he said, the deep timbre of his voice comforting as everything else was shattering. "I'd expect nothing less from you, even though your life is the one that's been turned upside down."

"Of course, I'm thinking of her. It's awful to be betrayed by your partner that way, especially when you're so young. If they've been together since high school, it could be her first big betrayal. My heart hurts for her."

Silence stretched through the phone before he spoke. "Do they teach you this selfless stuff in psychology class or were you born with it? Because it's pretty damn amazing, Teresa."

Chuckling, she gave her reflection one last perusal before heading to the kitchen to fry some eggs. "I'm not perfect, believe me. Didn't you hear? I'm a hussy and a tramp."

"You're nothing of the sort. I can't believe this is a scandal. Have the people of Lackawanna County *seen* half of the federal and state politicians we vote into office?"

"Scandals represent the mindset of the people. Although we're near Scranton, Battle Falls and Ardor Creek retain a lot of their small-town conventions. I think many still clutch onto their belief of traditional marriage and sex only being acceptable between committed partners, although things are slowly evolving. Change is slow the farther one is from bigger cities."

"I guess so. What implications are you expecting from this?"

"I don't know," she said, putting the phone on speaker and setting it on the counter so she could make the eggs. "I recently signed a social work contract with a local church community organization in Battle Falls. The contract has several clauses that one could argue were violated due to my public affair."

"Unbelievable. Do think that will happen?"

"I don't know," she said, shrugging. "I signed the contract to supplement my income from my clients to satisfy my debt faster. I anticipate losing several clients from my practice too. I just don't know how this will ultimately affect me."

"I'm meeting with my campaign manager at nine o'clock. He texted me this morning that he has several *scenarios* that can help us both. I'll call you once I've looked them over."

"Does one of them involve us running away and living on a tropical island forever? Because I'm down with that."

His chuckle reverberated through the phone. "Me too. I'd give anything to be stranded on an island with you, a cold drink and the sound of the ocean."

"Sounds romantic," she teased.

Silence crackled through the phone.

"I missed you on Thursday night," he finally said, causing her heart to slam in her chest. "I knew I would but it was more intense than I anticipated."

"I missed you too," she said softly. "I think we ended things so abruptly we didn't have time to process it."

"That's my fault. I didn't want to make a big deal of ending our arrangement because it was supposed to be casual. But, in the end, I'm not sure it was all that casual for me."

"What does that mean?"

His exhale traveled over the phone. "I don't know. Like I said, I'm not ready for marriage or a full-blown relationship but...," he hesitated, as if searching for the right words. "Our time together meant a lot. I haven't really reflected on what that signifies and I'm not sure I'm ready to."

"I'll let you off the hook, then," she said, grinning at the meaningful sentiments. "I'm not ready to dissect it either. And, well, we have a lot of crap to figure out."

"Do we ever. Okay, I'll call you when I'm done with Evan. Text me if anything else blows up."

"I've already informed my parents in Barcelona and my brother, who lives in California with his wife and two daughters. They're pretty progressive, thank god, so they're fine. In fact, I think my brother is rather enjoying this, the little shit."

"Yeah?"

"He's three years younger and tells me I don't get laid enough. Kind of weird for your kid brother but he wants me to be happy. I think he's excited I was getting some on the regular for a while."

Mark laughed. "Well, at least he has a sense of humor. My friend Peter is a ball buster with a wicked sense of humor and I can't wait to see what he has in store for me. I'm never going to hear the end of it."

"Yikes."

"Don't worry. He'll castigate me in such a loving way, it will end up being hilarious. That's kind of his thing."

"Sounds like a good friend."

"He is. Okay, hon, I'll call you later."

"Have a good meeting."

Scraping the eggs on a plate, Teresa headed to the table and sat down, taking a bite as she pondered. Although she should've been focused on the melee that now comprised her world, she found herself absently staring at the wall, remembering Mark's deep voice as he'd said tender words she'd never expected, but somehow craved, nevertheless.

Mark entered the diner and waved at Evan who sat in a nearby booth. Sliding in, he noted his campaign manager's morose expression.

"You don't look like you have good news."

"Nope," Evan said, spreading a stack of papers across the table. "We did some polling and there seem to only be a few options to salvage this."

"Let me hear them," he said, sitting back in the booth and preparing for the worst.

"At this point, you have three options you can consider, each of them with their own issues."

"Okay."

"Option one is you can throw Teresa under the bus. Paint her as someone who propositioned you and lured you into a purely sexual relationship even though you believe in more traditional relationships."

"Absolutely not, and I don't," Mark said, waving his hand through the air.

"You don't what?"

"I don't believe traditional relationships are 'standard' anymore. Being single, being with someone, or having a purely sexual affair should be completely fine in this day and age. Hell, if you want to be polyamorous or a swinger, go for it. But Teresa happens to be an amazing woman who met me on a hook-up app and doesn't deserve any of this. What are the other options?"

"For option two, you could leave the race and run again in four years."

Sighing, Mark ran his hand through his hair. "No. I mulled the run for a long time and I'm ready. Chisolm is a dick and we need someone who's not corrupt in the office. Someone who actually wants to help people. What's option three?"

Evan squirmed in his chair, causing Mark to frown.

"Just tell me, Evan."

"Option three actually polled highest among every demographic: seniors, youth voters, women, and men."

"That's promising."

Clearing his throat, Evan looked him straight in the eye. "You could announce your engagement to Teresa and move in together."

Mark's spine straightened as his eyes grew wide. "What?"

"Look, man," Evan said shrugging, "I don't answer the polls. I just postulate scenarios and see what people like. It turns out, people really like the idea of you and Teresa getting engaged. I guess there are more romantic hearts out there than I anticipated. Most responses indicated your engagement would turn even the most cynical voter around."

"Wow," he said, running his hand over his face. "Maybe I've lost touch with the romanticism of love and all that jazz. I just never realized this was such a big deal to people."

"You did tell me your mom gave you advice similar to this."

"Yes, but she's old school. I figured we lived in a more modern world."

"Romance can be modern," Evan said, grinning. "I like my wife most of the time."

Mark breathed a laugh. "Jocelyn is pretty great. You snagged a good one."

"Look," Evan said, leaning forward and resting his arms on the table. "The engagement doesn't have to be real. You could speak to Teresa and see if she'd be open to going along with the announcement until after the election. Once it's over, you could part ways. But she'd have to agree to move in with you, appear at public functions, and everything else being the candidate's fiancée would entail. I'll do my best to keep the appearances minimal for her, but she'd have to appear at some."

"You lost me at 'move in with me,'" Mark droned.

"It would cement the engagement narrative. I'm not sure I could sell it if you two don't cohabitate. Reporters would certainly snap pictures of her at her home, separate from you. I thought about it a lot and that's the only way I can be certain it would work."

"Good grief. This is ridiculous. I specifically searched for her on a hook-up app so I *wouldn't* end up in anything serious. And she'd never go along with it anyway. I'm pretty sure she values her independence and space as much as I do."

"You never know until you ask," he said, lifting his brows. "Maybe there's something that could make it worth her while. Can you think of anything you could give her in return that would incentivize her?"

Mark pursed his lips, recalling the debt Teresa had accrued. "Maybe, but it seems kind of untoward. What am I supposed to do? Call her and say, '*Hey, sorry I ruined your life but can you be my fake fiancée for this small recompense?*' It sounds insane."

"Public life and elections are insane, Mark. I tried to explain this to you." Sighing, he shook his head. "Look, I don't want to be an alarmist but if you can't convince her to do this, and if you don't want to take this engagement route, I think I might have to resign as your campaign manager."

"You can't be serious!"

"I believe in you, Mark. You're a good candidate with a heart of gold. But I don't run losing campaigns. It would ruin my reputation and my career is at stake. I'm sure you can understand that somewhere in that logical brain of yours."

Expelling a breath, Mark nodded. "I can. How in the hell did I ruin things so badly? I feel terrible for doing this to Teresa and wouldn't blame her if she decides to never speak to me again."

Evan's eyes darted between his as he pondered. After a moment, he said, "I don't want to overstep here, but you seem to carry affection for her, Mark. To me, it doesn't seem like the worst thing in the world to ask a woman you have a connection with to live together for a few months, especially if there's some way you can help her in return. And I certainly don't want to discuss your sex life, but it would allow you to continue that part of your relationship as well."

"I wouldn't pressure her in that regard at all," Mark said, slicing his hand over the table. "If I considered this, I would offer to take sex completely off the table. I don't want her to feel manipulated in any way."

"Fair enough," Evan said with a nod. "Take today and think about it and call me tomorrow with an answer. Unfortunately, time is of the essence." Standing, he patted Mark's shoulder. "I'm sorry this is happening, man. I really am. But remember it's a few months of hard choices to get to the ultimate goal." Gathering the stacks of papers, he gave Mark a salute and exited the diner.

Huffing a breath, Mark sat back in the booth and drank the lukewarm coffee the server set on the table half an hour ago, wondering what the hell to do.

Chapter 6

Teresa received the call from the director of the Battle Falls church community organization at noon. Mr. Dawson was very polite but quite terse as he explained the organization would be terminating her contract due to the recent events in the news involving her private life. Teresa accepted the termination, determined not to dwell on the missed opportunity.

Sitting in front of her laptop, she pulled up the spreadsheet where she'd tabulated her mountain of debt. The church organization's contract to provide social work services to their network of patrons would've contributed to her paying off the debt much faster. Now, even if she retained the private clients she had, the payoff date would be pushed back several years. Lips thinning, she also recognized she would surely lose some clients—perhaps the more provincial ones—who didn't want a therapist whose reputation was being dragged in the press.

Closing the laptop, she sipped the tea she'd made, inhaling deep breaths in between. Anger bubbled in her gut and she reminded herself that, although it was warranted, it wouldn't help her find a solution. No, she had to remain calm and attempt to figure out how to turn things around.

Her phone chimed and she read the text from Mark.

Mark: Hey. Met with Evan. I'd really like to speak with you in person. We could meet in public but it might result in more pictures if someone sees us. I could come to your place or you could meet me at mine. Sorry to be a pain but I don't want to add to the fodder.

Teresa: I get it. You can come here. 200 Robin Lane, Unit 34, Battle Falls. When should I expect you?

Mark: I'll be there at one o'clock. Thanks, Teresa. Excited to see you. Hope you don't hate me all the way. Maybe only ninety-nine percent?

Chuckling, she sent him a "hand on the chin thinking emoji" before typing.

Teresa: I could never hate you. But the apology is cute. See you soon.

After reading his confirmation text, she threw the phone on the table and groaned. Not because she was going to see Mark in an hour. No, the little butterflies in her stomach indicated she was rather excited about that. Instead, she was annoyed at the serious conversation they were sure to have. Teresa enjoyed her time with Mark as casual and fun, and hated their acquaintance had taken this serious turn.

Rising, she set her cup in the sink and headed to shower, wondering what Mark and Evan had discussed. Interested to find out, she applied makeup and slipped on her nicest pair of jeans and a silky top. After all, when one was going to discuss the details of picking up the pieces of their life, they might as well look like a million bucks.

Trailing to the living room, Teresa sat on the couch and waited for her former lover to arrive.

Teresa told herself to squash the nerves as she plodded toward the front door when the knock sounded. Inhaling a deep breath, she pulled it open to find a contrite, and very handsome, Mark Lancaster on the other side.

"Wow," he said, brown eyes roving over her like a caress. "You could write the book on how to look stunning while your life is imploding."

Laughing, she stepped back and gestured him inside. "I decided my comfy sweat pants weren't quite appropriate for the serious conversation we're about to have."

"Maybe not." He gave her a sheepish grin and looked around. "Nice place."

"Thanks," she said, waving him into the living room. "I like it and it's functional until I can buy a house, which might happen when I'm eighty at this point."

Sitting down, she gestured for him to do the same, noting his forlorn expression.

"Hey," she said, encircling his wrist as he sat beside her. "This isn't your fault, Mark. It's just a shitty situation. I know you feel bad but I'm not upset at you personally."

"You should be," he said, covering her hand. The skin of his palm was slightly rough, sending shivers through her body. "I feel awful. I'm so sorry, Teresa. I never thought this would happen in a million years."

"I know." She shook her head. "The world pivots on a five-second news cycle. This is an exciting and interesting story. Hopefully, it will die down soon."

Sighing, he sat back and ran a hand through his hair. "My campaign manager doesn't seem to think that will happen. His team did a ton of polling last night. If I don't employ a viable solution soon, he's going to resign and I'm going to withdraw from the race."

"No," she said, eyebrows drawing together. "I read up on your opponent once you told me the news. He's a scumbag. You can't withdraw."

"A scumbag who I'm sure has done a thousand more nefarious things compared to having an open, honest sexual relationship with someone. Unfortunately, the bad guys are harder to smear. The exposés just roll off them while the good guys get creamed. That's assuming you still think I'm a good guy at this point. I wouldn't blame you if you don't."

"I definitely think you're one of the good guys," she said, grinning. "Always. The platforms on your campaign site represent everything I believe in. Prison reform, decriminalizing minor marijuana drug offenses, advocating for fairer sentences for women who are in jail for self-defense against men who abused them. I'm all for it, Mark. What can I do to help you stay in the race? I'm sure Evan came up with some way I can help. Do I need to go on record and say I was your consensual sexual partner?"

Blowing out a breath, he shook his head. "I wish it was that easy. Believe it or not, in this day and age, people still have a problem with a purely sexual relationship. The polls were pretty clear on that."

"Yikes. And I thought we'd made such progress."

"Me too. After all the feedback Evan received, there was only one option that had a favorable outcome."

"Which was?"

His throat bobbed as he swallowed, making him appear nervous. Straightening, he ran his hands over his thighs as he contemplated. "Did you hear from the community organization?"

Nodding, she bit her lip. "They terminated my contract."

"Damn it," he said softly. "I can help you fight that, by the way. Regardless of the language, we can make a case that you did absolutely nothing illegal by having a consensual relationship with me."

"I appreciate that but the damage is done. A therapist requires complete trust from her clients. I wouldn't want to work with an organization where even one person questioned my integrity. It wouldn't serve any of the people I'm trying to help."

"Teresa—"

"It is what it is, Mark," she said, holding up a hand. "I'm not going to force them to work with me. Honestly, I have too much pride. I'm a damn good therapist and social worker, and if they're too farsighted to realize this and are so easily put off, it's not a good fit for me. After what happened with my IVF treatments, I promised myself I would tamp down the drama in my life. I don't want to be around people who judge me. I know my self-worth and I'm not ashamed of our relationship. If they're not on board, fuck 'em."

His lips curved into a smile, sending her heart into overdrive. Even now, with the terrible circumstances surrounding them, he was the most attractive man she'd ever been with. Clearing her throat, she smiled back.

"You're staring."

"Sorry," he said, reaching over and clutching her hand. "You're just pretty awesome. Fuck 'em is right. They don't deserve you."

"I agree. Still, it doesn't help my debt situation. Of course, that's not your concern, but it sucks, nonetheless."

"What if I made it my concern?"

Her brow furrowed. "In what way?"

Turning to face her, he grabbed both hands and held tightly. "I want to propose something to you and I want you to hear me out before you answer, okay?"

Dismissing how her heart skipped at the word "propose" while he was clutching her hands, she nodded. "Okay."

Licking his lips, he considered his words. "There was one scenario that every single demographic loved in the polling. It involved you and me...well, it involved us ending up together."

"Together..." she repeated slowly.

"Yes," he continued, a slight excitement in his tone. "It seems that if you and I got engaged, and furthered the narrative that our casual affair turned into something serious, voters of every demographic would not only accept it, it would most likely lift me in the polls."

Teresa swallowed thickly. "You want to get engaged?"

"No," he said quickly, eyes widening. "Definitely not—"

"Um, okay," she said, trying to pull her hands away.

"Wait," he said, tugging to retain his grip. "That came out wrong. What I meant to say was that, as we previously discussed, I know neither of us is in the right space for an engagement or marriage."

"Correct," she said with a nod, wondering where in the hell he was going with this.

"But," he said, lifting a finger, "if we created a fake engagement, we could both accomplish our goals and save our reputations."

"Wouldn't that be lying?"

"It would be a lie to further the common good. To allow me to win the election and to allow you to pay off your debt."

"How would I do that by entering into a fake engagement with you?"

"Because I'll pay it off," he said, his tone forthright and clear. "My life as a workaholic results in me doing very well financially, Teresa. I have more than enough to pay off your debt and I would be happy to do it if you agree to help me out."

Pulling her hands away, she stood, noticing how shaky her legs were. Striding to the mantel, she clutched it as she stared into the electric fireplace. "I won't take anyone's charity, Mark. I entered into the IVF rounds knowing full well how much debt I would accrue. It's mine to pay off."

"I understand your reluctance," he said, rising and slowly approaching. Sliding his hands over her shoulders, he gently urged her to face him. "I'm only offering because you would be helping me immensely and it's the only thing I can think of that I can even remotely offer you as a fair exchange."

"I don't want to lie to people and I don't want your money, Mark."

Sad eyes searched hers as he loomed over her. "I understand. I thought the idea insane when Evan suggested it. But the more I thought about it, the more it began to make sense in my mind. Maybe I'm just grasping at straws. Shit, I don't know." Rubbing his forehead, he backed away before sitting on the couch again. "I just don't know what to do here, Teresa. I figured it was best to at least present the scenario to you before dismissing it outright."

"Mark," she said, striding over and sitting next to him. "First of all, we'd be lying about our relationship. The entire reason I enjoyed our time together is because we were completely honest with each other."

"You're right," he said, lifting a shoulder. "It would be a lie to appease the public. Privately, I would tell my family and friends the truth, as I'd encourage you to do. But, regardless of whether we want to be truthful or not, the media is smearing us with lies and will continue to do so. In extreme cases like this, I don't think it's untoward to create a fake public engagement to counteract the media and my opponent's lies. Maybe that's morally questionable but I want to fight back. If they're going to fight dirty, I'm willing to roll up my sleeves too."

Teresa gnawed her lip, pondering the moral dilemma. On one hand, it felt wrong to enter into an engagement and publicly further a lie. On the other hand, Mark was right. Regardless of her moral compass, the people debasing them had no ethics whatsoever. What was the point of maintaining standards that would be shredded regardless?

"It's something I'd really have to think about," she finally said. "I need to make a pros and cons list and weigh the moral imbalances of entering into something like this."

"I understand," he said solemnly. "It's a huge decision and you've already indicated you hate the public spotlight."

"I certainly don't love it," she said, arching a brow. "How many events would I have to attend as your fiancée?"

"Evan assured me he'd keep it to a bare minimum. He's a straight shooter so I trust him with that."

"Like I said, I want you to win. I wouldn't mind appearing at some events if it helps you."

"Thank you," he said, smiling. "That means a lot, Teresa."

Gazing down, she stared at her fingers twining in her lap. "I wouldn't feel right taking money from you, Mark. Especially with the sexual nature of our relationship."

"I wanted to address that too." Straightening his spine, he latched on to her gaze. "You'd have to move in with me until after the election to further the fake engagement narrative but sex would be off the table until you want to discuss it. I'm going to be so busy with the campaign along with my regular clients, I can barely fathom having the energy to maintain a sexual relationship during the scant hours I'm home. And I figure you'd rather not have sex with a dude who has zero energy. Sleep sex hasn't quite caught on yet from what I've heard."

Throwing her head back, she laughed at his teasing. "Not quite yet. So, you wouldn't want to resume the sexual portion of our relationship if I agreed to move in and accept the fake engagement?"

"Not at first, at least, because I wouldn't want to create any sort of power imbalance or anything like that. And I need to focus all my energy on the campaign. Also, I feel like it will alleviate any concerns you have about me paying your debt. I don't want it tied to any sort of sexual agreement between us. I would be doing it as payment for your help with the fake engagement. That's all, Teresa. I swear."

She chewed her lip, contemplating. "And if we decided down the road we wanted to resume the sexual portion of the relationship? What then? It would be very different from meeting in a hotel room if we lived together. One argument between us could lead to a whole host of problems."

"Are you planning on arguing with me?" he teased. "Because I can't even imagine a scenario where we argue. You're pretty chill and drama free, sweetheart."

"True, but I've seen it all. If people want to find an opportunity to fight, they certainly will."

"Not us," he said, confident as he shook his head. "We've been extremely honest with each other so far and I don't see that changing. I think if we maintain that open communication, we'll be fine. And if you want to resume the sexual relationship down the road, once we've settled in, we can discuss it. I'll leave it up to you to bring up if and when you're ready. In the meantime, I'll pay off your loans up front so any hint of any sexual ties to the payoff won't be questioned."

"You can't pay me up front," she said, taken aback by the offer. "What if I don't fulfill my end of the bargain through the election?"

"It's a chance I'm willing to take. I trust you, Teresa. Those are the terms I'm comfortable with and I think they're the best terms for you too. So, that's what we'll do if you agree to this. I could probably have everything paid off by the end of next week. It's up to you. I definitely don't want to pressure you but Evan is pretty much going to fire me as his candidate if you take longer than an hour to decide." He winked.

"An hour?"

"Kidding," he said, reaching over and tucking a curl behind her ear. The sweet gesture shifted something inside and her shoulders softened. "Obviously, I'll give you as much time as you need to consider. If you decide not to do it, I completely understand and there will be absolutely no hard feelings."

"It's just so much," she said, lifting her hands and gesturing around. "What about my apartment? I'll still need it once we 'break up' in November." She made quotation marks with her fingers.

"I'll pay for the apartment too so you'll have it. It will give you a space to run to if I drive you crazy and you're right about needing it when we eventually part. No problem at all."

"I'm not destitute, Mark," she said, feeling her nostrils flare. "I charge my clients several hundred dollars per hour. I'm only in debt because of the fertility challenges."

"I know and I'm not offering to pay because I think you're destitute by any means. It's just that you'd be doing so much for me if you decide to do this and, unfortunately, the only way I can pay you back is financially. I wish there was something more I could do. I swear, if I could go back in time and help you with the fertility struggles, I'd do it. I hate that you had to go through that I want to help you move on from what must've been a very hard time in your life. If you're open to it. That's all, hon."

He looked so contrite, causing her bristle to soften. Teresa was no damsel in distress and had always provided for herself. Needing a man to do anything for her or contribute one dollar to her bottom line had never even been on the radar. Still, the thought of alleviating her crushing debt overnight did hold a certain appeal. After all, she'd be fifty soon and wanted to own a house before the mortgage term extended longer than any years she had left on the damn planet. Mulling it over, she lifted her gaze to his.

"Let me sit and think about this," she said, rubbing her palms over her thighs. "I'm going to weigh everything and get back to you by tomorrow evening. I think that's the soonest I can make a firm decision."

"Done," he said, tilting his head before standing. Extending his hand, he pulled her to stand when she took it. "Dr. Teresa Roe, I appreciate you considering my exceedingly strange and untoward offer." He shook her hand as she snickered. "Others might have punched me in the face but you've handled this with the grace I've come to expect from you. I'm grateful for it and appreciate it more than you'll ever know."

"You're welcome," she said with a cheeky grin, formally shaking his hand. "I will have my answer to you by tomorrow evening, sir."

After one last poignant smile, he turned to leave and she followed behind. She pulled open the door and he hesitated, turning to swipe the hair off her shoulder.

"You're really amazing, Teresa," he said, brown eyes sparkling in the midday sun. "No matter what happens, my life is so much better because I met you, even with all the crap that's happened over the past twenty-four hours."

"Thank you," she said, voice raspy as her throat tightened. "I think you're pretty amazing too."

Cupping her jaw, he slid his thumb over her cheek. "Talk to you soon, hon." With a slight nod, he pivoted and headed toward his car.

Teresa closed the door and rested her back against it, slowly sliding down until she sat on the floor. Brow furrowed, she pondered what the hell she was going to do. Running her fingers over her cheek where Mark had trailed his thumb, she couldn't contain her smile. The skin still tingled slightly and she admitted what she already knew deep inside: no matter how much she contemplated, and no matter how many cons to the pros, Teresa was going to help Mark Lancaster.

Because she wanted to, and because he was a good man. And, she thought, as she stood up from the hardwood floor, because she was powerless to say no to the man who smiled at her with such genuine longing and asked for her help. Denying it would be futile since it was irrevocably true.

Determined to make the list anyway, she headed to the kitchen and pulled out her notebook, wondering how long she'd spend on the task since it was irrefutably pointless. After an hour, the list was complete and so was her decision.

Dr. Teresa Roe was going to enter into a fake engagement with her sexy former lover who possessed a heart of gold. Resigned to her choice, she decided she'd call him in a few hours to give the appearance of extreme contemplation. In the meantime, she opened a bottle of wine and poured a glass. Lifting it in the air, she saluted the ceiling.

"Congratulations, Teresa. You're finally engaged."

Snickering, she lifted the wine to her lips and enjoyed the celebratory drink.

At precisely nine o'clock that evening, Teresa called Mark, who answered with a hopeful, "Hello?"

"Hi," she said, pleasantly buzzed from the most recent glass of wine. "I made my pros and cons list."

He expelled a loud breath. "Okay. Give it to me."

"The most important thing was speaking to my family before I made any decisions. Lucky for you, they're getting a huge kick out of this, which they'll pay for next time I see them in person."

"Yikes. Sorry to out your casual relationship to your parents. That's got to be uncomfortable."

"They're *very* European, thank goodness," she teased. "Just another scandal in the long chronicle of Europe's scarred history. And as I told you before, my brother will never let it go. It's endearing even though I want to strangle him."

"Is it weird that I want to meet him? He sounds like a pretty fun guy."

Chuckling, she nodded. "He is. He and my parents are fine with whatever I choose. They understand the engagement won't be real."

Silence stretched over the phone.

"So...you'll do it?"

"With some caveats," she said, sipping her wine. "Namely, we need to rethink the offer to pay off my loans."

"Yeah, I realized after I left that offer was laced with all sorts of misogynistic overtones which I totally didn't mean."

"I know." She traced her finger over the base of the glass, eyes narrowing. "Your intentions were good but I don't need you to save me, Mark. I'm very confident in my ability to knock out the debt."

"I didn't mean to imply otherwise, Teresa, I swear. I was just trying to come up with some way to make the proposition fair to you—"

"I get it," she interrupted, keeping her tone even but firm. "But I have a different proposal."

"I'm listening."

"Paying off my debt right away would be fantastic and would save me so much in interest. So, I'm willing to barter."

"All right..."

"I'd be willing to agree to let you pay my debt in one lump sum to save me the interest but I want it as a loan. I assume you consult social workers and therapists in your legal practice?"

"I do."

"Well, you've retained a new consultant, Mr. Lancaster. I will repay you in consultation hours on any cases you need until the loan is satisfied."

He was quiet for a moment. "Teresa, I wouldn't feel right about not paying you for your time on consults."

"You're paying me by satisfying my debt and saving me a boat-load of interest. I think it's a perfect option and the only one I'll consider. If you need time to think about it, that's not a problem."

"No, of course not. I'm just not sure you're getting the best end of the deal with that arrangement."

"I think it's a fantastic option. It will allow me to finally begin looking for a home. Hopefully, I can purchase one around the time we end our arrangement in November. I'll continue to pay my rent on this place in the meantime."

"I want to contribute to that, Teresa. Please. I feel terrible this situation is going to force you to leave your home."

Glancing at the walls, she realized her apartment wasn't really "home" at all. Yes, it was a comfortable place where she slept, but it held no sentimental value to her. Still, she understood the need to maintain a separate space, just in case something didn't work out with their arrangement.

"I'm not attached to this place so that's not really an issue. But, if you feel the need to purchase some nice bottles of red while I'm living with you, I certainly won't turn them down."

His deep chuckle drifted across the phone. "Done. I'm going to ply you with so much expensive wine, you'll never want to leave."

Biting her lip, she digested his words. Would she become attached to him if they lived together? Was it inevitable?

"Sorry, I didn't mean to make such a serious statement. I'll rarely be home, Teresa, so I doubt we'll see each other a lot. But if we do this, I'm rolling out the red carpet and will make you feel as comfortable as possible here."

"I have no doubt." Inhaling a deep breath, she slowly released it into the phone. "Let's do it. I want you to win this election, Mark. Let's get fake engaged."

She could almost see his cute grin on the other end. "Are you sure?"

"I'm sure. When should I move in? Tomorrow?"

"I, uh...well, I guess so. If we're going to do this, I'll call Evan and he'll probably want you moved in right away. We'll formulate a plan and a schedule of minimal appearances. I swear, hon, we'll make this as painless as possible for you."

"I know. I'm not worried about that in the least."

"I wish I could do more to repay you," he said, his voice soft and reverent.

"The terms I laid out are enough. Now, if you don't mind, I'm going to go veg in bed and watch everything on my DVR since I'll lose access to it tomorrow."

Deep laughter surrounded her. "Good call. Thank you, Teresa. I wish I knew how to express my gratitude but I have no freaking idea."

"No need. Let's beat this bastard. Good night, Mark. I'll text you tomorrow once I've packed."

"Sounds good. Sweet dreams."

Clicking off the phone, Teresa emitted a tiny squeal that was completely uncharacteristic of her calm, functional demeanor. But her life had been filled with quite a bit of heartache over the past few years and her time with Mark had been a bright spot. If she was honest, her life had become staid and a bit boring. Although she wasn't enamored with being dragged in the media, she acknowledged the turn of events was very exciting.

And what if she moved in with Mark and wanted to resume their sexual relationship? He'd mentioned he would be open to discussing that down the road. Understanding that was a topic that should remain off-limits until they settled in, Teresa shelved it to explore at a later date. For now, she would embark on this new phase of her life, free from the crushing debt that hung around her neck.

"I'm freeeee!" she exclaimed, standing and joyfully lifting her hands in the air as she twirled. Glancing at her phone, she noticed the alert that flashed with an update to the story on her and Mark's relationship.

"Well, somewhat free," she muttered, swiping away the notification. "Screw you, James Chisolm. We're coming for you, buddy."

Heading to her bedroom, Teresa brushed her teeth and donned her most comfy t-shirt before sliding between the sheets to binge the remaining Real Housewives episodes on her DVR.

Chapter 7

♥

Mark's phone rang on Sunday around eleven a.m. as he was placing fresh sheets on the bed in the guest bedroom. It sat down the hall from his room on the second floor of his townhome and he wanted Teresa to be as comfortable as possible there. Of course, having your life flipped upside down wasn't the definition of "comfortable" but Mark would do his best to ensure the place felt like home for her.

"What's up, Scott?" he asked, putting the phone on speaker as he stretched the fitted sheet over the double bed's mattress.

"Uh, hi..." was his friend's tentative response. "Ashlyn showed me the articles on her phone. Wow."

"Yeah," Mark said, grimacing. "It's a shit show. Chisolm must've had someone following me from the time I filed the damn papers. It's so intrusive and extremely unfair to Teresa."

"So, um, that's why I'm calling..."

"You sound weird, man. Just tell me what's up. Are you too scandalized by the situation to hang with me? I didn't foresee that judging by all the porn you told me you watched over the past years."

"Ha. Ha." Scott replied acerbically. "Actually, I know Teresa. She's my therapist, Mark."

Mark straightened as his eyebrows drew together. "Oh. Well, that's a bit...awkward."

"It's a strange coincidence, for sure. I wanted to let you know right away so it was out in the open."

Sitting on the bed, Mark lifted the phone, holding it closer. "I remember you telling me how much you liked your therapist and how helpful the sessions were."

"She's amazing. I can't imagine processing everything after the accident without her guidance. I also went back to her for several months when I met Ashlyn. She helped me unlock and release so many things. I'd recommend her to anyone."

Mark's lips curved. "She's pretty damn awesome. I couldn't believe it when I met her on Pure. I never imagined I'd find anyone so gorgeous, smart, and funny on a hook-up app."

"Is this thing between you more serious than the articles indicate?"

Mark pondered, running his fingers over the soft sheet. "I...don't know how to answer that, Scott. I wish I did. I'm hesitant to explore it right now for several reasons—the most important being that she's moving in with me in about two hours."

"What?"

Inhaling a deep breath, Mark relayed the events of the past few days and the subsequent solution he and Teresa had agreed upon. "When I told Evan last night, he was thrilled. He says this will save my campaign."

"Wow, buddy, your life took a turn in a matter of days. From single bachelor to public figure with a fake fiancée. My head would be spinning."

"It's not ideal but I'm in it now. I just..." he looked around the room at the dark blue walls he'd painted himself. "I want her to feel comfortable here. I feel terrible she's stuck in this situation."

"Makes sense. I obviously don't know her on a personal level but she seems practical and level-headed to me. I'm sure she doesn't blame you."

"She says she doesn't but things have happened so fast. I hope she doesn't come to resent me. In the meantime, I'm going to try and make this lovely townhome you built as welcoming as possible. And, I can cook for her on the weekends, so that's something."

"I still say you make the rest of us look bad with your cooking skills. You're almost as good as Ashlyn and that's saying something since I'm pretty sure she's on Emeril's level."

"Her food truck is a gem. You lucked out with her, man. I'm proud of you for not blowing it so far."

Scott's chuckle traveled over the phone. "She says she's stuck with me now that we have Grant but, deep inside, she's mad for me. I'm not buying her tough love for a second."

"You two are damn near perfect for each other." Reflecting, he digested the words that ran through his head. *Kind of like me and Teresa...*

He didn't say the words out loud, for they indicated a level of commitment Mark wasn't even ready to contemplate. Still, they rang true. He and Teresa had such an easy, fun connection and he hoped it didn't change once they began cohabitating.

"You still there?"

"Yeah," Mark said, standing and setting the phone down so he could spread the comforter over the bed. "Just need to get back to prepping the house for her arrival."

"I'll let you go. Just wanted to get it out in the open that she's my therapist. I'm not currently seeing her but would never rule out seeing her again in the future. I assume you're going to bring her to the first barbeque of the season we're having in April."

Mark pursed his lips, pondering. "I'd like to bring her but I'm not sure what she does on the weekends. Maybe she has some epic social life I'm not aware of. But I'll invite her if that's cool with you and Ashlyn."

"Definitely. I'd love to hang with her outside of the office as long as she doesn't think that crosses any boundaries. Maybe you can ask her. I don't mind you telling her we spoke about this."

"Okay, I'll discuss it with her and get back to you. Hopefully, we'll have warm weather in April. I always love the first cookout of the season."

"And the first cookout where Carrie and Peter are married. Finally. I've never seen two people who were destined to be together fight it so hard."

"I'm so happy for them," Mark said, smiling as he straightened the fabric. "And the boys are elated."

"They are. Ashlyn has them on this chase to dig up treasure and letters that Sally Pickens supposedly buried around the house. We love having them over. Ashlyn says Grandma Jean swore the stories were true but, so far, no luck."

"Those kids have limitless energy for that kind of stuff so I'm sure they'll find it if it exists. Okay, man, let me hop off here. I'll talk to

Teresa and let you know. Thanks for calling and getting this out in the open."

"Sure. I hope you beat the asshole who did this to you, Mark. Whatever I can do to help, please let me know. We've all got your back."

"Thanks, Scott. I'm determined to win. Talk to you soon."

Straightening, Mark observed the freshly made bed and surrounding room. It was sparse, with minimal furniture, but clean and tidy. Hoping Teresa would be satisfied with the closet and drawer space, he flipped off the light and headed downstairs to arrange the charcuterie he'd purchased at the grocery store earlier that morning.

As he arranged the meat and cheeses, he noticed the nerves that tightened his chest. Teresa was giving up so much to save his campaign and he was honored at her willingness to help. Determined to repay her in tiny gestures of gratitude, he finished prepping and opened the very expensive bottle of cabernet he'd procured on the way home.

Pouring it into the decanter, he waited, soaking up the silence. It would be the last time he was alone in his home for several months. In the past, the notion had always seemed daunting. Mark craved his space and independence, and had always rather loathed the idea of giving it up to cohabitate with someone else. But Teresa was so chill, and they got along so effortlessly, he wondered if it would be a chore. Noting there was only one way to find out, he glanced at his phone, realizing she'd arrive within the hour.

When the doorbell chimed, he swung open the door with a rapt sense of anticipation he hadn't felt in...well, he couldn't quite remember *ever* feeling the tiny pricks of excitement that raced through his veins. Smiling at her as she held two suitcases in her hands, his heart skipped when she beamed at him.

"I hear you've got an opening for a shameless hussy who frequents hook-up apps."

Throwing back his head, he laughed and ushered her in. "Only if they're extremely beautiful and exceedingly smarter than me. Looks like you fit the bill."

"Thank you," she said softly, eyes sparkling as she stepped inside and lifted the suitcases. "Should I just put these here? They're a bit heavy."

"Oh, sorry," he said, taking them from her. "Let me set them upstairs in the guest bedroom and we'll head into the kitchen. I prepared some charcuterie and wine to welcome you."

"How fancy," she said, arching a brow.

Chuckling, he pivoted to head up the stairs. "Be back in a sec."

Once the bags were deposited in the guest room, he charged back downstairs and extended his hand. "I'll give you the tour later but, for now, let's sit and chat."

She slid her palm over his, the skin so soft against his. "Lead me to the wine, sir," she said, winking.

Tugging her toward the kitchen, he gestured for her to sit on one of the island stools. Sliding over the stool across from her, he settled into the conversation as they discussed logistics over the next few months.

"I'm liquifying one of my investment accounts tomorrow," he said, taking a bite of the goat cheese before sipping the wine. "I plan to pay your debtors directly so you don't have to accept a deposit and pay taxes on it. I'm going to meet with my friend Peter tomorrow, who's a very savvy accountant, and he'll help us."

"That's perfect," she said, running her finger along the base of her wine glass. "I can't believe I'll be debt-free by the end of the week."

"If all goes well," he said with a nod. "And Evan has set our press conference for nine-thirty on Tuesday morning. I figured that would work for you since you mentioned your office hours start at eleven on Tuesdays."

"Good memory," she said, throat bobbing as she sipped the wine. "Are you one of the few men on the planet who actually listen when a woman speaks?"

Arching a brow, he shrugged. "Not quite sure since I've rarely been around one woman long enough to test it out. Guess you'll be my first subject."

"Well, I'm excited to analyze the results."

The words, said in her raspy, sexy voice, did all sorts of things to his insides. Feeling himself harden, he strove to keep his desire in check. She'd been here for barely an hour and his system was already going haywire. Was it already a foregone conclusion they would eventually resume their sexual relationship?

Searching deep within, he realized he vehemently wanted that to happen. It was futile to deny it and an extreme waste of time. Still, he didn't want them to be involved in anything remotely sexual until he paid off her debts. Something about that didn't sit well with him and he wanted the gesture to be free from any sort of sexual entanglement.

Accepting the excuse to deny his attraction—for a few weeks at least—he settled into their discussion, thoroughly enjoying it as always. After a while, he gave her a tour of the townhome, showing her how to work the TV in the living room and telling her she could use the desk in the home office that sat near the front door.

"I want you to feel at home here, Teresa," he said, gesturing around the office. "Please don't feel like you have to ask me before you make any decisions. My home is your home now."

"That's a lovely sentiment," she said, gazing around the room. "The home office is a bonus and I'll certainly use it. Does the whole 'make myself at home' statement extend to the DVR?" she asked, making quotation marks with her fingers.

"Oh, shit." His features contorted into a mock grimace. "Are you going to DVR The Bachelorette?"

"And Real Housewives, buddy," she said, poking him in the chest. "It's a fair amount of reciprocal torture for the upheaval in my life."

"Fair enough," he said, showing her his palms. "DVR whatever you want. If I'm feeling adventurous, I might even watch some of it with you." Waving his hand, he gestured toward the stairs. "Let me show you your room."

"I think you might secretly enjoy The Bachelorette more than you let on," she said, trailing up the stairs behind him. "Don't worry, your secret is safe with me."

"God forbid," he murmured, leading her into the guest bedroom. "The sheets are fresh and the drawers are empty. The closet's pretty big and you have your own separate bathroom right next door. My room has an adjoining bathroom so you'll have your privacy."

"Thank you," she said, glancing around the room. "I like the deep blue."

"Thanks. It seemed like the perfect color when I bought the place."

"Well, I guess I should start unpacking. Unless you wanted to show me something else?"

"Nope, we're good. Take your time and feel free to change into sweats. I put on jeans and a button-down to welcome you, but I like being comfortable and am about to throw on a t-shirt and sweatpants for the rest of the day."

"You're speaking my language," she said, grinning. "Comfy is my jam when I'm at home."

The thought of seeing her luscious curves in comfortable clothing sent a jolt of desire down his spine. Something about the image was lascivious, as if he was the only one who might get a glimpse of the relaxed Teresa she rarely showed to the outside world. It made him feel...special in a way...and maybe a bit creepy, so he decided to let her have her privacy. Backing toward the door, he stood in the frame as she bent over to lift the suitcase on the bed, her gorgeous ass filling out every crevice of her tight jeans.

"I'm making chicken marsala with green beans and sweet potatoes for dinner. Would love for you to join me if you're hungry."

"Oh, my," she said, straightening and waggling her brows. "He cooks too?"

"I love cooking but usually only have time to do it on the weekends," he said, pleased at her excitement. "My mom is an excellent cook and taught my sister and me from when we were young. I usually make enough to have leftovers for a few days and when they run out, I pick up Italian or sushi until I can make something again. Anyway, you're always welcome to join me anytime I make dinner."

"Well, this deal just got a whole lot sweeter. I'll certainly be taking you up on that."

"Can't wait," he said, winking. "See you later, hon. Just holler if you need anything."

Closing the door, he headed downstairs to wrap up what was left of the charcuterie and do a bit of prep for dinner. Smiling at the thought of her settling in upstairs, Mark felt content. Even with the onslaught of negativity that was sure to appear in the press next week, something about having Teresa under his roof made him feel calm and steady.

He realized it was her demeanor, so trusting and open, and her willingness to navigate through the situation without anger or fear. Grateful for her, he thought of the other women he'd dated or met on Pure—ones who could've been outed like this in similar situations. Not one of them would've handled it with the grace Teresa had exhibited so far.

Thanking his lucky stars, he rummaged around in the fridge, determined to make her one hell of a dinner. That, at least, was within his control and he looked forward to the evening with rapt anticipation.

Chapter 8

Mark rolled into Monday relieved he had a plan to move forward. He rose early and made a full pot of coffee, leaving some for Teresa when she woke. Since he left before dawn, he jotted a quick note and left it beside the coffee pot.

Headed out early. Text me if you hate the creamers in the fridge and I'll pick up something different on the way home tonight. Please eat the leftovers since I'll be home late. Have a good day. – M

Rushing through the door, he hopped in the car and grabbed a bagel at the deli before arriving at his office. He'd chosen to set up a solo office in Ardor Creek, along with the room in the satellite office he rented in Scranton. The rented room allowed him to be near the courthouse without having the overhead of a full-fledged office. Mark had lived in Ardor Creek his entire life and planned on keeping his headquarters there even if he won the election. The commute to Scranton was only thirty minutes, which he didn't mind since it allowed him to catch up on Howard Stern on Sirius.

Striding into his office, he sat at his desk and scarfed the bagel while he sifted through emails. Afterward, he pulled up the documents he needed for his meeting with Peter and complied them before stepping outside to make the two-block walk to Grillo Design and Construction.

The bell rang above as Mark entered Scott's office and he was met with a beaming Carrie Stratford.

"Well, hello, Mr. Lancaster. I assume you're here for the appointment with my husband? Although I'm a bit hesitant to let you near him. Perhaps you'll pass on salacious pointers about these hook-up apps I've suddenly become familiar with. Do I need to be worried?"

"Hilarious," he said, rolling his eyes at her teasing. Leaning his forearms on the counter, he grinned down at her as she sat behind the large computer monitor. "I don't think you have anything to worry about. Peter's not looking at any woman but you. In fact, I think he mentioned you two are into some pretty kinky costume fetish roleplay?" He rubbed his chin.

"Shhh!" she scolded, slicing her hand over the keyboard. "He wasn't supposed to tell anyone that. Good grief. Now I'm wondering who else knows..." her voice trailed off as she squinted at the ceiling.

"Sweetie, it's Ardor Creek. You can probably count on one hand the people who *don't* know at this point."

"Uggh," she said, resting her head in her hand. "Why do I love this town so much?"

"We all love it, whether we admit it or not."

"So true," she said wistfully. "And now Peter seems to love it too. It's a damn miracle. Anyway, he's not in yet but should be here any minute. He had to swing by Edna's house to have her sign a few places she forgot on her tax returns. You can go sit in his office if you like." She gestured down the hallway. "And if you need to use his desktop to pull up anything, the password is CareBear1234."

Laughing, he nodded. "I'll do that. The password's adorable, by the way."

"I know," she sighed, biting her lip. "I think I have to keep him at this point. I kind of love him."

"I think you always have," he whispered loudly, lifting his hand to his face to mimic telling her a secret. Pushing open the divider, he headed down the hallway. "Thanks, Carrie."

"Sure thing," she called before her fingers resumed flying over the keyboard. "And don't think I'm letting you off the hook about the mysterious and gorgeous psychologist and the fake engagement. Ashlyn told me everything you told Scott. I'll be grilling you soon. Ta ta!"

"Fantastic," Mark muttered, realizing his friends were going to tease him mercilessly. Resigned to that inevitable fate, he sat at Peter's desktop and pulled up the account information on the investment fund he was going to liquidate to pay off Teresa's loans.

"Hey, bud," Peter said, rounding the corner. "Sorry, I'm late. Edna Schultz forgot a ton of signatures."

"No problem," Mark said, standing and giving Peter the seat before rounding the desk and sitting across from him. "I made hard copies here," he pulled out a manilla folder, "and pulled up the account on your computer."

"Sweet," Peter said, moving the mouse around. "Let me study this for a sec."

An hour later, Mark was set with the logistics and felt comfortable with the decision he'd made. Since he was selling stock, there would be minimal taxes owed and the money could be liquidated quickly.

"I told Teresa it would be liquidated by the end of this week," he said to Peter.

"I'd give it three weeks in total for the entire liquidation, mailing the checks and the banks satisfying the loans. She'll be debt-free by mid-April at the latest."

"Awesome. Thanks for helping me with this, man."

"Sure," Peter said, sitting back and lacing his hands behind his head. "You're really going out of your way for her. Interesting."

"You've got that turned around, my friend. She's upended her entire life to save my campaign. And, remember, the payoff is actually a loan. She's going to pay me back with consultations for my clients although I wish she'd just let me pay her debt off scot-free. But she was adamant and I don't want to create some sort of weird imbalance."

Peter squinted, studying him as the corner of his lips curved. "You like this broad."

"I'm not sure that's an appropriate term but, yes, I like this *woman*. She's an amazing person who has handled this better than I probably deserve. She wants me to win and thinks I'll be a better D.A. than Chisolm."

"Damn straight. What an ass. Want to toilet paper his house like we did Lester's in seventh grade when he tried to steal Scott's turtle?"

"Uh, I'm good, but thanks." Rising, he gathered his papers. "I'll update Teresa on the timeframe and appreciate you helping me with this, Peter."

"Sure. When can I meet her? Want to double date? Karaoke night maybe?"

"Look, man, this thing with her isn't a relationship. It's strictly to save my campaign. She's as busy as I am and, from what she's told me along the way, she's about as interested in dating as I am. I appreciate the sentiment but I'm going to be crashing during the few scant hours I get away from work and the campaign."

Peter's grin deepened, furthering his frustration.

"Dude, it's not like that. Stop making it weird."

"Sorry, man, but there's no way in hell you're going to convince me you have no interest in the woman living in your house, who you've mentioned is amazing about a hundred times over the past hour. I'm not buying it."

"Interest, maybe. Acting on that interest?" he asked, lifting a finger. "Not right now. I've fucked up enough shit in my life. I need to let that settle before I even contemplate anything else."

"And after it's settled?" Peter asked, arching a brow.

"Maybe," Mark said, trailing to the door and pulling it open. "A soft maybe. There's a lot to think about if we go down that path again. On that note, I'm leaving before you grill me on anything else. See you later." Giving a salute, Mark exited the office, waving to Carrie as she smiled at him while speaking into the headset.

After a solid workday with several calls from Evan updating him on Tuesday's press conference details, he lifted his phone to respond to the text Teresa sent him that morning.

Teresa: Thanks for the coffee. The cream was perfect. I love hazelnut and French vanilla.

Mark: Sorry it took me so long to respond. Busy day. If you need me to grab anything on the way home from dinner with my parents tonight just text me.

He grinned at her cheeky answer.

Teresa: Perhaps a new reputation? Kidding. I hope I can joke with you about this. I think it will keep me sane.

Mark: Always. The key I gave you worked fine in the deadbolt this morning, right? Sometimes it sticks.

Teresa: Worked like a charm. If I crash tonight, I'll probably lock the deadbolt too. Is that okay?

Mark: Definitely. Want you to feel safe. And please eat the leftovers. I'll go to the grocery store later this week.

She sent a "yum smiley face" emoji.

Teresa: You've ruined me for the next guy I have a scandalous affair with. I'm sure he won't have your cooking skills.

Chuckling, he shook his head.

Mark: One small thing I can do to repay you. I'll update you on the payoff timeframe tomorrow morning. A few weeks longer than I thought but not too bad.

Teresa: I'm grateful regardless. Also, I expect some consultations to come my way soon. This is a loan, mister. I want to pay it off in an honest fashion.

Mark: Got it. I'll have something for you soon, I'm sure. See you tomorrow.

Teresa: See ya.

Sighing, Mark delved into the rest of his paperwork while mentally prepping to confront his parents' concerns about the fake engagement he'd entered into.

Chapter 9

That evening, Mark stepped into his parents' home on the outskirts of Ardor Creek, inhaling the fantastic smell that wafted from the kitchen.

"Hey, son," his dad said, foot elevated in a cast on the stool in front of him as he lounged on the couch. "You're late."

"Five minutes," he muttered, leaning down to kiss his brown hair. "And I'm sure Mom already told you my life is imploding. You're lucky I didn't have to cancel."

"Seems like you might have an ulterior motive," his dad said, eyes sparkling as he grinned. "Mom said you're going to take your grandma's ring."

"Yep," Mark said, straightening and glancing at his ankle. "How's the recovery from the ankle surgery? Your color's good."

"It's fine," he said, waving his hand. "I just hate being immobile. Mom's been a good nurse. I'm sure she's going to finagle another cruise out of this once I heal."

Chuckling, Mark nodded. "I'd expect nothing less. I'm going to go check on her. Do you need anything?"

"I'm good. She's cooking lasagna."

"Yum."

Striding into the kitchen, he found his mom leaning over the stove, basting bread with melted butter. "Hey," he said, leaning down and kissing her soft white hair. "Dad seems to be recovering well."

"He's ornery as a hornet but I'm happy he feels okay."

"Brenda!" a voice called from the living room. "Can I have more iced tea?"

Mark grinned and showed his palms. "I swear, I checked to see if he needed anything."

"He's getting a kick out of having me wait on him," she said, rolling her eyes before setting down the butter and rummaging in the fridge for the tea. Pouring a glass, she handed it to Mark. "Be a good boy and take this to him."

"Brenda!"

"For god's sake, Joseph! Your son is bringing you the tea. Relax."

"Ah, married bliss," Mark teased, saluting her with the glass. "So exciting."

"You need to hush, young man," she said, swatting him with the towel. "I'm still not sure I'm going to give you mother's ring for this *fake* engagement. The poor dear might roll over in her grave."

"Okay, let's squash the dramatics," he murmured, taking the tea to his dad before returning to the kitchen. "If you're not open to it, I can buy a ring. I just thought it would be a nice touch to let Teresa wear it."

"Well, I'd like to meet this Teresa," Brenda said, donning oven mitts before sliding the garlic bread on the top rack. "Why didn't you bring her tonight?"

"I told you, Mom, this is an engagement in name only. I don't have any autonomy over her time or schedule. She values her independence and alone time as much as I do."

"Well, I'm sure she has to eat. I want you to invite her next time you come over for dinner."

"Okay," he said, unable to control his smile. "I can't guarantee she'll come but I will. On that note, I'm assuming Justine isn't coming?"

Sighing, Brenda sat on one of the island stools and shook her head. "Dean is working late and she wants to have dinner ready when he gets home."

Sliding onto the other stool, Mark rubbed her upper arm. "I'm pretty sure Dean isn't working. Terry told me he's been spotted around town with Olivia on more than one occasion recently. Justine needs to leave him."

"It's so hard when you have kids," Brenda said, cupping his cheek. "You'll understand when you have your own babies one day. Justine stays with him because she loves him and because of Avery."

"I'm pretty sure he's rough with them, Mom. Last month when I had Sunday lunch with them, Justine had a huge bruise on her forearm. She said she walked into the stairwell but I see this all the time with my domestic abuse clients. I'm pretty sure Dean caused that. What if he hurts Avery? How far are we going to let this go?"

"It's her life, son. Of course, my heart breaks for her, but she's going to have to find the will to leave him on her own."

Mark shook his head. "I'm going to talk to her again. I'm having lunch with them on Sunday. Dean is never there on the weekends anyway. Says he's golfing but I have my doubts."

"You're sweet to check on your sister," Brenda said, patting his face before standing to check the oven. "Dinner's almost ready. Can you help your dad to the table?"

Grimacing, Mark stood. "Isn't it easier to let him eat in the living room?"

"Not for dinner when our son is visiting. Go help him and I'll consider giving you the ring without nagging."

"Done." Striding to the living room, Mark helped Joseph amble his ankle over the tiny scooter and supported his shoulders as they shuffled to the kitchen. Dinner was heavenly and Mark made sure to call dibs on the leftovers.

"Make sure you wash these by hand and not in the dishwasher," Brenda said a few hours later as she packed the plastic containers full of food in a bag. "You melted the last ones I lent you."

"Yes, ma'am," he said, leaning on the island. "And I think there's something you still need to give me."

Scrunching her features, she sighed. "Be right back."

After a moment, she padded back into the kitchen, holding a ring box. Mark reached for it and she drew it back. "Your grandmother passed this ring onto me to give to my son for his future wife. I don't like the idea of you using it for nefarious purposes."

"Mom," he said, sliding his hand over the juncture between her neck and shoulder. "If you don't want me to take it, I won't. But this fake engagement is going to help cement my position as D.A. I'm going to be able to help so many people who aren't served by the current jerk in office. What's nefarious about that?"

"Nothing, I guess," she sighed, handing him the box.

Grasping it, he stuck it into his jacket pocket. "Thank you," he said, kissing her on the forehead.

"I'm taking it back if you don't bring her to dinner next time, young man. Do you hear me?"

"Yes, Mom. I think you'll really like her. She's a good person and doesn't deserve the treatment she's getting in the press."

"Go solidify your fake engagement, then," she said, swiping her hands over his jacket to straighten it. "And let me know once you've checked on Justine and Avery. I worry about my girls. She and I haven't always had the easiest relationship, but I love your sister, Mark."

"She knows. Love you, Mom."

With one last peck, Mark headed home, leftovers and engagement ring in tow. After placing the food in the fridge, he headed upstairs noting Teresa's closed door and the late hour. Tomorrow morning, they would announce their engagement to the world. Craving sleep, Mark prepped for bed and passed out as soon as he hit the sheets.

Chapter 10

♥

Teresa awoke Tuesday morning nervous but resolved. Several news alerts had appeared on her phone overnight, and she read them before slamming the device on the bedside table. Rubbing her eyes, she hoped today would be the day she set things right.

As she showered, she laughed at the absurdity of the stories. One stated that she used the hook-up apps to find unlucky-in-love men and cultivate them into therapy clients.

"So fucking absurd," she muttered, stepping from the shower and wrapping the towel around her wet hair. "Although several of the men I met over the years could've used some therapy." Nodding at her reflection, she wondered if Mark could hear her talking to herself in the bathroom. Wiping the condensation off the mirror, she began applying her makeup, determined to look like a million bucks for the press conference.

Once back in her room, she pulled out her nicest skirt-suit, black and fitted, and donned a silky purple blouse underneath. Black pumps completed the ensemble and she gave herself one last glance in the long mirror against the bedroom far wall.

"Not bad, Dr. Roe," she said, sliding her hands over her hips. "Screw 'em."

Teresa had always possessed confidence in her abilities and her appearance, but she certainly didn't love the spotlight. Unfortunately, if she wanted to save her career and reputation, she had little choice. Embracing her inner fortitude, she headed downstairs.

"Hey," Mark said, smiling as he poured coffee into a mug. "Want some coffee?"

"Sure," she said, sitting at the small table in the corner. He poured her a cup and trailed over with both mugs in hand.

"I added hazelnut," he said, setting it in front of her.

"Perfect." Sipping, she noticed his cheeky grin. "You're awfully chipper for seven in the morning."

"I'm ready to get this campaign back on track. Evan is waiting at the diner and we'll do the press conference inside Ardor Creek Town Hall. Chad's staff will take care of the sound equipment, podium, and all that jazz."

"Awesome. I'm ready to get it over with."

"Me too." He sipped the coffee. "So, I have something I want to give you to make this more official."

"Okay," she said, arching a brow.

Pulling a box from his pocket, he opened it to reveal a silver ring with three small diamonds nestled together on top. "It's an engagement ring."

"I can see that," she said, frozen as she stared.

"Actually, it was my grandmother's engagement ring. She left it to me and wanted me to give it to the woman I eventually proposed to one day."

Teresa drank the coffee as tiny tingles of anxiety buzzed over her skin. "And you want me to wear it?"

"I, uh..." Rubbing his forehead with his fingers, he nodded. "Yeah, I thought it would make it more official or something. My mom told me it might be too sentimental for what we're, uh, well, what's going on here, but I plowed ahead like I always do." Giving a sheepish grin, he shrugged. "Guess I should've listened to her."

Teresa's eyes darted between his as she struggled with what to say. "It's a lovely gesture...I...it's just so...."

"Real," he said, closing the box. "Maybe it's too real. Yikes. I've never really been a sentimental person so I don't get the gravity of these things. I didn't mean to make you feel uncomfortable. I can buy a different ring that's for show."

"Wait," she said, extending her hand and sliding it over the box. "Let me see it." He handed it over and she flipped open the lid, admiring the band. "It's really beautiful, Mark. I just..." Latching onto his gaze, her eyebrows drew together. "Don't you want to wait and give this to the woman you *actually* propose to?"

His features drew together as he pondered. "I've always imagined getting married and having kids one day, but it seemed so far away. I guess I didn't realize that whoever was on the other end of that vision might want to be the only one who wears this ring."

"Yeah," she said, closing the box and handing it back to him. "If it were me, I'd like to be the only one, for sure." Winking, she tried to lighten the mood. "Although it's a really sweet gesture."

"Thanks," he said, stuffing it back in his pocket. "Sorry if I made it weird. I do want you to have a ring, though. I think it will help solidify the story."

"I have a pretty emerald ring my parents gave me years ago. I'll stop by my apartment and get it on the way to the diner. It could easily pass as an engagement ring."

"Perfect," he said, seeming relieved. "Just a note that I'm probably going to make several more mistakes like that. I'm kind of dense with romance. Probably why I eventually gave up on having a relationship. I just never really got it."

"What's to get?" she asked, smiling over her cup. "You're not so bad. You're honest and sweet and pretty darn handsome. It's a good start."

"Well, thank you. And that opens the door for me to tell you how amazing you look today. You're going to knock their socks off."

"Thanks," she said, fluffing her hair. "I had to make it believable you'd fall for this older woman."

"Forty-five is barely older."

Teresa bit her lip. "I'm actually forty-six. I'll be forty-seven in August. I fibbed just a tiny bit on the app." She held her thumb and forefinger an inch apart.

"Wow, I never would've guessed. Doesn't matter to me. I think you're gorgeous."

Teresa's heart slammed in her chest. "Thank you," she whispered.

"Since we're driving separately, I'm going to go ahead and meet Evan and let him know you'll be a little late since you're picking up the ring."

"Sounds good," she said, rising and placing the cup in the sink. "I also think we should sit down and discuss the appearances and events Evan wants me to attend. I'm a planner and need to keep things organized in my calendar."

"We can discuss tonight if you like. Mom made lasagna and garlic bread and I brought home a ton of leftovers."

"Yum. Sounds like heaven after a long day of fighting the press. Let's do it. I should be home by seven."

They headed upstairs to finish prepping for the day before sliding on their jackets in the foyer. Mark locked the door behind them before they walked to their cars. A man stood at the end of the driveway, taking pictures before he called, "Mr. Lancaster! Dr. Roe! Are you continuing your illicit affair after the allegations of Dr. Roe's sexual practices with her therapy clients?"

Mark dropped his briefcase, his hands forming fists before Teresa grabbed his forearm.

"It's not worth it, Mark," she said, gently tugging him toward the cars. "We'll set everything straight at the press conference."

"Are you the P.I?" Mark yelled. "I know your name, Robinson. If I see you on my property again, I'll file a complaint and ensure you lose your license indefinitely."

The man stepped off the driveway and onto the street. "You can't file a complaint if I'm on a public road, Mr. Lancaster."

"Watch me, asshole!" he spat, gesturing with his finger. "I'll call the cops so fast your head will spin. Do yourself a favor and get a new boss. Chisolm is going down and I'm going to prosecute him for every shady business deal he's been involved with over the past eight years!"

"Mark," Teresa said, drawing him between their cars. "If he gets video of you screaming, it's not a good look."

Groaning in frustration, he shook his head. "I know. Damn it. It's just so infuriating."

"Hey," she said, unable to resist swiping away the strand of hair that had fallen over his forehead. "We're tougher than anything these assholes throw at us."

He cupped her jaw, causing her to shiver. "I know but I still want to defend you."

"That's sweet but not needed. Let's give him a different show instead. He can be the first one to learn about our engagement." She waggled her eyebrows.

"How so?"

"Um, I think you should kiss me so he can photograph it."

Palming her other cheek, he tilted her face. "Yeah?"

"Yeah," she said, nodding.

Those gorgeous eyes stared into her soul before he lowered his mouth, cementing his lips to hers. Only days ago, she'd thought the opportunity to kiss him might be gone forever and she relished in the feel of his firm lips against hers once again. Extending her tongue, she pushed against his lips, breathing a soft moan when he opened them.

Surging inside, her tongue found his...sliding...battling in a war where they both were victorious. Dropping her bag to the ground, she encircled his neck, drawing him close as their bodies aligned. The hard ridge of his erection jutted into her abdomen, causing her body to flush as slick moisture coated her core.

His deep groan vibrated through every pore as she trembled in his arms, knowing the kiss was supposed to be for show but enjoying it too damn much to care. The strokes of his tongue turned to nibbles as he took delicious nips of her bottom lip.

"I missed kissing you," he murmured against her mouth.

"Me too. So damn much."

"Do you think he got the shot?" he teased, arching a brow as he gestured with his head toward the man who was overtly photographing them.

"Uh, yeah, I think he got it."

Uttering a soft laugh, Mark rested his forehead against hers. "Maybe we should also discuss this kissing thing tonight over lasagna. I really like it."

Teresa's eyes searched his. "We said sex is off the table for the first few weeks."

"Kissing isn't sex. We can pretend it's for the cause."

She damn near giggled. "I'm not sure you're that great of an actor."

Drawing back, his features condensed into mock mortification. "You've wounded this former high school drama player terribly. I played Tree Number Eight in the production of A Midsummer Night's Dream and killed it."

Throwing back her head, Teresa devolved into laughter. "Oh, no. Sorry to squash your dreams there, Denzel. Okay, you can pretend. I might enjoy having you kiss me every once in a while."

"Me too," he said, placing a sweet peck on her lips. Bending down, he grabbed her bag and placed it over her shoulder. "See you at the diner, hon."

"See you there." Turning, she slid behind the wheel of her black sedan and backed out of the driveway, perhaps a tad aggressively so the asinine P.I. knew she'd hit him if he didn't move. Glancing in her rearview mirror, she saw him get into his car and begin to follow her.

"Jerk," she said, annoyed. He followed her to her apartment, parking on the street while she ran in and grabbed the ring. Once back in her car, she flipped him the bird after backing out of her parking spot. Still, his tenaciousness proved Evan was right about her needing to move in with Mark. If she continued to live in a separate apartment, people might have trouble believing their hook-up sessions had turned to true love. Sighing, she lamented on how cynical the world had become.

Pulling up to the diner, she found a spot and applied lipstick in the mirror. It had been smeared in the spontaneous make-out session with Mark. Closing her eyes, she remembered the kiss for one poignant moment before reminding herself she had an important day ahead and it was fruitless to be stuck in the clouds. Grabbing her bag, she exited the car and entered the diner.

Chapter 11

♥

Teresa liked Evan immediately and felt they were in good hands with his advice and direction. He seemed to genuinely care about Mark but had a firm practicality that would serve him well as the campaign progressed. They spent some time discussing the next few months, the appearances Teresa would make, and her overall duties as Mark's fiancée.

"All in all, I think it will have a minimal impact on your life," Evan said, sitting back in the booth and studying her. "Mark and I are extremely grateful you agreed to do this."

"Chisolm seems like a Grade-A jerk from everything I've read and now he's personally attacking me. I want to see him go down in flames. I'm committed to getting Mark elected."

"Fantastic," Evan said, beaming. "I hope once things calm down you'll accept my invitation to come to dinner at our home. My wife, Jocelyn, loves to entertain and she's always up for a glass of red wine."

"I might have told him you love a good red," Mark said, grinning.

"I'd love to, Evan. Thank you."

Once they'd discussed everything at length, they headed to Town Hall where Mayor Chad Hanson was waiting to greet them.

"Hey, buddy," he said, shaking Mark's hand. "I guess I was wrong when I pegged you as the most drama-free of our friend group. Yikes."

"I'm not sure I even remember what drama-free is anymore," was Mark's acerbic reply. "Chad, this is Dr. Teresa Roe, the woman who's saving my campaign."

"Hi, Dr. Roe," Chad said, extending his hand. "It's a pleasure to meet you. All of us are really interested in this little situation Mark's gotten himself into."

Laughing, she shook his hand. "Teresa is fine, Chad, and I'm not quite sure what you mean, but I'm guessing it involves some sort of humorous and deprecating torture for Mark."

"You bet your ass it does—"

"Okay," Mark interrupted, stepping closer. "Can you at least let me finish the press conference before you start ribbing me?"

"Sure, man. There's plenty of time to gang up on you when I'm with Scott and Peter. Come on," he said, waving his hand, "let me show you the setup."

They walked through the large foyer to the press area and Teresa noted the podium with the plethora of microphones. Clenching her hands together, she felt the nerves settle in.

"Hey," Mark said, leaning down so his lips barely brushed the shell of her ear. Sliding his palm over hers, he laced their fingers. "You're going to do fine. As we discussed with Evan, I'll do most of the talking. If they ask you a question and you don't want to answer, just nod to me and we'll move on to the next reporter."

"Okay," she said, squeezing his hand. "I didn't think I'd get so nervous."

His lips formed a compassionate smile. "I'm so sorry you have to go through this. I wish—"

"It's okay," she whispered, covering his lips with her fingers. "Like I said, I'm tough. Let's just get it over with."

He nodded against her fingers before Evan called his name. Retreating to check on the equipment, Teresa observed his broad back as she took several deep breaths, attempting to reign in the nerves.

Eventually, the reporters filtered in, forming a circle around the podium as several of them set up cameras on tripods. Others held microphones in their hands as they furiously scribbled notes on the pads they held. With one last nod to Mark, Evan stepped to the podium and cleared his throat.

"Good morning. I'm Evan Gold, Campaign Manager for Mark Lancaster. As many of you have reported, Mr. Lancaster filed the necessary paperwork to run for Lackawanna County District Attorney last week. Almost immediately after, he experienced an invasion of privacy that was unwarranted and extremely unfair. Since Mr. Lancaster's private life is being detailed in the press, he wanted to set the record straight. I'll now turn the podium over to him and he will take a few brief questions afterward."

Evan stepped back and Mark took his spot at the podium, grasping the sides as he gazed upon the crowd.

"Good morning. First of all, let me take this opportunity to formally announce my candidacy for District Attorney of Lackawanna County. Over the last eight years, we have been stuck with a D.A. whom I believe is evil and corrupt." A murmur filtered through the crowd of reporters. "You heard me correctly. James Chisolm is a stain on the office and the people of Lackawanna County deserve better. My goal is to win this election and institute a wave of reform that will enhance the lives of each and every person who lives in our county."

Bulbs flashed as he paused, assessing the crowd.

"More than his corruption, Chisolm is a petty, mean-spirited person who not only began a vicious wave of attacks against me as soon as I declared my candidacy, but he unleashed unwarranted attacks on someone who does not deserve them and isn't even a candidate in this race. However, she's someone I've chosen to spend the rest of my life with so Mr. Chisolm has decided that makes her a target."

Facing her, he extended his hand and Teresa took it, grasping for dear life as he drew her to stand by his side. "I would like you all to meet Dr. Teresa Roe. She is a psychologist who has served the Ardor Creek and Battle Falls areas for several years, positively impacting the lives of numerous people in our county. Not only does she practice private family therapy, but she is heavily involved in social work and community organizations. And, she has agreed to be my wife."

Murmurs buzzed around the room as Mark glanced down at her, giving a reassuring smile. "We met on an app, as most people do these days, and it's the best thing that's ever happened to me. Although I have no interest in discussing my private life with the press, I understand a certain amount of scrutiny comes with a public campaign so I would like to give you all the opportunity to meet Teresa and let her speak a bit about her practice. Once we wrap up this press conference, I'm sure you'll see we're like any other engaged couple in their forties, just trying to have a relationship in this sometimes lonely world."

Turning to her, he gestured to the microphones. "Teresa, the spotlight is yours."

Stepping forward, she cleared her throat and tapped one of the mics. "Hello? Is this thing on?"

Laughter emanated through the crowd.

"Thank you, Mark, for that kind introduction. Now that you all know who I am, and how Mark and I met, I'd like to take this opportunity to assure you I'm actually quite boring. The stories you fabricated about me and my practice were entertaining," she said, holding up a finger, "I'll give you that. But the only truth to them was that he and I did meet on an app. As a therapist, I can tell you this is by no means scandalous in this day and age, and I assume it won't further any of your journalistic careers."

Several of the reporters smirked at the cheeky comment.

"Now that we've announced our engagement, I hope this will all die down and you'll leave us to carry on in peace. Before I leave you, I do want to address something that's been heavily discussed in the media over the past few days."

Clenching her hands on the sides of the podium, she straightened her spine. "Many of you have written stories discussing whether I use sex therapy in my practice. I don't, but I would like to take this opportunity to validate the therapists who do and the wonderful benefits of that type of therapy. Many people use sex therapy to break down negative programming from previous sexual abuse, PTSD, physical disabilities and so much more."

Glancing over the crowd, she attempted to make brief eye contact with as many reporters as possible. "I'll assume those reporters who attempted to smear me—or any other therapists who do practice sex therapy—didn't know how ignorant they sounded or how much damage they could do. Now that you know, I hope you'll end the shameful practice of denigrating a legitimate form of therapy and all those who benefit from it. Slut-shaming has no place in a person's journey to heal themselves and anyone who employs it moving forward is a sensationalist rather than a journalist in my opinion." With a firm nod, she stepped back. "Mark? I think my damage here is done."

His gaze was reverent as he gave an almost imperceptible nod. "Well, folks, I think you can see why I fell head over heels. She's a straight shooter and a wonderful therapist. My public life is open game and I want you to keep me honest, but I hope you'll be respectful of my fiancée and let us retain our privacy. With that, I'll answer a few questions."

Teresa observed him handle the questions from the reporters with ease, showcasing his political skill. Something welled inside her chest as he answered with his deep, confident voice and she realized it was pride. She was exceedingly proud to be his fiancée...well, his *fake* fiancée. After their blazing kiss earlier that morning, she'd do well to remember that fact. Settling into her new role, her lips formed a smile as her fake future husband cemented the narrative of their burgeoning relationship.

Chapter 12

After the press conference, Teresa headed to her office, located off the highway in an office complex between Ardor Creek and Battle Falls. She'd rented the space for years and loved the homey office development. Each window had white painted shutters and a wooden fence surrounded the complex, which had five offices in total.

She met with several clients, a few of whom mentioned that morning's press conference. Teresa politely steered the focus back to them, thankful she'd retained their business. So far, she'd only lost three private clients from the debacle, each of whom had canceled their appointments later that week, and she figured it was for the best. She'd rather spend her time helping clients who trusted her and wanted her assistance.

That evening, she arrived at Mark's home, pleased there was no one at the end of the driveway waiting to take her picture. Perhaps the press conference had worked, after all. Noting Mark's car in the driveway, she found the door unlocked and headed inside.

"Hello?" she called, locking the deadbolt behind her. "You just leave your door unlocked?"

"Hey," he called, breezing down the hallway as he dried his hands with a dishtowel. "When you've lived in Ardor Creek all your life, you just trust people, I guess."

"Right. Well, this former Philly girl is someone who always locks the door, especially when a creepy dude was waiting to photograph us outside this morning."

"Noted," he said, giving a salute. "I already threw on sweats if you want to do the same. Lasagna should be ready in five minutes."

"Awesome. I'm starving." Heading upstairs, she donned her comfy sweatpants and t-shirt and headed toward the kitchen. "Man, it smells so good."

"Mom's lasagna is the best," he said, gesturing to the table with his head as he pulled the tray from the oven. "Poured you a glass of wine."

"Thanks." Lowering to sit at the table, she swallowed a hefty gulp. "Well, we survived today."

He carried over the tray, setting it on the hot pad, before bringing over garlic bread and his own glass of wine. Sitting across from her, he held up his glass. "To surviving."

Clinking, she took a sip before inhaling the luscious dish. "I'm already warning you, I'm going to have seconds."

Chuckling, he spooned out a portion and handed her the plate. "I'd be offended if you didn't."

They caught up on their day as they ate, Teresa once again marveling at how easy conversation was with her handsome dinner companion.

"So, there's something else I need to tell you. It's a bit weird so I've been waiting for the right time."

"Uh oh," she said, cutting the lasagna to have her second helping. "I'm not sure I can take any more bombs."

"I don't *think* this one will be so bad."

"Okay. Lay it on me."

"So, you've heard me mention my buddy, Scott. The one who built this place. Chad also mentioned him this morning."

"Mmm-hmm," she said, chewing.

"Well, it turns out, Scott was in therapy for a while."

Teresa's eyes grew wide. "Was he now?"

"Yep," Mark said, grinning. "He had a pretty great therapist."

Swallowing, Teresa squinted as she contemplated. "Someone is coming to mind but I can't say anything due to HIPAA rules."

"Right. Well, he said I could bring it up to you and gave permission for me to discuss it with you."

"If you proactively mention it, I'm not bound by HIPAA."

"I figured. It's Scott Grillo."

Teresa smiled. Scott was one of her favorite clients who'd come to her over the years after the loss of his wife and daughter, and subsequent newfound relationship with his current wife, Ashlyn. "I had a hunch."

"You did?"

"Yep," she said, taking another bite. "He's around your age and an Ardor Creek lifer. You all seem to stick together."

"He's a really good friend. The four of us—me, Scott, Chad, and Peter—are really close. Along with Carrie and, well, Ashlyn now."

"That's awesome. Lifelong friendships are so hard to cultivate. My dad was an engineer and moved to the states before I was born to join the US Army Corps of Engineers. That landed us in a few places but I went to high school in Philly. I'm still in touch with a few friends from there on social media, but it's hard to maintain the connections in our busy world."

"Definitely," he said, sitting back and rubbing his stomach as he sipped the wine. "We all somehow stayed in Ardor Creek. I was never enamored with city life for some reason, although I do love the occasional weekend getaway in New York."

"Me too. I'm a huge Broadway fan."

"Really? Musicals?"

"Yep. I've always loved them. I'm a terrible singer but in my dreams, I'm Mariah Carey."

Laughing, he nodded. "I'm terrible too but most of my friends have surprisingly good voices. We'll have to join them for karaoke at the pub one night. It's fun, especially after a few beers."

"Sounds like it. In the meantime, please tell Scott I'm thrilled he was open to discussing our professional connection. If he's okay to hang out socially, now that he's not seeing me anymore, I'd love to meet Ashlyn. She sounds like an amazing woman."

"She is and I might have just the opportunity for that."

"Okay," she said, lifting her brows.

"They're having a barbeque at their house the third Sunday in April. It's the first one of the season and barbeques are big deals for our group. We have a lot of them when the weather's warm. Sundays are better because Carrie and Peter's boys play sports on Saturdays."

"Sounds fun. I have Sunday brunch once a month with my female entrepreneurs' club, but I should be free the third Sunday in April. The club is supposed to be this fancy group of women who deliberate important topics, but we usually end up getting tipsy and discussing Real Housewives."

"Sounds exciting," he teased, rolling his eyes.

"Hey!" Wadding up her napkin, she threw it at his head. "It's extremely fun, thank you very much."

"I'll take your word for it." Standing, he cleared their plates before sitting down and distributing the rest of the bottle of wine evenly in their glasses.

"I have to work tomorrow," she murmured, lifting the glass to her lips.

"I won't tell if you won't." His sexy tone sent shivers down her spine, and she emitted a small hiccup. Realizing she was pleasantly tipsy, she snickered.

"You're adorable when you giggle like that," he said softly.

"Mark," she said gently, placing her chin in her hand as her elbow rested on the table. "We agreed not to involve sex in this extremely strange new situation we're navigating."

His eyes roved over her face as he studied her. "I know. Why did we decide to take it off the table? I forgot."

Breathing a laugh, she squinted. "I think you didn't want to pay off my loans while we were boning. It's very Edward and Vivian."

His eyebrows drew together. "Who?"

"Edward and Vivian? From Pretty Woman?" When he just stared at her with confusion, she took a huge gulp of wine. "Lord help me, he's truly a bachelor. The man has never seen Pretty Woman."

"I mean, I've heard of it," he said, a bit exasperated. "I just don't know the characters' names or the storyline by heart."

"She's a prostitute and he's a rich, handsome businessman who rents her for the week."

"And that's romantic?"

Giving a *pfft*, she waved her hand. "*Men*. You wouldn't get it unless you see it. But yes, it ends up being extremely romantic."

"Sounds kind of misogynistic and creepy to me, but whatever."

"Well, it was made in the '90s but the sentiment holds up. Anyway, you didn't want me to be your Vivian so that was one reason we took sex off the table."

"Until the loans are settled anyway," he said, arching a brow.

"Yes, but there's still the fact that we're living together now. It creates a completely different dynamic in our relationship. What we had was casual. It's very difficult to maintain a casual relationship when you live with someone."

"True," he said, tracing the table with his finger. "Although I did tell you I contemplated asking you to date me."

"And now we're fake engaged. What a leap."

Laughing, he nodded. "Seriously."

Gliding his hand across the table, he rested it against the surface, palm up. Butterflies flitted in her stomach as she slid her palm over his. Staring into her eyes, he rubbed the skin of her hand with his thumb.

"I agree with keeping sex off the table until the loans are paid off. It's less messy and will make us both feel more comfortable. After that, I'm open to exploring something, but it's completely up to you. I'll leave the ball in your court and you can come to me if and when you're ready."

"I might not want to chance it," she said softly.

"And I'm completely fine with that. It has to feel right for both of us, hon."

Mesmerized by the feel of his skin caressing hers, she played with her lip as she pondered. "I want to be honest with you here, Mark."

"I'd expect nothing less from you, Teresa."

Gently extricating her hand, she sat back and lifted the glass, swirling the remaining liquid. "Several years ago, I moved to this area to settle down. I was in my mid-thirties and was ready to hopefully find a husband and have kids. I thought leaving the city and slowing down a bit would recalibrate my life so I could begin a new chapter."

He listened intently as she continued.

"I dated a lot but no one ever clicked. As every year slipped by, I realized my chances of finding someone were diminishing. Eventually, I accepted finding a life partner to have kids with probably wasn't in the cards for me."

"I find it incredibly hard to believe that someone as amazing as you couldn't find a partner."

Her lips twitched. "That's sweet. I'll take some of the blame because I think I was too picky. I wanted it all: good looks, a sense of humor, a guy who would buy me ice cream after a bad day and rub my feet while I ate it."

Tapping his temple, he grinned. "Ice cream and foot massages. Got it."

Laughing, she shook her head. "That wasn't meant as a suggestion for *you*. I just wanted someone who got me, I guess. When it didn't happen, and my window to have a child was running out, I decided to do it on my own."

"That's an incredibly brave decision."

"Maybe," she said, shrugging. "Regardless, I was in my forties at this point and knew it wouldn't be easy. Each time the fertilized embryos didn't implant successfully, I experienced what I can only describe as a very intense, small mourning period. Then, I picked myself up and did it again until it was no longer viable."

She thought she saw the slight sheen of wetness in his eyes. "I'm so sorry," he said, his voice thick and raw. "I wish I could've been there for you. I can't imagine going through that alone."

"My family was really supportive and I do have a few close girlfriends, mostly from the entrepreneurs' group I was telling you about, and they were extremely supportive. But, in the end, I had to accept I'll never have a biological child. It was heartbreaking."

His expression was filled with such sorrow, she felt the urge to comfort him, causing her to smile. "I'm fine now, Mark, honestly. Thankfully, I'm a therapist and I know all sorts of fantastic grief and coping mechanisms. But I'm telling you this because I want you to understand I can't have kids."

His features drew together. "Okay…"

"I want to be up front about that because if we resume our sexual relationship while we live together, I can't guarantee I won't develop feelings for you, nor that you'll develop them for me. There would always be an extra layer of finality to our relationship if you wanted to eventually settle down with someone you could have biological children with."

Leaning on the table, he stared at his hands as his thumbs twirled together. "I understand."

"You've mentioned a few times you see yourself settling down, getting married, and having kids one day. I assume you want everything that entails. You'd want to find someone who can conceive the old fashioned way, and that's completely understandable. Unfortunately, that's not an option with me. I need you to process this up front because I think if we resume our sexual relationship, we have a good chance of developing feelings for each other."

Lifting those brown eyes, he stared deep into her soul. "I think you might be right."

Wanting to alleviate some of the heaviness that permeated the air, she lifted an eyebrow. "They don't pay me three hundred and fifty dollars an hour for nothing. I'm pretty good at this stuff, buddy."

His mouth fell open. "Three hundred and fifty an hour? That's more than I charge."

"What can I say? I'm a pro."

"Damn," he said, exhaling as he sat back in the chair. "You're going to pay off my loan in no time."

Chuckling, she nodded. "Yep. I'm ready for those billable hours."

His shoulders softened and she relaxed into her chair. "I wasn't trying to get into a heavy discussion. I just wanted this out in the open, Mark. We have a few weeks to think about it. Once my debtors are paid, we can revisit it."

"Okay," he said, gazing at her over the table. "Like I said, whenever you're ready to discuss it, you can come to me. I'll leave the door open and I certainly don't want to pressure you."

"Thank you. You know, you're a really good guy."

Palming his chest, he rubbed his hand over his heart. "It makes me really happy to hear that since I basically ruined your life."

"You did no such thing. At the moment, I'm happily tipsy and full of lasagna. I'd say I'm winning in this situation."

Settling into their banter, they talked for another hour, getting to know each other better as they finished the wine. Afterward, he led her upstairs, holding her hand although she wasn't really drunk enough to need the guidance. When they stood outside her bedroom door, he placed a kiss on her forehead.

"Thank you for everything today, Teresa. You were amazing at the press conference. I'm so...well, I just feel pretty lucky to have you in my life."

"I was just happy I didn't freeze or mispronounce anything. I did use the word 'sexual' a lot. Is that weird?" She rubbed her chin.

"I don't think so, but let's revisit when we haven't polished off a bottle of wine. Night, hon."

"Night."

Closing the door behind her, she prepped for bed and slid in between the sheets, comforted by the fact he was only feet away.

<h1 style="text-align:center">Chapter 13</h1>

Now that the crisis had been averted, Mark barreled through the rest of the week. Throwing himself full force into the campaign and his law practice, he barely made it home to sleep before rising at the crack of dawn to do it all over again. This meant he rarely saw Teresa, although indications of her presence could be seen throughout his townhome when he chose to look.

She had a habit of leaving cute pink athletic slip-ons by the front door, spurring him to wonder if she left them there for when she needed to step outside. The dollar store soap in his downstairs half bathroom had been replaced with some fancy soap that smelled amazing. Reusable shopping bags had appeared in the cabinet under his coffee pot with a note that read: *Let's use these so we can save a tiny piece of the world, okay? The plastic's got to go. Love, Your New Roommate, Fake Fiancée, and Detester of Plastic Bags.*

The note prompted a chuckle when he found it on Thursday evening and he wrote one back early the next morning: *Message received. Also, thanks for the soap. I smell like a bouquet of magnificent flowers which doesn't make me question my masculinity at all. Love, Your Fake Fiancé and Newfound Environmentalist.*

Friday evening, he arrived home late after a long day in Scranton. He'd argued two cases in the courthouse and couldn't wait to rip off the uncomfortable suit as soon as he walked in the door. Entering the darkened foyer, he noticed Teresa on the couch as the TV droned in the background. Quietly approaching, he found her fast asleep, lightly snoring as her mouth hung open.

It certainly wasn't the most attractive position to find one in but, for some reason, Mark felt a tug toward her. Black curls snaked over the small pillow as air flowed through her full lips. Longing to touch her, he restrained himself from reaching down to stroke the apple-ripe curve of her cheek.

She stirred under the blanket before slowly lifting her lids. Gazing up at him with sleepy eyes, she smiled. "Hey. Are you watching me sleep?"

"Yes," he said, lowering to sit on the couch. "I'm sorry because it's probably super creepy. You just looked so peaceful."

Wiping her mouth with the back of her arm, she smirked. "I'm pretty sure I was drooling."

"That's hot. Don't let anyone tell you differently."

Laughing, she squirmed under the blanket as her lips curved. "How was your day?"

"Good. Busy. Exhausting." He shrugged. "But, hey, it's only going to get busier, right? I signed up for this."

"You did," she said, nodding as her hair dragged across the pillow. "If you ever want to talk, I know a good therapist."

"That's a kind offer, but I think you're already doing enough."

Her gorgeous hazel eyes roved over his face. "Okay, then we can just talk as friends. I think we're at the friend level, right?"

"Definitely," he said, unable to stop himself from brushing a curl from her forehead.

"If you hate the soap, I can throw it out. Don't want to give you a complex."

He breathed a laugh. "I like it, actually. It smells fantastic. Not as good as your Ariana Grande perfume but close."

She bit her lip as mirth swam in her eyes. "Are you flirting with me, Mr. D.A.?"

"Yes," he whispered, winking. "Is it working?"

"Maybe." She squinted one eye closed. "I'll report back once I've figured it out."

"Can't wait." Standing, he stretched. "I've got to get out of this suit. I feel like a caged animal."

"I'm going to watch the rest of the Real Housewives episode I missed when I crashed. Is that okay?"

"Yep. I'm heading to bed. I'm going to the store tomorrow—reusable bags in tow—so text me if you need anything. I'm going to make beef stew for the upcoming week."

"Yum. I'm volunteering at a health fair tomorrow and have brunch with the ladies on Sunday so I might not see you a lot this weekend."

"I'm visiting Justine and Avery on Sunday so I'll be out as well. The stew will be in the fridge whenever you want some. Sleep well, hon."

"Night," she said, settling into the couch and lifting the remote to resume the show.

Mark prepped for bed, unable to control his grin as he milled about his bedroom. He'd always lamented the idea of living with someone because the thought of giving up his space wasn't palatable. He valued his privacy, along with his independence. Although he'd sporadically dated in the past, he'd never come close to considering cohabitation.

But coming home to Teresa snuggled into his couch had seemed...*right*, somehow. As if she belonged there. Perhaps as if she belonged with *him*. Staring at himself as he brushed his teeth, Mark wondered why it didn't feel strange or awkward. Was he finally ready to contemplate something more serious? Perhaps turning forty had quelled his reservations. Unsure, he slid into bed, deciding he could analyze it later since he was exhausted.

S aturday's grocery store run and subsequent stew prep were uneventful, giving Mark a rare day to relax. On Sunday, he slipped on his jacket in the foyer as Teresa headed down the stairs.

"Wow," he said, noting her dark jeans, heels, and silky blouse. "You look amazing. Heading to brunch?"

"Sure am and thank you." Reaching for her leather jacket, she slipped it on. "You're heading to your sister's, right?"

He nodded. "I'm going to try to speak to her about possibly leaving her husband. Not really looking forward to the conversation, but I think it's time."

"Conversations like that are hard," she said, sliding her hands under her hair to free it from the jacket. It fell down her back in a wave of black curls and Mark felt himself harden. *Down boy.* "As I've said before, I'm here if you need me. The offer's always open. Hope you have a good visit."

Giving a wave, she exited through the front door.

Half an hour later, Mark stuck his head through the unlocked door of his sister's two-bedroom home, located in a cul-de-sac in Southern Ardor Creek. "Justine? Avery? You guys here? I got pizza."

Striding inside, he set the pizza on the round table in the kitchen, wondering where they were. Opening the back sliding door, he trailed to the tiny shed Justine used as her studio.

"Awesome job, baby," Justine said as Avery held her hands to the pottery wheel. "You're going to be better than Mommy. You're so talented."

"Hey," Mark said, smiling. "Do we have a future famous artist on our hands here?"

"I'm making a bowl," Avery said, smiling under a mop of blond hair as she held up red-clay stained hands. "Mommy says I'm really good."

Mark glanced at the bowl, which looked like a glob of clay, but who was he to argue? "Looks great, sweetheart."

"Okay," Justine said, wiping her hands with a cloth before wiping Avery's. "I think Uncle Mark brought pizza. Let's get inside and wash these hands so we can eat."

Avery ran toward him, arms outstretched, and Mark decided the shirt and jeans he was wearing weren't his favorite anyway. Crouching down, he hugged her, anticipating the clay would get everywhere. "I missed you, munchkin," he said, squeezing.

Avery emitted a small grunt and he pulled back. "You okay?"

She nodded before glancing at Justine.

"Go inside and wash your hands," his sister said, gesturing with her head.

Avery disappeared through the shed door as Mark's hands fisted at his sides. "Please tell me she wasn't grimacing because she's hurt, Jus. I swear to god, if he hit her, I'll kill him."

"She fell," Justine said, lifting her chin. Mark noticed three long bruises on the skin between her neck and shoulder and he slowly approached.

"You have bruises on your neck," he said, feeling his nostrils flare. "Did he hit you too? This has to stop, Jus. I won't let this continue."

"He was drunk and felt terrible afterward," she said, tears welling in her eyes as she stared up at him. "And he didn't hit Avery. He accidentally shoved her when she ran toward me while we were arguing. She fell and barely bruised her side. She'll be fine, Mark."

"No," he said, slicing his hand through the air. "I won't stand by and watch you be abused. Watch your *daughter* be abused. I represent domestic abuse clients for a living. I'm going to help you get away from him."

Her chin trembled as she shrugged. "I love him, Mark. I don't know what you want me to say. I'm not ready to leave him. He *swears* this was the last time."

"I don't give a damn!" Mark yelled, feeling his heart shatter when she flinched. "Good god, you're terrified. How can you live like this? What if he hurts her? What if he *kills* you? I can't let this happen, Justine."

Blowing a breath through puffed cheeks, she ran her hand through her hair. "I just don't know what to do. He promised it wouldn't happen again."

"I understand this is hard," Mark said, tentatively sliding his hands over her shoulders. "But I love you and I love Avery and I want to help you. Mom and Dad want to help too."

She rolled her eyes. "Mom and Dad have never accepted Dean or my decision to become an artist. You'll never convince me they're supportive."

"Well, I support you and we need to find a solution. He'll be playing golf for several more hours today right? We can pack and you can stay with me until we figure something else out."

Her lips formed a faint smile. "Even with your new fiancée?

Expelling a breath, he laughed. "Yep, even with the shit show I've made of my life. She's a therapist, Jus, and she's awesome. It would probably benefit you and Avery to talk to her."

Inhaling, she pursed her lips. "Let me think about it for a few days," she said, lifting her finger when he tried to argue. "Please. It's a huge decision. I need to truly contemplate if I can leave him. I'm sorry. I know that's disappointing. I've always been the disappointment in this family. We can't all be heroes like you."

"Um, have you seen any of the news articles in the past week? I've made a royal mess of not only one, but two lives. I think you're ahead in the tally here."

Grinning, she cupped his jaw. "You're still pretty perfect. I truly appreciate how worried you are for us, but I need time to process."

He exhaled a resigned breath. "Okay. I'll give you a week and, then, I need an answer. This doesn't have to be a huge ordeal. People gain the strength to leave abusive relationships every day. I know you can do it, Jus."

Gnawing her bottom lip, she nodded. "Maybe I can." Stepping back, she wiped her hands on her jeans. "In the meantime, please tell me you got pineapple on my half of the pizza."

Sliding his arm over her shoulders, they began to walk toward the house. "I did, although Antonio razzed me about it like he always does. You're pretty weird, you know?"

Gently punching his side, he made a goofy face as she laughed. "Us Lancasters have always been a bit weird but it makes us interesting."

"No doubt."

Avery lifted her freshly washed hands above the sink and exclaimed she was starving before they all sat down at the kitchen table. Reveling in her sweet smile, Mark tried his best to suppress the concern, although it still simmered as they devoured the pizza. He was determined to extricate his sister and niece from the abusive situation and wouldn't rest until they were safe.

Chapter 14

Teresa settled into her life as Mark's fiancée, thrilled the transition was rather effortless. She had to appear at a fundraising event during the second week and a Saturday fundraising brunch a few days later but, otherwise, her schedule was unencumbered. Mid-April arrived along with warmer weather and the promise of spring. She'd always loved the change in seasons and felt it signaled hope and renewal.

Mark approached her one evening as she was bent over the dishwasher, loading in the last of the plates and silverware from the leftover rigatoni he'd made earlier that week. His desire to cook scrumptious meals was certainly a bonus to their situation. Sensing his presence, she straightened and arched a brow.

"Were you, uh...staring at my ass as I loaded the dishwasher?"

His resulting grin was a perfect amalgamation of sexy and sheepish. "If I said 'yes' would I be in trouble?"

Wrinkling her nose, she lifted a shoulder. "Not sure. How was the view?"

Throwing back his head, he broke into joyful laughter. "Pretty damn amazing. You have a gorgeous body, Teresa. I thought so from the first night we met."

Desire racked her body as she told her pounding heart to calm down. "Thank you. I'm a bit curvy here and there but I've always rather liked it. Women are supposed to have curves."

Stepping closer, he stopped only inches away. Teresa could almost feel the heat emanating from his tall frame. His tongue darted out to lick his lips and her knees almost buckled. "Honey, you have curves in all the right places. It's sexy as hell."

Feeling her throat bob as she swallowed, she released a ragged breath. "The last of the loans cleared today. I'm scot-free...well, except for the time I owe you. You saved me tens of thousands of dollars in interest, Mark. I'm grateful."

Anticipation entered his eyes, along with the simmering lust that lurked in the brown orbs. "So, I'm no longer Edward to your Vivian."

Squinting, she pondered. "I guess not. I don't consider the consultations something that creates an imbalance since I often do them for other attorneys."

His lips curved as he studied her. "Then, maybe we could—"

He was interrupted by the chirping of his phone. Lifting it from his pocket, he answered. "Hey, Justine. You okay?"

He held up a finger and Teresa nodded before he trailed to the living room. Sighing, she resumed loading the dishwasher and popped the soap pod inside before starting it. Glancing at her watch, she realized it was almost nine o'clock and she needed to get up early for a last-minute fundraising breakfast Evan had planned with a group of donors. Heading upstairs, she heard Mark's deep voice as he spoke to his sister.

Once she was in bed, her phone dinged and she picked it up from the bedside table.

Mark: Well, that was the worst timing in the world. Sorry. As we've discussed, I'm trying to get Justine to leave her husband but she's stalling. It's a shitty situation.

Teresa: I understand. I hope I get to meet her and Avery one day soon. I'd love to offer them a safe space to talk.

Mark: That means so much. I hope they'll be ready soon. In the meantime, I'm pretty sure I blew an opportunity to kiss you and I'm super bummed.

Chuckling, her thumbs moved over the keypad.

Teresa: You were within range, for sure. I'm considering.

Mark: I know you have reservations. I do too. But if you're open, I'd love to be with you again. I think we'll be okay if we're honest. We were pretty good at that before so I'm optimistic.

Smiling, she closed her eyes, remembering the feel of his broad hands against her skin. Mark was an amazing lover. Sweet, thoughtful, and never selfish. Every time they'd been together, he'd always ensured she experienced pleasure before finding his own. Rubbing her legs together under the soft sheets, she admitted how much she missed his caresses.

Teresa: Let's see how things go over the next week. Maybe I'll blow it with your friends at the barbeque on Sunday and completely turn you off.

Mark: No way. They're going to love you. Can't wait for you to meet them. Well, you've already met Scott but can't wait for you to meet the others.

Teresa: Me neither. Looking forward to it. Sweet dreams.

Mark: You too, honey.

Setting the phone on the nightstand, she clicked off the lamp and snuggled into bed as trepidation pulsed through her frame. Closing her eyes, she lost herself to the memories of all the times they'd loved each other, knowing deep within she would most likely develop feelings for him if they resumed their sexual relationship. Before, when they'd had defined boundaries, the lines had been clear. Now that they were becoming friends—and lived together—the lines were blurred and erratic.

Still, knowing she would most likely fall, she wanted to dive off the cliff anyway. It wasn't often a sexy, kind man fell into your lap and offered you magnificent sex. Hell, she would be fifty in a few years. Who knew if everything would shrivel up and wither away at some point?

Snickering at the silly thought, she inhaled a deep breath and cemented her decision: she would resume her sexual relationship with Mark the next time the moment felt right. It might end in disaster or, at the very least, a severely broken heart, but Teresa had survived worse. In the end, you only lived once, and after her heart-wrenching struggle with fertility, she wanted to experience some happiness.

Maintaining steady breaths to calm the anxiety, she eventually settled into the decision as her lips formed a soft smile. Falling into slumber, she clutched the pillow, yearning for the days to come when she could fall asleep against Mark's chest as he gently stroked her hair.

Chapter 15

♥

The day of the barbeque arrived and Teresa dressed in comfortable yet fashionable jeans, a cute, light sweater, and strappy sandals she'd gotten for a steal during a sale at the mall. The sun was already high in the sky and she buzzed with anticipation at meeting Mark's friends. He'd come home late last night and she'd already been in bed so this was the first time she'd seen him since Thursday.

Striding into the kitchen, she found him cutting sandwiches into small slices.

"Finger sandwiches? How European."

Chuckling, he nodded as he loaded them onto a tray. "Carrie's kids love them and I do too, although I pretend it's just for them. I did ham and cheese, mozzarella and tomato, hummus and lettuce, and peanut butter and jelly for Charlie. That's his favorite."

"Impressive. I just bought two bottles of wine and the spiked seltzers in the fridge."

"The ladies will definitely help you drink them, don't worry," he said, grinning. "Peter doesn't drink, and Scott rarely does, which works out pretty well for Carrie and Ashlyn since they have built-in designated drivers."

"I remember Scott mentioning he didn't drink after the accident," Teresa said, opening the fridge and pulling out the box of seltzers before loading them in a bag with the wine. "I didn't realize Peter didn't drink."

"He's been sober for several years now. It's an awesome story, actually. He's pretty open about being a recovered addict and we're all so proud of him."

"I love stories like that. Can't wait to meet him. And I'm obviously dying to meet Ashlyn."

"Well, I think this is ready," he said, snapping the cover over the tray. "By the way, Ashlyn puts me to shame. She runs a gourmet food truck on Main Street and is the best cook I've ever known. She'll probably make something super fancy."

"Yum. Glad I wore my eating jeans." He laughed before she asked, "Do you want me to drive?"

"Nah," he said, waving his hand. "I'll drive. That way you can drink copious amounts of wine and I can drive home."

Arching a brow, she bit her lip. "I'm sensing an ulterior motive here."

Extending his free hand as he held the tray, he shook his head. "No way. I'll be a perfect gentleman. Ready?"

Sliding her palm over his, she let him lead her to his luxury sedan. On the way, they discussed the polls, which were soaring for Mark since the announcement of their engagement.

"Do you think Chisolm has something else up his sleeve? He must be furious you're ahead."

"I'm sure he does," Mark said, turning onto the gravel road that led to Scott and Ashlyn's house. "I'm doing my best to stay aware, but you never know with someone as crooked as him. I'm defending a few clients right now that he's prosecuting and he's asking for more than the maximum sentences. It's most likely an attempt to get to me through my clients."

"That's terrible."

"It is, but I'm going to win each case. All three are clear instances where the client had extenuating circumstances and charges should be dropped or reduced. Still, he's a dick to pursue them so aggressively. Par for the course, I guess."

"I look forward to the day when you take office and actually prosecute people who deserve it. A corrupt D.A. certainly doesn't serve the people effectively."

Glancing over, he smiled. "Your background comes in handy since you know how the social work and government systems function. Evan told me yesterday you poll even higher than me. I might be a bit jealous." He held his thumb and forefinger an inch apart as she laughed. "Have you ever thought of running for office? You'd be great."

"I'm not a politician," she said, observing the sprawling front porch as they approached the house. "I value my privacy too much. But I'll continue in my therapy practice as long as I can because I love helping people."

"That's really noble."

"Thanks, but it fulfills something for me too so it's definitely not a chore." Removing her seat belt, she gazed at the house. "Nice home. I remember when Scott told me he was going to ask Ashlyn if he could move in. I loved that choice, by the way. It represented a new beginning for him."

"Their back yard is awesome and a perfect place to grill and watch the kids play soccer. We can just walk right back."

Grabbing the bag with the wine, she followed Mark around the corner, taking stock of the expansive back yard. A long table was set up by the grill, covered with various pasta salads, chips, and soda bottles. A man stood at the grill maneuvering ribs over the grate beside Scott Grillo, who was holding a red solo cup.

"Doc!" Scott said, grinning when he saw her. "You guys made it."

Setting the bag on the table, she walked over. "Hi, Scott. It's so nice to see you outside the office."

He lifted his brows as he opened his arms. "Can I hug you? Is that weird? Am I violating some sort of code or something?"

Laughing, she stepped into his embrace and gave him a strong hug. "Not at all. I was thrilled when you permitted Mark to discuss our professional relationship. What a small world, huh?"

"Small, indeed," he said, smiling as she stepped back. "This is my buddy, Peter. He's the master griller at these things."

"Hello, Peter," she said, extending her hand.

"Well, hello, strikingly gorgeous therapist who's fake engaged to our very good friend. Man, am I happy to finally meet you."

He was extremely handsome with a dimple below his straight nose and blue eyes. "Oh, boy. I assume you're the jokester Mark told me about."

"Me?" Peter asked, pointing to himself with the tongs. "No way. Although I'm not as serious as Scott. This guy's favorite pastime is watching paint dry. I've verified this multiple times, by the way," he murmured, features contorting into a mock grimace.

"I stop by construction sites to ensure the paint is dry before hanging fixtures, yes," Scott said acerbically. "He likes to twist things."

"Hey, man, whatever floats your boat," Peter said, flipping a rib. "Thank god you married Ashlyn before you froze in a boredom coma."

"Okay, leave him alone," Mark said, patting Peter's shoulder. "Scott's demeanor has been much more palatable since marrying Ashlyn, but we still loved him when he was surly."

"Are you all making fun of Grumpy Scott?" a chipper voice asked. Teresa turned to see a striking raven-haired woman striding over with what looked to be a tray of tacos beside a smiling redhead. "Because you all know I adore Grumpy Scott."

"You must be Ashlyn," Teresa said, excitement welling in her chest. "I feel like I already know you."

"It's so nice to meet you," she said, setting down the tray and throwing her arms around Teresa. "I hope it's okay to hug you because I'm going all in."

Squeezing, she chuckled. "It's totally fine." Drawing back, she extended her hand. "And you must be Carrie."

"Hi, Teresa," she said, smiling as she shook. "We're so glad you're here. Mark can't stop talking about how amazing you are. You have quite a reputation to live up to."

"They're intent on torturing me for the foreseeable future," Mark said, glowering. "You'll probably have to play along. And, yes, she is amazing, so leave me alone, okay?"

Before Teresa could answer, two boys came barreling around the corner of the house. Breathless, one of them held up what looked to be a dirty box. "Mom! We found this on the side of the house! We can't get it open though. We need a key."

"Wow," Carrie said, surprise lacing her features. Taking the box, which spanned about two palm widths, she examined it. "This is really cool." Glancing at Ashlyn, she whispered, "Did you bury this?"

"Nope," Ashlyn said, eyes wide as she shook her head. "I swear. Grandma Jean always said Sally buried letters and trinkets around the house so her husband's ghost could find them if he came looking. Man," she said, rubbing her arms, "I'm getting chills. This is so cool."

"We need the key, Ashlyn," the youngest boy pleaded.

"I don't know where it is." Narrowing her eyes, she contemplated. "I need to do a deep search of the attic and a few other places. I promise, guys, I'll look in every corner until I find it. In the meantime, can you tell Teresa hello? She's a very special friend of Mark's and Scott's too."

"Hi, Teresa," they said in unison, waving.

"Hello," she said, finding them adorable. "Let me guess. You're Sebastian?"

He nodded and extended his hand. "Nice to meet you."

"Well, aren't you a gentleman?" She winked at Carrie as she shook.

"This is Charlie," he said, gesturing with his head.

"Hi, Charlie."

He gave a timid wave and sank into Carrie's side.

"He's only shy in the beginning," she said, sifting her fingers through his hair. "Give him five minutes and he'll talk your ear off."

Nodding, she smiled at the boys. "It's so nice to meet both of you. I hear you're both soccer stars in the making."

"I'm going to get a scholarship!" Sebastian said. "My coach says I already play at a high school level."

"Impressive," Teresa said, sparing Carrie a smile. "That will come in handy when it's time to pay for college."

"Don't I know it," she said, holding up crossed fingers. "Every little bit counts."

A wail sounded from the baby monitor on the table and Ashlyn picked it up.

"Well, the peanut is awake," she said, holding up the monitor so Teresa could see Grant in the crib. "He screams like this for a few minutes after he wakes up but, otherwise, we're really lucky. He's such a good baby."

"Maybe he can teach Carrie how to stop screaming when she wakes up," Peter teased beside the grill. "She's a monster."

"Well, *someone's* sleeping in the guest room tonight," she said, batting her eyelashes. "That way, you can wake up all by yourself. Have fun!" Pivoting, she began to follow Ashlyn inside.

"Whoa!" Peter called, setting the tongs beside the grill and rushing to grab her wrist. "I take it back. You're a perfect princess when you wake up." He leaned forward, attempting to kiss her.

"Go away," she said, palming his face before he maneuvered around and planted a wet kiss on her neck. "I'm going to help Ashlyn." Tugging free of his grasp, she stuck her tongue out at him before heading inside.

"She can't keep her hands off me," Peter said, winking at Teresa. "Don't listen to a word she says." Flashing a grin, he resumed his spot at the grill.

The boys tugged Scott toward the yard to show him the soccer goals they'd fashioned from two-liter soda bottles and Teresa beamed up at Mark. "Your friends are awesome."

"Right?" he asked, grasping her hand and squeezing. "Thank you for coming with me."

"Thank you for inviting me." She squeezed back before Scott waved them over to play with the boys.

Half an hour later, Chad Hanson arrived along with another couple, Terry and Brian. Teresa learned she'd been a server at the local pub since high school.

"I just always fit there and Brian and I got pregnant senior year, so I just ended up staying there," Terry said with a shrug. "Now, it's home and I can't imagine working anywhere else."

"I'll have to come eat there one day," Teresa said, sipping wine from her solo cup. She loved that the setting was relaxed enough they didn't need fancy drinkware. "How many kids do you have?"

"Two," Brian said. "A boy and a girl, but they're nineteen and twenty-one with their own significant others and busy lives so we rarely see them anymore."

"Except when they need money," Terry muttered.

Chuckling, Brian kissed her temple. "Truer words, honey."

The food was magnificent and the alcohol flowed, and before Teresa realized it, the sun began to set behind the trees.

"Okay, boys, let's help Mom pack the leftovers in the bags," Peter said, maneuvering various dishes on the table. "I've got some groveling to do when we get home. Chop chop!"

Snickering, Teresa shook her head. "He should take his act on the road. He's hilarious."

"I'm not sure Carrie always agrees with that sentiment, but he is pretty funny," Mark said, smiling down at her. "I'm ready to pack up some leftovers and head home too. If you're ready."

Gazing up at him, Teresa was overcome by how handsome he was in the waning sunlight. His height was extremely attractive to her, and she loved how he loomed over her as his eyes simmered with lust. He didn't try to hide it or play coy. No, her forthright lover...fake fiancé...friend...whatever he was becoming, didn't trade in hidden desires or clandestine games. The smoldering arousal that laced his features was on full display and it was alluring. She'd always hated games and was terrible at playing them. Why hide what you covet deep inside?

Desire, thick and heavy, began to hum in her veins as her breathing became slightly labored. "I'm ready," she almost whispered.

His lips curved into a sexy smile. "Your eyes are so pretty right now. They have so many colors in them."

Nodding, she cleared her throat. "Heterochromia."

"Huh?"

"Multi-colored eyes. I have yellow, green, and brown all swirled together. You can see it best outside. I just call them 'hazel' because it's easier."

His nostrils flared slightly and she noticed the vein pulsing in his neck. "I want to see them in the moonlight."

She exhaled a ragged breath. "I want that too."

"Uh, am I interrupting something?" Peter asked, approaching. "Or maybe I'm not understanding the definition of 'fake' in this relationship?"

"You're fired as my friend," Mark said, scowling.

"Hey, I packed leftovers for you guys," he said, lifting the bag in his hand. "Come on."

"Okay," Mark said, taking it. "You're forgiven—for now—but you're on thin ice."

"Story of my life, brother," Peter said, patting him on the back.

After saying their goodbyes, Teresa folded in the car, her body pulsing with equal parts desire and warmth from the wine. They chatted about the day as she affirmed how much she'd enjoyed meeting everyone.

When they arrived home, they unpacked the leftovers and placed them in the fridge. Mark lifted the bottle of red from the counter and gently shook it. "Want another glass before bed?"

Pulse thrumming with anticipation, she shook her head. Striding over to the light switch, she flipped it off, flooding the kitchen with darkness. Extending her hand, she wiggled her fingers.

White teeth flashed in the dim room as he trailed over and grasped her hand. "Are you sure, sweetheart? I wish I could promise it won't get messy but I can't."

"Life is messy," she said, tugging his hand. "Let's go."

She led him to the bottom of the stairs before he halted and bent down, lifting her in his arms as she squealed.

"Mark!" she said, threading her arms around his neck. "I'm too heavy to carry up the stairs."

"No fucking way." He placed a sweet peck on her lips. "Hold on, hon." He carried her to his room, gently laying her across the bed, his body bracketing hers. Lowering, he nudged her nose with his.

"Teresa," he whispered, brushing his lips against hers ever so softly. "I've missed you."

"I missed you too," she said, sliding her fingers in his thick hair while fighting the insane urge to cry. Something about his poignant words stirred up every emotion she'd vowed to keep in check when they resumed their sexual relationship.

Touching his lips to hers, he pushed them open and devoured her mouth. Teresa moaned, wrapping her leg around the back of his thigh, pulling him into her as he kissed her. Cupping her head in his broad hands, he maneuvered his lips over hers, jutting his erection into the juncture of her thighs. Arousal slammed into her core, coating it with slick honey as she squirmed underneath.

Grunting in frustration at the clothes they were still wearing, she clutched the fabric of his polo shirt, tugging it over his head before he resumed kissing her again. Sliding her palms over the smooth skin of his back, she felt her skin flush with desire.

"Let me see those pretty breasts, honey," he said, grabbing the hem of her sweater and dragging it over her head. Tossing it to the ground, he freed the clasp of her bra and tore it from her body.

"Yesssss..." he hissed, kissing a trail down her neck and between her breasts as his hands cupped the sensitive mounds. Massaging them, he licked the valley between, spurring goosebumps to rise along her skin.

"Mark," she cried, thrusting her fingers in his hair.

Lifting his head, he stared deep into her eyes as his fingers toyed with her nipples. "There they are," he murmured, gazing at her so reverently. "Those gorgeous eyes in the moonlight as I tug your sexy nipples."

Teresa's body bowed, so aroused from his words and hands. "God, I'm so wet," she cried, pushing her core into his thick cock underneath his jeans. "I want you inside me."

"Soon, hon," he said, trailing kisses down her stomach as he slid his hands to unclasp her jeans. "Let me take these off." Rising to his knees, he tugged off her sandals before shrugging her jeans and underwear down her legs, tossing them to the carpeted floor.

Inhaling a deep breath, he slid his hands along her inner thighs and rested them behind her knees. Lifting them high, he gazed at her wet opening.

"Look at that sexy pussy," he said, resting her calf over his shoulder while still holding her other leg high. Lowering his hand, he touched two fingers to her core. Eyes locked with hers, he glided the fingers inside as she bit her lip, suppressing a ragged moan as he surged within.

He circled his fingers deep, stimulating her quivering walls, before slowly dragging them out and lifting them to his lips. Staring into her eyes, he licked her essence.

Closing his lids, he moaned. "Do you know how good you taste?" he rasped, reclaiming her gaze. "I could lick every drop."

Lifting her hand, she traced his cheek. "I want that but, right now, I need you to take off your pants and fuck me, Mark."

He nipped her finger. "I want to make you feel good, honey."

"You are," she said, joy evident in her words as she smiled and shook her head on the bed. "So damn good. Please."

Growling, he stood and tugged off the rest of his clothes before sliding back between her legs. Lifting them again, he palmed the backs of her knees as he held her open.

Teresa reached for him, craving the connection, cupping the sides of his jaw as he slid the head of his cock over her opening, coating it with her wetness.

"Fuck…" he moaned, clenching his eyelids together as he glided his shaft over her core. "You're drenching me, baby…"

She whimpered his name, spurring him to open his eyes, his gaze lasering deep into her soul. Locked onto her, he began to nudge inside, inch by inch, until she thought she might go mad. He was tall and broad-shouldered, and his shaft was certainly proportional. Reveling in the fullness as he filled her, she emitted a small giggle.

"Are you laughing?" he asked, breathless. "That's not a good sign."

"It's a good laugh." Groaning as he surged deeper, she threw her head back on the bed. "You're big. It's...oh, god, it feels so good."

Leaning down, he released her legs and balanced on his palms as they rested beside her head. "Keep going. You were telling me I have the biggest cock you've ever seen." Working his hips against her, he smiled.

"Did I say that?" she teased, grasping his face. "It's certain-ly...*ohhhh...*"

Words escaped her as the head of his shaft jutted against the tiny bundle of nerves deep within. Each thrust of his hips sent a jolt of pleasure through her body and she lowered her hand, gliding between them. Gathering some of her wetness on her fingers, she began to rub her clit as he fucked her.

"Do you want me to—"

"Keep doing *exactly* what you're doing. I love playing with myself while you fuck me."

"God, that's so hot," he rasped, increasing the pace of his hips. "You're so sexy, honey."

Her fingers dug into the back of his neck, her nails spearing the skin, as her other hand worked her engorged nub. Feeling herself begin to fall, she reveled in the muscle that ticked in his jaw as she held on for dear life.

Lowering his head, he captured her mouth in a torrid kiss, spearing his tongue inside as he undulated into her. They were so in tune, his torso moving with hers as if they inhabited one shared body. Tossing her head back on the bed, she wailed.

"I'm close...*harder*...right there..."

The orgasm blinded her, shooting her off the precipice of reality and into a pleasure-filled dream. Small sparks of desire burned her skin as she writhed below him, shuddering when he cried her name. He began to spurt inside her, the jerks of his cock pulsing against her quivering walls as she reached for the stars. Floating high, she rode the wave, thrilled to be in his arms once more.

Mark buried his face in her neck, mumbling words of arousal and tender endearments as he emptied inside her trembling frame. Lost in the moment, she wrapped herself around him, wanting to capture every shudder and quake of his gorgeous body.

Eventually, he was replete and collapsed over her. He was heavy, but not uncomfortably so, and she snuggled into his embrace. Sighing, he placed his lips over the shell of her ear and whispered, "I think I'm dead."

Throwing her head back, she laughed, the sound joyful as it surrounded them. Mark joined in, the two of them damn near giggling like teenagers. Resting his face on his hand as his elbow dug into the mattress, he stroked the hair from her forehead.

"I've never really laughed during sex. It's fun."

Biting her lip, she nodded. "It is kinda fun."

They gazed softy through half-lidded eyes as he gently stroked her face. "God, I missed that. You're not going to relegate me to two days a week again, are you? Because I think I need more."

Chuckling, she rubbed her smooth leg over his hairy one. "Remember the whole 'messy' thing? The more we do this, the more that has a chance to happen."

"Right now, I just don't give a damn, sweetheart." Caressing her face, he grinned. "Not when you look like that and I'm still inside you."

"Honestly," she said, shifting underneath and pushing her body into his, "I don't give a damn right now either."

Their chuckles mingled as he kissed her again, slow and lazy as their tongues slid in languid patterns. Drawing back, he asked, "Want to hang in here and watch whatever trashy show you loaded on the DVR? I'll watch with you until I can go again." He gestured to the TV mounted on the wall.

"One man's trash is another woman's award winner," she teased, arching a brow. "And, yes, I'd love that."

Slowly extricating from her embrace, he stood and offered his hand. "I swear to god, if I become addicted to these shows, I'm never forgiving you."

Laughing, she followed him into the bathroom, noting the dual sinks. They cleaned up and trailed back to bed, where she snuggled into his side and turned on the most recent Bachelorette. He stroked her hair as her cheek rested against his pec, reminding her of all the times he'd done it before. If she was honest, this was always the favorite part of their loving: the times when they were sated and they held each other as their heartbeats intertwined.

Attempting to focus on the show, Teresa felt her eyes droop and told herself to stay awake.

Five minutes later, she was dead to the world.

Chapter 16

♥

Teresa climbed toward consciousness, compressing her eyelids at the shaft of sunlight that was trying to pierce through. Craning her head, she stretched, wondering why the muscles in her neck were so sore. Hell, her whole body was stiff, but not painfully so, and she racked her sleepy brain, trying to remember why. Suddenly, the images from last night's steamy lovemaking flitted through her head and she gasped. Opening her eyes, she shifted on the pillow to find a grinning Mark Lancaster.

"Good morning," he said, his deep baritone laced with a sleepy eroticism that sent a shot of arousal straight to her core.

"Shit," she whispered, palming her forehead. "I fell asleep in your bed. I'm so sorry. That must violate about a hundred ground rules of our non-serious sexual arrangement. Or, do we need to set new ground rules? Damn, we probably should—"

He slid over her, aligning his naked body with hers as he covered her mouth with his fingers. Lips curved in a sexy smile, he asked, "Do you always talk this much in the morning? Because I'm kind of an 'I *need a cup of coffee before I can have a coherent conversation*' sort of person."

Teresa grinned beneath his hand and nodded.

"Noted." He gazed at her with lazy eyes and she noticed the stubble that had grown over his jaw while they slept. God, he was handsome. Feeling her brain turn to mush, she told her pounding heart to relax.

"Sorry," he said, sliding his hand from her mouth to cup her jaw. "You were just freaking out there." Caressing her face with his fingers, he shook his head. "There's no reason to freak out, Teresa."

"I...you're right," she said, trying to amalgamate the emotions swirling inside. Fear. Lust. Anxiety. Elation. "I didn't want to violate your space. I meant to go back to my room after we were together again. Sleep had other plans, I guess."

His eyes darted between hers as he inhaled a slow breath. "I get it. We're in uncharted waters here but I assure you, I don't read anything into you falling asleep in my bed. I certainly don't mind it right now." He pushed his erection into the soft skin of her thigh.

"We need to establish ground rules so we're on the same page." Sliding her arms around his neck, she pulled him close. "But we can do that another time—"

She yelped as he flipped them over, causing her arms to flail as she sprawled over him. "Yes..." he murmured, grasping his cock and sliding it against the folds of her core. "Let's discuss that another time."

Straddling him, she slid over his engorged shaft, balancing her palms on his chest as she loomed over him. "Or maybe we should discuss it now," she said, the tone of her voice sultry and low. "I think you might agree to anything right now."

"Anything in the goddamn world, honey," he said, surging his cock between her wet folds before drawing back and plunging again. "This might be the best morning of my life."

Overcome with laughter, she undulated atop his strong frame, losing the ability to keep up the playful banter. Giving in to his passionate caresses, she let him take her to heaven once more before they both had to return to reality.

Teresa eventually rolled out of Mark's bed and dressed, unable to suppress the nervous anxiety that ran through her frame. One night together and she felt off-balance and unsure. For someone so stable, it was a bit disconcerting. Determined to give Mark space, she dressed and headed to the local coffee shop for breakfast. It was a comfortable place to wade through the pile of charts she needed to update in her electronic medical records before heading to her office.

As she worked, she realized she'd overreacted. She and Mark had always been extremely honest with each other. Even though they were living together and involved in a public fake engagement, they were the same two consenting adults who'd always communicated clearly and effectively. Adding sex back into the mix was a new factor, but it didn't warrant extra significance. People had been having casual sex since the beginning of time, and she was determined to keep it light and fun.

She returned home that evening to a cute note from Mark stating he'd had an amazing time with her, and to eat the leftovers since he'd be home late. Smiling at his thoughtfulness, she devoured the ribs and pasta salad before eventually retiring to her room.

The rest of the week was busy for both of them and she barely saw Mark, except for the mid-week fundraising lunch Evan scheduled. On Friday, he arrived home around eight p.m. and found her drinking wine at the kitchen table as she toiled on her laptop.

"Hey," she said, smiling as he squeezed her shoulder.

"Hey, stranger." He strode over to the counter and poured himself a glass of wine before sitting down. "To a long freaking week."

Clinking her glass against his, she sipped. "Seriously. I wasn't sure you still lived here."

"I shot my first campaign commercial this week and it was intense. But I'm now an expert at the phrase, '*I'm Mark Lancaster and I approve this message.*'"

"Well done. I firmly believe you are, indeed, Mark Lancaster."

Grinning, he swirled the wine. "So, I was hoping you'd be downstairs when I got home. The weekend's coming and I'd kind of like to spend it with you."

Her heart skipped a beat. "You would?"

Nodding, he shrugged. "I was never into dating because I thought it would be so much work. You know, having to expend effort to ensure you had great conversation and possibly great sex afterward."

"Yes, those things usually require a small bit of effort," she said, arching an eyebrow.

"Touché." He playfully rolled his eyes. "I think I built it up in my head that it was a waste of time because I never really enjoyed it. I just never really clicked with most of the women I dated and found them needy and shallow. I know that probably sounds judgmental but it was my honest experience." Sliding his hand across the table, he extended his fingers and she slid her palm over his. "It's just different with you, Teresa. I don't why, but it is."

"Are you saying I'm low-effort? I'm not sure how I feel about that."

Throwing back his head, he laughed. "Man, I'm blowing this. I think what I'm trying to say is that I don't feel the need to define this further than what it is. I enjoy spending time with you and I definitely enjoy making love to you. I know you want to set ground rules and I'm all for that. I just don't want to overthink things since they're already so easy between us. Does that make sense?"

Licking her lips, she studied him. "It does. I just hesitate to leave things undefined in the instance one of us finds ourselves wanting more."

His thumb gently caressed her skin. "I'm still not there yet, mostly due to how chaotic life is with the campaign, maintaining our engagement, and trying to help my sister. I'm fine with casual but monogamous like we were before. I'd like to just go with the flow since we live with each other now."

"And what does that mean to you?"

Lifting a shoulder, he said, "If you fall asleep in my bed you don't freak out, and if I sneak into yours, you'll let me kiss you."

He was so cute as he waited for her response, a hopeful glint in his eyes. "Only kiss me?"

He squinted. "Maybe a *bit* more. You're kind of irresistible, Teresa, but I think you know that."

Biting her lip, she could barely contain her grin. "I'm glad you think so. I'll be forty-seven soon. I'm hoping I don't age out during our fake engagement."

"No way. You're gorgeous, honey. And I'm secretly enamored you're the older woman. It's got an exciting vibe to it."

"Uh, if you say so." She playfully scrunched her features. "Okay, I'm fine with going with the flow and spending time with each other when we're able to. But if things change—if you feel it's getting too serious for you—I want you to tell me, and I'll do the same."

"Done." He squeezed her hand. "Now that we've gotten that out of the way, I really need to explore the whole kissing thing." Tugging her toward him, she yelped as he dragged her to straddle his lap.

"Oh, yeah, that's good," he said, cupping the globes of her ass as she threaded her fingers through his hair, grasping for balance. "Come here, Dr. Roe. I need a consultation."

Giving in to the laughter and the onslaught of feelings, Teresa cemented her lips to his.

Chapter 17

♥

Mark began the week extremely pleased with how his life was progressing after the scandal that could've upended everything. Instead, the near-disaster had created something so magnificent in its wake, he thanked the universe for his fortuitous stroke of good luck. He was now living with a sexy-as-hell woman who appeared at fundraisers with him, doubling the haul because she was extremely popular. She wasn't needy or vapid and gave him space in the home she treated with respect.

Oh, and there was one other thing: Mark was having the best sex of his life with the remarkable and stunning Dr. Roe.

Never had he been with someone who made him laugh but also made him feel so comfortable. Perhaps comfortability was a strange thing to covet in a lover, but he'd found it with Teresa and it was pretty damn awesome. Mark had always thought relationships were time-consuming and extremely difficult. Although his parents had a wonderful marriage, they were the exception to the rule and he'd seen too many instances of messy divorces and unhappy couples.

But with Teresa? They just fit, somehow. It was easy and fun and...*free.* He felt free with her, which was definitely not something he'd ever anticipated. Even though he believed he would settle down and have kids one day, he understood that final step would require intense energy and dedication.

"Maybe you were wrong, buddy," he said to himself as he tossed a salad in his kitchen one Friday evening a few weeks after the cookout. He'd mixed a homemade Caesar dressing and couldn't wait to try it. Teresa was due home any minute and he hoped she'd sit down and eat with him...before he carried her to bed and did all sorts of naughty things to her exquisite body. Grinning at the thought, his head whipped when he heard her heels on the hardwood in the foyer.

"I'm making a chicken Caesar salad," he called, hoping like hell she'd be open to wearing the heels to bed again. That had been *hot* and he was suddenly anxious to recreate it.

"Awesome," she said, striding into the kitchen as his phone rang. "I'm starving."

Checking the caller ID, he noticed it was Justine. "Let me take this. Go ahead and make a plate." Lifting the phone to his ear, he said, "Hey, Jus, what's up—"

"He's not breathing, Mark!" his sister's agitated voice said on the other end. "He hit his head on the counter and there's blood everywhere."

A wave of fear for her and Avery washed over him as blood pounded through his veins. "Justine," he said, ensuring his tone was calm. "I need you to breathe. Just take a few deep breaths. Are you and Avery okay?"

"He hit her, Mark," she sobbed, sounding so distraught he wanted to reach through the phone and pull her through so she could escape. "I can't believe he hit her. We were fighting and she ran into the kitchen and he...oh, my god..."

"What happened next?" he asked, clenching the counter.

"I wanted to protect her. I grabbed the knife from the block and I swiped at him. I sliced his arm open and he lunged at me. I dodged and Avery screamed and then I cut his other arm as he advanced. He...he lost his balance and hit his head on the corner of the island, Mark. *Ohmygod*, I think he's dead."

Teresa cupped his shoulder, concern in her eyes as she gazed up at him.

"Justine, I need you to listen to me. Is Avery still in the kitchen?"

"Yes."

"Okay, first, call 911. Tell them there was an accident, he fell and hit his head, and that it was self-defense. Don't say anything else. You're not required to divulge any details. Then, take Avery to her bedroom and pull up a movie on the tablet. It's better to remove her from the scene if it's bloody. Then, come back downstairs and wait for me. I'll be there in ten minutes. If the cops get there first, don't say anything else. Do you understand?"

"Yes," she whispered.

"Good. Okay, hang up and call 911. Do you know CPR?"

"I learned years ago but I don't remember."

"Okay. Once Avery's upstairs, hold pressure to his wounds to stop the bleeding. Then, wait for the ambulance to arrive."

Uneven breaths skated across the phone.

"Justine. Call 911 and get Avery upstairs. I'll be there soon."

"Okay."

The phone went dark and he lowered it to his side, needing a moment to gather his thoughts.

"My god, Mark. What happened?"

"Dean hit Avery and there was an altercation with Justine. He fell and hit his head on their kitchen island."

Lifting her fingers to her mouth, she shook her head, eyes wide. "I can go with you."

"No," he said, striding to the counter and grabbing his keys. "I've already involved you in one too many scandals."

"What about your niece? I can watch her if you need me to."

Rubbing his forehead, he nodded. "Let me go there and assess and call you afterward. I'm sorry."

"Don't apologize," she said, following him when he turned and stalked down the hallway. "I mean it, Mark. I want to help and I'm equipped to handle crisis situations. Once you've figured everything out call me."

Facing her as they stood in the foyer, he cupped her cheek. "I will. I have to go." Leaning down, he placed a soft kiss on her lips. "I'll call you when I know more." Opening the front door, he headed to his car.

On the way to Justine's, he called his friend Gary Lincoln, who was an Ardor Creek police officer.

"Hey, Mark," Gary said, answering on the second ring. "We already got the call."

"Holy shit, Gary. I have no idea how injured he is. It's possible he died upon impact. I told her not to say anything. It was self-defense."

"That piece of garbage has been rough with them for a long time," was Gary's angry reply. "I'm pissed as hell, Mark. I'm on my way now. I'm off duty tonight, but I told Chief I wanted to go to the scene since she's a family friend."

Mark huffed out a breath. "I guess we are kind of like family at this point. Forty years in Ardor Creek will do that to you."

"Damn straight. I should be there in two minutes."

"I'll be there in five. See you soon."

Several minutes later, Mark parked on the street outside Justine's house, noticing the ambulance and police cars with lights circling. Entering the house, he found her in the living room, sitting beside Gary as he stroked her arm.

"It's okay, Jus," his friend said as she cried into her hands. "He's still alive."

Mark's eyes widened. "He is?"

Gary nodded. "They're loading him on the gurney now and are going to take him to the hospital. He's unconscious and the head wound is severe."

Mark turned to see two paramedics wheeling a stretcher out the front door, Dean atop it as he lay under a white blanket.

"Where's Avery?"

"She's upstairs," Justine said, staring up at him with wet eyes. "She's watching cartoons on her tablet with headphones on. I told her to stay there until I come upstairs."

Crouching down, he pulled her into his arms. "Give me a hug and I'll go see her." Justine squeezed him as she sniffled in his ear. Turning to look at Gary, he asked, "Has anyone questioned her?"

Gary shook his head. "Jim and Susan are the two deputies on duty. They're in the kitchen examining the scene. I told them you were her lawyer and to wait until you got here."

Drawing back, Justine wiped her cheeks. "Are they going to arrest me?"

"Most likely," Gary said, his tone resigned but supportive. "I'll stay with you as long as you need me, Jus."

Mark observed the reverent way his friend gazed upon his sister as realization slammed through him. Gary was in love with her. Mark wasn't sure how, but he just *knew*. It was evident in the way he stroked the hair from her temple and stared at her with emotion-filled eyes. Curiosity flamed deep within as he wondered how long Gary had hidden the feelings, but now was certainly not the time to explore it. Rising, he squeezed Justine's shoulder.

"Let me go check on Avery. Can I take her home with me tonight if they hold Justine?"

"I'll make sure you can," Gary said. "Child Protective Services is going to want to process her in the system, but we'll figure it out."

"Thank you," Justine whispered, clutching his hand. "Please don't let them put my baby with anyone else besides Mark. I don't want her to be placed with strangers."

"I won't," Gary said softly. "I promise, Jus."

Sucking in a breath, Mark headed upstairs to find Avery. She was sitting on her bed, lounging as she watched her tablet wearing cute pink earphones. Noticing him, she sat up and tugged them off.

"Daddy hit Mommy and then he hit me," she said, appearing so small in the bed. Fear laced her blue eyes and he hurt for her.

Sitting down, he noticed the red marks on her cheek as fury threatened to choke him. Opening his arms, he asked, "Can I hug you? I just really need a munchkin hug right now—"

She flew into his embrace, knocking the air from his lungs. Squeezing, he forced himself to let her go, remembering she might be hurt in other places as well. Drawing back, he held her upper arms. "Did Daddy hit you anywhere besides your face, sweetheart? Did he push you hard enough to make a bruise or create any painful spots?"

She shook her head, chewing on her bottom lip.

"It's okay. Do you want to tell me something?"

Tears filled her eyes, shattering his heart into a million pieces.

"He hit Mommy really hard. Like this in her side," she said, gently touching her fist to his abdomen, "and then like this." She tenderly touched her fist to the side of his throat. "I tried to help her."

Mark recalled the bruises he'd seen on Justine's neck downstairs. Clenching his fists, he imagined heading to the hospital and finishing the job of murdering Dean Rodgers. What a fucking bastard.

"That was really brave of you to try and help her," he said, stroking her hair. "We're going to go to the police station with Mommy and some nice people are going to ask you what happened. I'll be there the whole time."

"Is Daddy hurt?"

Mark nodded. "He's going to the hospital right now."

Avery's eyes darted between his as she contemplated what to say. The blue orbs were filled with heartache and fear that a five-year-old should never have to fathom. Hating she'd experienced violence, he tried to lift his expression, hoping to soothe her.

"Hey," he said, smiling as he rubbed her arm. "Mom and Dad will be okay, munchkin." He had no idea if the words were true, but felt it more important to comfort her.

"I don't like him."

"Who?"

"Daddy," she said as her chin trembled. "He's mean and hits Mommy a lot."

"I bet that's scary."

She nodded. "If he gets better maybe he can live somewhere else. Mommy and I have fun when he's not here."

Cupping her cheek, wetness clouded his eyes, and he told himself to stay strong. "You're never going to live with him again. I promise you that, sweetheart. Do you hear me? I'm going to take care of you and your mom, and you'll never have to live with him again."

"Can we come live with you?"

His throat tightened at the heart-wrenching question.

"I'm going to take you home with me tonight," he said, determined to accomplish that feat. "We'll have a sleepover at Uncle Mark's house. Would you like that?"

Nodding, she grabbed the plush bunny that sat against the far pillow. The stuffed animal had seen better days and one of its ears was missing. "Can I take Carrot with me?"

Smiling, he stood and lifted her in his arms. "You sure can. I'm going to bring you downstairs to talk to the policemen and police ladies. They're going to be really nice and ask you questions about what happened. Mom's friend Gary is here and he's a policeman too. You remember Gary, right?"

She nodded.

"Okay. If you're scared or have any questions, you just let me know." Situating her against his hip, he carried her downstairs to begin the process of overseeing his sister's arrest.

Chapter 18

♥

By three a.m., Mark was exhausted. Standing in the staid interrogation room, he waited for Gary to appear. Teresa had called him as he drove to the police station and insisted she wanted to help. Since she was a social worker, she had many contacts at CPS and Mark was thankful for her assistance.

She'd arrived at the station, a determined look on her face as Gary brought her up to speed. They'd worked together to expedite Avery's meeting with CPS while Mark oversaw Justine's questioning by the detectives on duty.

There was no doubt it was self-defense. Unfortunately, the D.A. was Mark's sworn enemy and he felt a sense of foreboding that Chisolm would take special interest in Justine's case to hurt him. It was terribly unfair to Justine, but such was life, and Mark would do his best to represent her and get any charges dropped.

Eventually, Justine was taken into custody and charged with involuntary manslaughter. Mark had a feeling Gary had a hand in garnering that charge instead of attempted murder. Dean was in a coma at the local hospital fighting for his life due to the severe head injury and deep cuts on his arms. Mark hoped the life support malfunctioned and he went to hell where he belonged.

"Your arraignment is set for nine o'clock Monday morning at the county courthouse in Scranton, Jus. I'm going to propose they let you out on bail," Mark said, speaking to her in the interrogation room before they placed her into custody. "You're not a flight risk and have no prior offenses. Unfortunately, you'll have to stay in county jail until Dean can make a statement."

"He'll say it was my fault," Justine said, tears welling in her eyes. "That I tried to hurt him. He'll never admit he hit Avery or me."

"You let me worry about that," Mark said, feeling his nostrils flare. "I deal with scumbags like him all the time. The truth always comes out eventually."

She gave an almost imperceptible nod. "Were you able to ensure Avery can come home with you?"

"Yes," Teresa said beside him, her features laced with compassion. "Gary and I were able to get CPS to sign off on Avery coming home with us. I can also try and have your parents added to the list of approved guardians."

"No, I only want her with Mark," Justine said, hands clenched atop the table. "Dad's recovering from surgery and Mom can barely handle that. They don't have the capacity to take care of her. You have to take care of her, Mark. Please."

"I will, Jus," he said, sliding his hands in his pockets as he leaned against the cement wall. "I promise."

Her lips formed a tender smile. "Hope you're ready for a crash course in parenting, big bro. And you too, Teresa. Man, you really stepped in it when you met my brother on that app. We're supplying you with a constant stream of scandals. Sex addict politician and prospective murderer. Welcome to the family."

Teresa breathed a laugh. "Well, I remember thinking life had become a tad boring before I met Mark. Maybe I manifested this in some strange way. Regardless, your brother is pretty awesome and I'll help him take care of Avery, Justine."

"Thank you," she whispered. "I'm so sorry, guys."

"Don't apologize for protecting yourself and your daughter from that asshole," Mark said, straightening. "I'm going to get every fucking charge dropped, Jus. I mean it."

Gary opened the door and trailed inside the room. Lifting the handcuffs from his belt, he sighed. "I have to cuff you to take you to the county jail in Scranton, Jus. I'm sorry. It's standard procedure. I convinced Jim and Susan to let me ride in the back seat with you and I'll help process everything when we arrive."

Rising, she blew a breath through puffed cheeks. "Okay." Extending her arms, she approached him. "Go ahead."

Gently encircling her upper arm, he turned her. "Cross your wrists behind your back." She complied as clicks echoed off the walls while the cuffs were secured.

"I love you," Mark said, hugging her one last time before pulling back and stroking her face. "Don't worry. You've got the best lawyer in Lackawanna County." He winked, hoping to reassure her.

"I love you too," she whispered. Giving Gary a nod, she let him lead her from the room.

Exhaling, Mark ran his hand through his hair. "Son of a bitch," he muttered.

Teresa approached, sliding her arms around his waist and clutching. Resting her head on his chest, she squeezed, giving him the comfort he so desperately needed. Grateful, he embraced her, resting his cheek on her soft curls as she held him.

"I'm so honored to be your fake fiancée," she said, causing him to smile at her gentle teasing. "You handled this brilliantly, Mark."

"I swear," he said, stroking her hair, "I was a fairly normal, boring person before I met you, Teresa. There wasn't one criminal act or hint of scandal in my family."

Chuckling, she burrowed into him. "This is much more exciting. And, we get to bring your adorable niece home." Drawing back, she grinned. "She's so sweet, Mark. I can't wait to get to know her."

Cupping her cheek, he shook his head. "I don't deserve you." His voice was raspy with emotion, and he was humbled by her acceptance and understanding.

"None of that," she said, wrinkling her nose. "I'm happy to be here for you. Now, if you're ready, there's a little girl who's scared and tired waiting for us. Let's take her home." Extending her hand, she lifted her brows and wiggled her fingers.

Mark grasped them for dear life, thankful he had a companion on this uncharted journey. Never had he craved a partner to handle tough situations in his life but, now, knowing Teresa was by his side, he was armed with the most powerful ammunition in this new battle: her unwavering support.

Following her from the interrogation room, they trekked to find Avery and head home.

When they arrived at Mark's house, he carried a sleeping Avery inside and placed her in his bed. Pulling the covers over her, he kissed her forehead and trailed to the kitchen, where Teresa was making tea.

"Here," she said, placing two cups on the table. "It's decaffeinated so hopefully we can still sleep afterward."

Sitting across from her, he sipped the warm liquid. "Thank you. I put her in my bed and I'll sleep on the couch. Suddenly, my two-bedroom townhome isn't ideal."

"You've gained a fiancée and a kid in the span of a few months. I think your single status might be shattered."

Chuckling, he blew on his fingers and opened them wide. "Gone with the wind. Shit got real tonight."

Studying him as she drank, she narrowed her eyes. "Avery can have my bed and I'll sleep on the couch. I don't mind."

"No way. I'm perfectly fine on the couch." When she tried to argue, he lifted a hand. "Non-negotiable, hon. At least I can still let you have a comfortable place to sleep."

"Okay." Her full lips formed a tender smile as she sipped the tea. "What is Evan going to say about all this? We need to form a plan. I'm sure Chisolm is going to take advantage of your sister's situation."

"I have no doubt he's going to exploit the hell out of it. Justine will get dragged in the press even worse than we were because he'll spin her into some sort of revengeful attempted murderess. I fear it's going to devolve quickly."

"Then, we'll just have to fight." Reaching over, she encircled his wrist. "I'm in this now and I'm determined to help you beat Chisolm. We'll do it together, Mark."

His lips formed a slight frown as he covered her hand atop his wrist. "I'm not sure it's fair to ask you to do that."

"You didn't ask. I'm offering and I'm pretty tough when I'm laser-focused on something, so let's get to work." Drinking the last sip of her tea, she stood and placed the cup in the sink. "After I sleep, that is. I'm beat."

Striding over, he placed his mug in the sink. Cupping the juncture between her neck and shoulder, he felt his heart thrum as she gazed up at him with those multi-colored eyes.

"This puts a damper on our newly resumed sexy shenanigans. I was *really* looking forward to them during the rest of our cohabitation."

Licking her lips, she placed her hand over his cheek. "People with crazy lives have sex all the time, Mark. If we want to figure out a way to make it happen, we can."

"I want it to happen," he all but growled, causing her to laugh. "I've never wanted anything so much in my damn life."

"Then we'll find a way. Let's get everything settled for Justine and Avery and we'll pick up where we left off." Sliding her arms around his neck, she flashed a gorgeous smile. "I want you too, you know? Maybe I'll just sneak into your room while you're showering since I can't seduce you on the couch. Oh, that sounds fun." She waggled her brows.

"Are you trying to give me blue balls?" he asked, drawing her closer. "Because that's the obvious result when I think about you in the shower."

Lifting to her toes, she brushed a kiss across his lips. "Maybe for tonight but not forever. Let's make it a reality one day soon. Good night, Mark." Running her thumb over his lips, she blew him a kiss and turned to head to bed.

After placing the cups in the dishwasher, Mark lowered to the couch, unable to keep his eyes open. Drawing the blanket over his body, he closed them, dreaming of Teresa's wet olive skin as he loved her in the shower. Hell yes, that was happening. But first, he had to figure out a plan. Already anticipating the plethora of tasks he needed to accomplish tomorrow, he fell into a depleted slumber.

Chapter 19

Teresa awoke early and was unable to get back to sleep. Figuring it was a sign, she got up with the sun and headed to the grocery store. She and Mark usually ate egg white omelets for breakfast and, although they were great, she didn't foresee a five-year-old enjoying them quite as much as she did. Searching the aisles, she found the yellow pancake mix container, thankful it was labeled "Shake and Pour." That she could certainly do.

She also grabbed some turkey sausage links and syrup and headed home to cook breakfast. Once she'd thrown back on her sweatpants and t-shirt, she got to work in the kitchen. As she stood over the stove assessing which pancakes to flip, she noticed something out of the corner of her eye. Turning, she saw a sleepy Avery in the doorway clutching a stuffed bunny that only had one ear.

"Hi, Avery," she said, noticing the t-shirt that fell past her knees. "I bet Uncle Mark gave you that comfy shirt to sleep in. I thought I heard you two talking early this morning before going back to bed."

Avery nodded.

"Well, it looks very comfortable. I'm making pancakes and sausage. I took a guess you'd like pancakes. Was I right?"

She padded over on bare feet and strained to look at the stove. "I like them a lot. Mommy makes them really good."

"Sweet," she said, flipping one over in the pan. "I'm not a great cook, but I think they look okay. I'll load them on a plate and we can eat at the table. Do you like sausage too?"

A gap-toothed smile accompanied her nod.

"Fantastic. Want to reach inside the drawer there and grab us three forks? You can set them on the table and hopefully Uncle Mark will wake up and eat them with us."

"That would be great because Uncle Mark is starving," a deep baritone chimed from the doorway.

Avery ran toward him and he picked her up, placing sloppy kisses on her neck as she giggled. Their obvious affection for each other was endearing and Teresa tamped down the images that flitted through her brain. Images of having her own little girl and husband to cook breakfast for. Sighing, she flipped another pancake.

"Hey," he said, eyes hooded from sleep as he smiled down at her. "You didn't have to cook. This is amazing."

"It's only pancakes and sausage. Nothing as intense as the meals you whip up." A tuft of hair stood straight on his head, mussed from sleep, and she ached to run her fingers through it. God, he was sexy like this, his voice still gravelly as he slowly awoke. Telling herself to get a grip, she gestured with her head.

"Want to help Avery set the table? The syrup's right there and I'll load everything up and bring it over."

"Thanks," he said, squeezing her wrist before following her directive.

They had an easy, relaxed breakfast as Teresa got to know Avery better. She learned that Carrot was her best friend, although her neighbors Kate and Roxanne were a close second. She would start kindergarten in September and was excited to go to school.

"I can already read," Avery said, chin jutted proudly as she finished the last of her pancakes. "Mommy says I'm really good."

"Whoa, that's awesome," Teresa said, winking at Mark as he chewed. "We need to buy some books so you have some here at Mark's house."

Licking her lips, she looked at Mark. "Can I go back home with Mommy soon?"

"You already tired of me, kid?" he teased, smoothing his hand over her hair.

"No," she said, giggling. "But I miss Mommy."

Teresa's heart lurched at the sweet statement.

Sitting back, Mark exhaled a deep breath. "Mommy is going to go before a judge and explain everything that happened with

Daddy on Monday morning. Once she does, we'll see if she's able to come home. I really hope she is. If she's not, you can stay with me and Teresa a while longer. Would that be okay with you?"

Avery nodded.

"Good." Standing, he stacked the plates and took them to the sink. "In the meantime, Grandma and Grandpa want us to come over tonight and have dinner with them. She's going to cook spaghetti and garlic bread." Rubbing his chin, he squinted at the ceiling. "If I remember, there's a little girl I know who really enjoys spaghetti and garlic bread..."

"Me!" she called, raising her hand. "I love it when Grandma makes spaghetti."

"Whew," he said, wiping his forehead. "I thought it was you. Thank goodness." Lifting his gaze to Teresa's, he arched a brow. "I'd love for you to come with us. If you're free, that is. I don't want to infringe on your private time. You might be tired of us."

Inwardly thrilled at the invite, she leaned her head on hand as her elbow rested on the table. "I'd love to," she said, unable to keep the wistfulness from her tone.

His grin threatened to shatter her heart. Did he think she wouldn't accept?

"I have to warn you, my mother will grill you about everything. It will probably be pretty intense. You can think about it and back out any time before we leave. I was thinking of heading over around five."

Breathing a laugh, Teresa shrugged. "I have to meet her someday, right? She did make you promise to bring me to dinner. Why not today?"

"Fair enough. In the meantime, I need to head to the office and then the police station and process some documents for Justine's arraignment on Monday morning. I'm going to go visit her in Scranton tomorrow, and Carrie and Peter have agreed to watch Avery so you can have a break from our insanity."

"I'm happy to watch her, Mark. I think we're becoming friends, right?"

Avery bit her lip, adorable as she nodded with excitement beside Teresa.

"That's amazing but you still deserve your space."

"I'll take it, but we're a team now, Mark. I hope you realize I'm in this and want to help."

His gaze was reverent as his throat bobbed.

"Thank you," he whispered.

With a nod, Teresa cleared the rest of the table and headed upstairs to shower and dress. Afterward, she sat in the living room updated the EMRs on her laptop while Avery played games on her tablet. Sounds of the shower running upstairs spurred images of Mark naked...with rivulets of water sliding over his muscular body...and she cleared her throat. Now that the shower fantasy had entered her head, she was becoming a bit obsessed.

In the afternoon, they took a walk around Mark's neighborhood, enjoying the warmth of May, before loading in the car and driving to Mark's parents' home. When they entered, Avery ran to a woman with short, white hair and embraced her in the foyer.

"How's my darling grandbaby?" she asked, kissing Avery's head. Straightening, she extended her arms to Mark, and Teresa noticed the sheen of tears in her eyes. "My sweet girl is in jail, Mark. How did this happen?"

"Don't cry, Mom," he said, embracing her. "I'm going to go see her tomorrow and I'm going to try like hell to get her out on bail."

Avery sucked in a breath below them. "You can't say 'hell'. It's a bad word."

Mark grimaced. "I meant 'heck'. Sorry, munchkin." Turning, he waved Teresa closer. "Mom, this is Teresa. Please don't give her the Spanish inquisition. She's here to have a nice, relaxing dinner with us."

"Oh, stop," she said, swatting his chest. "Brenda Lancaster," she said, extending her hand. "So nice to meet you. My son says such glowing things about you every time he stops by."

"Such a pleasure to meet you, Brenda," Teresa said.

Craning her neck, she looked at Teresa's left hand. "Where's mother's ring?"

"Long story," Mark said, ushering her to the kitchen. "It's in a safe place, Mom. Relax. Can we help you set the table?"

"Oh, fine," she said, pivoting to walk to the kitchen. "You all never tell your mother anything anyway. I wish Justine would let Avery stay with us but she seems adamant she wants her to stay with you.

I'm perfectly capable of taking care of a child. After all, I raised you two, didn't I?"

"Brenda!" A deep voice called from the living room. "Bring them in here so I can see Avery and meet Teresa. Damn it, I can't move from the couch."

Mark arched a brow. "You were saying?" he said sardonically to his mother. "I think you have your hands full."

"Oh, posh," she said, waving them toward the living room. "Go on and hang with him so he'll calm down. Dinner will be ready in twenty minutes."

Teresa found Joseph lovely with his sparkling brown eyes, so similar to Mark's, even if he was a bit surly at being relegated to the couch. Eventually, they sat down to eat at the long wooden dining room table and she enjoyed the meal immensely.

Several hours later, once the sun set behind the horizon, they loaded into the car and headed home.

"I gather from the dinner conversation that your parents' relationship with Justine is a bit strained," she said to Mark from the passenger seat as Avery sat in the back, watching her tablet.

"Yeah," he said, sighing. "They had this vision for us. Graduate high school, get a college degree, and get a professional job. Justine is a brilliant artist and always wanted to pursue that. Add in her tumultuous relationship with Dean, and it created some tension."

"Understandable. Hopefully, once everything is settled, she'll move on from him. That should at least ease the strain on that front."

"Hope so."

Pulling into the driveway, they ambled into the townhome and eventually began prepping for bed. As Teresa slid in between the soft sheets, she thought of Mark sleeping downstairs on the couch so his niece could have his bed. It was a selfless act, affirming his decent and loving nature. He would make an excellent father to his own children one day. Running her hand over her abdomen, Teresa allowed the tears to well, saddened at the thought of what he would create with someone else.

Deep in her heart, she acknowledged the desire to be the one to give him children. Allowing the tears to fall, she processed them, understanding she needed to let the pain surface. After a while, she wiped them from her face and expelled a deep breath, releasing the yearning.

The sentiments were serious and perhaps that should've worried her. Instead, they gave her a strange sense of peace. She was on the precipice of falling in love with Mark. The realization reminded her that she still had the ability to feel...the ability to love...that she was human. Although they had no future, it was comforting since she'd lost so much. Embracing the feelings, she turned to her side, placed her wet cheek against the pillow, and fell to sleep.

Chapter 20

♥

Mark embraced a positive outlook, barreling head-first into representing his sister and getting Avery settled in his home. When he visited Justine on Sunday, she reaffirmed her desire that Avery stay with him and not their parents, although she was open to them taking care of her if Mark needed a break. Wanting to ease her, Mark agreed. He loved Avery with all his heart, so the decision was effortless.

Teresa was a champ, embracing the situation with graceful poise. Mark was awed by her easy acceptance of their new normal and often wondered how she remained so balanced. The more time he spent with her, the more enamored he became, and he realized he was developing feelings for her.

In the past, he hadn't dated one woman long enough to truly get to know them on a personal level. Usually, after the lust waned, he would lose interest and cut ties, hoping they found someone they felt a connection with. But his situation with Teresa made cutting ties impossible. It forced him to maintain a relationship based on agreement instead of lust. Of course, there was lust—Mark couldn't remember ever being more attracted to someone. But more than that, they'd developed a mutual respect, and he was awed by her kindness and acceptance.

On Sunday evening, Mark received a call that Dean was awake and talking to detectives. Mark held no illusions that James Chisolm would hold back a vicious media assault against his sister and spin her into the culprit instead of her shitbag husband. Resolved to fight tooth and nail, he would dedicate every effort to getting her charges dropped and ensuring she reunite with Avery.

Unfortunately, he didn't have to wait long for the battle to begin.

When Mark walked into the courtroom Monday morning, he saw James Chisolm at the prosecutor's desk and his throat tightened with anxiety.

"This is a minor arraignment hearing," Mark said, approaching him. "There's no reason for the D.A. to oversee this case."

"A pleasure to see you too, Mark," Chisolm said, features contorted as he tilted his gray head. "A D.A. must take all cases under their jurisdiction seriously. You wouldn't understand since you'll never reach that position."

"My sister is charged with involuntary manslaughter. It's hardly murder."

"Oh, didn't you hear? Dean Rodgers is awake and he's quite talkative. Seems he was the innocent party and your sister attacked him. I'll be amending the charges to attempted murder and you can bet I'll prosecute this case to the fullest extent of the law."

Mark's hand fisted as he saw red. Inhaling deeply, he forced himself not to punch the bastard in the face right there in the courtroom. "He's an abuser, Chisolm. You know it was self-defense."

Chisolm shrugged. "Make the case then. It's his word against hers. We'll see."

Furious, Mark set up at the defendant's desk and smiled reassuringly at Justine when she was brought in wearing an orange jumpsuit. Kissing her forehead, he updated her on Chislom's plan.

"Attempted murder?" she whispered. "That's insane. He hit me and then he hit Avery. I only pulled the knife because I thought he was going to hurt her. Mark, this is crazy."

"Chisolm's using you to get to me," he gritted, feeling a muscle tick in his jaw. "It's disgusting but I expected this. I'm going to do my best to get you released on bail, but if the escalation of charges is accepted it will be more difficult in the short term. But don't worry, Jus. I won't rest until you're released and the charges are dismissed."

"I understand," she said, nostrils flaring as her chin warbled. "I should've left Dean years ago. I'm such an idiot. You tried to tell me and Gary always urged me to file restraining orders when he was rough with me..." Closing her eyes, a tear slid down her cheek.

"I fucked everything up. I believed him every time he said it was the last time."

"He's the one who was wrong here, Jus. Not you. It might take some time but justice will prevail. I truly believe that."

Lifting her lids, she gave a warbled smile. "You've always fought for the good guy and been the optimist. I love that about you. Thank you for doing this, Mark. I'm sorry I've brought another scandal on your campaign."

"Don't worry about that. I'm going to beat this jerk and Teresa's my secret weapon. We won't let him win."

Her eyes skated between his. "You glow when you talk about her, you know?"

Mark smiled. "How can I not? She's amazing."

"Holy shit," she almost whispered. "I'd almost given up."

"On what?"

"That you'd find your person. I think she's your person, Mark."

Squinting at the ceiling, he pondered. "It's an interesting notion for your independent and slightly commitment-phobic brother. Regardless, I'm thankful for her support, and Avery has really taken to her as well."

"Thank god. I'm so thankful you're taking care of her. Nothing against Mom and Dad but, well, it's just easier with you."

"I get it. I'm still going to accept help when they offer. Maybe this is a good opportunity for you all to mend your relationship. You always thought they were so disappointed at your decision to become an artist but I don't think they understood it, Jus."

"They never *tried* to understand it," she said, annoyed. "Mom just kept telling me I could make my sculptures in my spare time once I got a real job."

"Well, maybe they can change."

The conversation ended as the judge entered the chamber. Mark and Chisolm went back and forth, debating the escalation of the charges and the reasons for bail. He did his best to outline the truth and Dean's history of abuse. Unfortunately, Chisolm had a sworn affidavit from Dean stating he was the victim and Justine had attacked him. After much debate, the judge made his decision.

"I'm always sorry to see these types of cases. Domestic abuse is a serious allegation and I understand your plight, young lady," he said to Justine. "But Dean Rodgers disputes this allegation and it's important we have all the facts and hear from all parties before a decision is made. I accept the escalation of charges to attempted murder and deny bail at this time. If any other extenuating evidence comes to light, I want to be made aware immediately. Understood?"

Mark and Chisolm uttered their agreement as Justine placed her head in her cuffed hands, unable to control the tears.

"Has the child been assigned a temporary guardian?"

"I've submitted a court order to be named temporary guardian until a verdict is announced," Mark said, gently rubbing Justine's back as she sobbed beside him. "CPS completed the documentation the night Mrs. Rodgers was taken into custody and we'd like a confirmation ruling from you."

"Do you have any objection?" the judge asked Chisolm.

"No objection, Your Honor."

"Then I accept the temporary custody arrangement and it will remain in effect until a verdict is determined in this case. I'll hear arguments in three weeks on June 12th at nine a.m. Good luck, young lady. I'm sorry for this turn of events and wish you the best." Banging his gavel, he stood and court was adjourned.

Mark hugged her before the guard came to lead her away. "I need you to be strong, Jus. We're going to fight this with everything we've got and I'll take care of Avery. I'll bring her to see you as much as you want."

"Let me think about it," she said as the guard led her away. "I'm not sure I want her to see me in jail."

He nodded as she disappeared through the wooden door. Pivoting, he stalked to James Chisolm as he was stacking papers into his briefcase.

"Denying bail is ridiculous. You know she's not a flight risk or a threat to society. You're doing this to hurt me and it's despicable!"

A menacing chuckle escaped his lips. "Good luck winning an election when your sister is on trial for attempted murder *and* you're raising a little girl. I'm thrilled at that little turn of events, by the way. Having more responsibility in your life means less time to campaign. Not sure you thought that one through, Lancaster."

"Not everything is about the damn campaign," he hissed. "She's my niece. Of course, I'll take care of her. What the hell is wrong with you? Don't you have a family you care about? There has to be some speck of humanity inside that hardened shell you show to the world."

"I care about winning, my boy. It's all I've ever cared about. Your sister's actions have vastly increased my odds and I'll exploit them to the fullest extent." Grabbing his briefcase, he began to walk away before turning back. "You know? I messed up by outing your sexual relationship. I never thought you'd gin up the fake engagement and the voters love Dr. Roe."

"Because she represents intrinsic honesty and integrity," Mark said, jaw clenching. "Voters still appreciate that whether you want to believe it or not."

He shrugged. "Maybe. I was pissed I underestimated you and thought it might be over, but this new opportunity is gold. I won't rest until your sister is in prison for attempted murder, Mark. You messed with the wrong guy when you decided to run against me. Think about that next time before you make decisions you're not ready for." With a final nod, he pivoted and stalked away.

"Fucking asshole," Mark muttered, repressing the urge to throw his briefcase against the wall. Straightening his spine, he headed to face the day and figure out a way to save Justine.

Chapter 21

♥

The week was hectic as Mark and Evan tried to do damage control while Chisolm continued his assault. On Wednesday morning, Dean Rodgers appeared beside Chisolm at a press conference, head wrapped in a large white bandage while he balanced on a crutch. The image portrayed a man who was severely injured by a vindictive wife, although that was far from the truth.

"Dean Rodgers is an upstanding family man and loves his daughter," Chisolm said into the microphone. "This is just another example of how Mark Lancaster's family isn't up to the mantle of the austere position of District Attorney. Even now, Mr. Lancaster fights for his sister's freedom knowing she stabbed and almost murdered my client. I won't rest until she's locked away where she can't hurt anyone else."

Mark's hands almost crushed the phone as he watched the live stream and he reminded himself getting angry wouldn't help Justine. Cooler heads always prevailed in these situations, although maintaining calm was extremely difficult.

Dean stepped toward the mics and extolled a sob story regaling how much he loved Avery and Justine, assuring the reporters he would never hurt them.

"Lying bastard," Mark murmured to the phone. "Your day is coming, buddy."

After the press conference, he visited Justine at the county jail, reassured by her quiet optimism.

"I've thought about it a lot and I know we're going to win, Mark," she said into the receiver of the phone attached to the wall as he observed her through the glass that separated them. "I'm doing a lot of meditating and am visualizing the best outcome."

"I'm so proud of you, Jus," he said, placing his palm on the glass. "We'll get there."

Resting her palm against his through the divider, she smiled as a tear slid down her cheek. "Don't bring Avery to see me, okay? I don't want her to see me in here. Just keep doing what you're doing and ensuring she's happy. The hearing is only three weeks away and I know you're going to get me out of here."

"Are you sure?"

Nodding, she swiped away the tear. "They're going to ask for Avery's statement, right?"

"Yes," he said, glancing at his notes. "An assigned social worker will sit down with her to hear what happened in her own words. Teresa can't be assigned because she lives with me, but court-ordered social workers are very professional. She'll be in good hands."

"I don't want her to relive it, but I feel her statement will exonerate me."

"It will. I've also got a stop on Dean's custody request. That will never happen. Avery's staying with us until you're released so don't worry about that."

Smiling, Justine's eyes searched his. "My newly domesticated brother—fiancée, kid and all. It looks good on you."

"It's not so bad," he said, winking. "I love her so much, Jus."

Arching a brow, she asked, "Avery or Teresa?"

"Ha. Ha." Rising, he stacked his papers. "June 12th will be here before you know it. Love you, sis."

"Love you too."

Blowing her one last kiss, he headed home.

Teresa did her best to settle into the new normal—which certainly wasn't anything *close* to normal. Still, she was an expert at crisis management and knew Avery needed positive reinforcement in her life. Rebounding from her father's abuse and her mother's incarceration would require a lot of observation and care, and Teresa was determined to ensure the process was as smooth as possible.

Luckily, the three of them settled into a pattern that was rather effortless. One warm early-June evening, as they ate dinner in the kitchen, Mark brought up the idea of traveling to the lake on Saturday.

"Peter loves fishing and he can teach you," Mark said to Avery. "I think it would be fun to spend the day up there. What do you say?"

"Okay," she said, nodding as she ingested a bite of the paella Mark had prepared. "I've never been fishing."

"I used to go a long time ago with Grandpa but haven't been in years. It will be fun. Maybe Teresa will catch one too."

Teresa's eyebrows lifted. "I...oh, I wasn't sure if it was a family thing. If you all want to go with Peter's family that's fine. I have a ton of work to catch up on."

Mark's expression fell and she realized she'd inadvertently hurt his feelings.

"I don't want to infringe on your private time," he said, pushing the food around on his plate. "You've been spending so much time with us you probably need a break."

"You should come, Teresa," Avery said.

"I...oh, dear, well...of course, I'd love to. But I don't want you all to feel obligated to spend time with me."

"What's obligated?"

Teresa chuckled. "It's when you have to do something even if you don't want to."

Her lips formed an adorable pout. "You don't want to come to the lake with us?"

Lifting her gaze to Mark's, she noticed him pursing his lips to contain his laugh.

"I'm really bungling this. You could help me, you know?"

"I'm getting a kick out of it," he said, white teeth flashing as he smiled. "And, honestly, she feels the same way I do."

"If you really want me to come, I will. I just don't want to impose, Mark."

"I'd love for you to come," was his soft reply.

"Please come, Teresa," Avery pleaded.

Smiling, she nodded. "Okay. I'd love to join you guys."

Avery gave a cheer as Mark grinned. In truth, Teresa was happy to spend every waking hour with them, but she also was wise enough to foresee the impending issues. After all, not so long ago, she'd been ready for marriage. When that hadn't worked out, she'd tried like hell to have a child. Now, a relationship and a child had been placed in her path and she feared she was becoming attached.

She and Mark hadn't resumed their sexual relationship since Avery moved in, but Teresa felt them slowly dancing toward that inevitable conclusion once things were a bit more settled. It would add one more link in the chain that tethered her to him, and the more "family" activities she embarked upon, the more she would covet them.

Until it was over. Teresa often reminded herself of the expiration date of her current situation. Once Mark hopefully won the election in November, she would move out and they would resume their separate lives. If all went well, Mark would win Justine's case, allowing Avery to move back home. The temporary family unit they'd formed was born of necessity, not emotion.

And yet, knowing all that, Teresa longed to enjoy her time with these two people who were slowly occupying every inch of her heart. It was reckless and uncharacteristic of the careful, systematic way she usually approached life, but she'd done things that way for forty-six years and where had it gotten her? Alone and barren with a mountain of debt. At least now, she was debt-free with a handsome lover and an adorable kid to spend time with. Maybe reckless was exactly what she needed, if only for a while.

After dinner, as she was loading dishes into the dishwasher, Mark shimmied up behind her, bracketing her body with his. Placing his lips against the shell of her ear, he murmured, "Thank you for agreeing to come on Saturday."

Turning, she smiled, reveling in the feel of his warm body so close to hers. "Thank you for inviting me. I don't want you to feel like you have to. Unless you think there will be photographers there. Maybe it's good for them to see us in social situations."

"There's been some renewed interest in us since Justine's case, for sure, but that's not why I invited you."

"No?" Her tone was sultry as he drew closer.

"Definitely not." Pressing his lips to hers, he emitted a soft groan as he kissed her. "Avery's deep into the game on her tablet in the living room and I'm taking full advantage of that little snippet of good fortune."

Unable to resist, she slid her arms around his neck and lifted her lips to his. Gliding his arm around her waist, he drew her close, tangling his fingers in her hair and tilting her head to grant him access.

Their tongues warred and mated before he ended the kiss, placing tender pecks across her neck and resting his cheek against hers. "God, Teresa, I miss you. I need to be with you again soon."

She shuddered at the poignant words. "I miss you too."

Drawing back, he gazed at her, eyes swimming with desire. "Carrie and Peter offered to have Avery stay over tomorrow night. They have a guest bedroom she can sleep in, although the boys want to build a tent fort outside and sleep there. Carrie thought it might be fun for Avery to stay over."

Teresa considered. "It will probably do her good to be around other kids. I mean, she has been relegated to spending time with two proclaimed single adults. Being around the boys will be fun for her."

"And it will give us a night alone."

Stroking his scalp with her fingernails, she arched a brow. "Why, Mr. D.A., what would you do with me if we were alone?"

A sexy growl escaped his throat as he pushed his body into hers. "Well, something naughty in the shower comes to mind. I haven't been able to stop thinking about you in the shower since you mentioned it to me."

"Oh, my, that sounds dirty. You'll have to make sure to clean every inch of my body—"

"Uncle Mark," Avery cried, entering the room and holding up the tablet. "It's broken."

Sparing Teresa a frustrated glare, he extricated from her embrace and crouched down. "Let me see." Turing the tablet in his hands, he tried to turn it on. "The battery's probably dead, sweetie. Let me find a long cord and we'll charge it."

They began rummaging through a drawer as Teresa resumed loading the dishwasher, sad their sexy banter had ended. Eventually, they all retired to their separate rooms and she lifted the phone when it dinged.

Mark: Avery will be getting a tablet with unlimited battery life, by the way. I'm not taking any more chances.

Teresa: Good luck finding that. But I'm excited to have you all to myself Saturday night.

Mark: You have no idea, honey. I'm going to make you feel so good.

Teresa shivered underneath the covers, imagining his broad hands skating over her body.

Teresa: Counting on it. You always do. Sweet dreams.

Sending him a kiss emoji, she pulled up one of the recently published psychology articles a colleague had emailed over since reading it would send her right to sleep.

Chapter 22

♥

Teresa had a fantastic time at the lake on Saturday. Peter was hilariously self-deprecating as he encouraged the kids to fish, and Avery seemed to enjoy the activity. Sebastian appeared annoyed Peter was trying so hard to enroll him, but Charlie was excellent and caught several fish. After he caught his third, he and Peter threw it back and Sebastian rolled his eyes.

"I'm over this, Dad. I just want to play Nintendo Switch."

"Okay, buddy," Peter said, cupping Sebastian's shoulder. "I've tortured you long enough. You're free."

"Thank goodness," Sebastian said, relaying exasperation as he grabbed the handheld video game system and trailed to a large rock nearby. Sitting atop it, he began to play, shutting out the rest of the world.

Mark patted Peter on the back as he observed Avery spin the reel of the rod in her hand. "It's okay, man. We can't all be perfect dads. At least Charlie likes you."

"Hilarious," Peter muttered, leaning down to help Charlie. "Keep your day job and leave the jokes to me. Sebastian will fall in love with fishing one day. Mark my words."

"Holding my breath," Mark teased, eyes widening when Avery got a tug on her line. "Hey! You've got one! Let's reel it in."

Teresa sat beside Carrie on the blanket spread atop the grass, smiling as she observed them.

"They have the comradery of old friends," she said wistfully.

"They do," was Carrie's soft reply. "We've all known each other forever. The Ardor Creek boys are my family."

"How lovely." Teresa trailed the tip of a stick across the grass, wondering how to broach the subject on her mind. "If Sebastian ever wants to speak to someone, I'd be happy to talk to him, Carrie. He's a kind, sensitive little boy who will be transitioning to a teenager soon and that's always difficult, no matter how well adjusted you are."

Carrie's lips curved. "He's such a good kid, Teresa. I think the divorce and my ex-husband's desertion were hard on him. He holds a lot of anger inside, but he's also so sweet and funny."

"He is," Teresa said, encircling her wrist, "and I hope you don't think I'm overstepping. Therapists have an annoying habit of inserting themselves in situations and wanting to fix everything. I'm sorry if I crossed a line."

"Not at all," Carrie said, shaking her head. "I've thought about taking him to see someone for a while now. He probably should talk to someone neutral just to get the feelings out. Peter's presence in our life has been helpful but it only goes so far."

"Well, you just let me know." Teresa leaned back on her palms, inhaling the fresh air. "I'll do it for free."

Her eyebrows drew together. "I wouldn't ask that of you. Of course, I'd pay you for your time."

"I insist," Teresa said, her tone firm. "Friends don't exchange money for helping each other out. I hope we're becoming friends, Carrie. I really like hanging with you guys."

"We're definitely friends," she said with a tilt of her head. "And I love seeing you with Mark. He always kind of skulked through life solo but you two seem to fit somehow."

Inhaling, Teresa observed Mark's broad shoulders as he loomed over Avery, helping her with the fish that now dangled from the hook on her pole. "It's easy between us. I'm not sure I've ever felt that before. It doesn't sound romantic or exciting but maybe I'm too old for that stuff anymore," she said, her tone teasing.

"No, you're not. How old are you anyway, if you don't mind me asking? You look around our age. I'm forty and trying to have another baby so maybe I'm old too."

"I'll be forty-seven in August but you can tell everyone I'm your age." She winked.

"Well, you look amazing." Biting her lip, she seemed to ponder her next words. "Now I might be overstepping but Mark mentioned you tried to have a child through IVF. He didn't divulge any details, don't worry, but I'm curious about the process in case Peter and I can't conceive naturally. I'd love to pick your brain, but I don't want to invade your privacy or make you feel uncomfortable."

"It's fine," Teresa said, sitting straighter and crossing her legs beneath her. "Ask away and I'll try my best to answer honestly."

They talked for several minutes, Teresa relaying her experience and the different steps she took. Eventually, she informed Carrie of her inability to have children and her sadness at the loss.

"Oh, Teresa," she said, tears swimming in her green eyes. "I'm so very sorry. I wish I could change that for you."

"Thank you. The pain was almost unbearable when I accepted the inevitable truth but it eventually lessened, as all pain does. Now, I do my best to live with positivity and gratitude for what I still have."

"Wow." Carrie blew a breath through puffed cheeks. "You've *really* got it together. It's impressive."

"Well, thank you. It's a bummer because I'll never be a mom, but I'm still able to help children through my practice. It's such a gift."

Her brow furrowed. "Why can't you be a mom? I mean, you could adopt, right? Is that something you're open to?"

Sighing, she trailed her fingers over the grass. "I don't know. Maybe. I was open to having a biological child in my mid-forties on my own because I wanted it so badly. But adopting a child without a partner holds a different dynamic in my mind. I'd have to really think about it."

Curious eyes darted between hers as Carrie contemplated. "Have you asked Mark if he's open to adoption?"

"Oh, no." Teresa waved her hand. "He's mentioned a few times he wants a traditional family and I would never ask him to sacrifice that for me. Once he wins the election, I plan on buying a home and letting him resume his life. I truly hope he finds someone who can give him everything he wants."

"Teresa," she almost whispered, "that's assuming a lot from a few comments made during casual conversations. Don't you think it's worth at least discussing?"

"It's not our deal," she said, shrugging. "I understand what we entered into. He helped me immensely by paying off my debt and saving me tons of interest. We both benefit from this temporary arrangement and the least I can do is let him resume his life and seize his dreams when it's over."

Squinting, Carrie made a "*hmmm*" sound before glancing toward Mark and the others by the lake. "We'll see. I'm not sure your arrangement will end up being temporary, but okay."

Chuckling, Teresa wiped her hands together and stood. "All right, let's table this and join the others. What do you say we show these guys how to fish?"

Standing, Carrie grinned. "Do you know how to fish? I'm terrible at it."

"No damn idea but let's try anyway."

Arm in arm, they walked to the water to join the revelry.

That evening, when they returned home, Teresa got a call from a colleague who was dealing with a patient who needed to be hospitalized. Muting the phone, she addressed Mark.

"I need to take this consult in the office," she said, gesturing with her head toward the den. "It will probably take about twenty minutes."

"No worries," he said, smoothing a hand over her upper arm. "In the meantime, I'm going to head upstairs and enjoy having my room back for the night. Carrie just texted that the kids are nestled into the tent fort and having a grand old time."

"Nice. Want me to come find you in your bedroom when I'm done?"

Leaning down, he growled in her ear. "Hell yes. The door will be open."

Chuckling, she unmuted the phone and winked before heading into the den. Sitting at the desk, she helped her colleague navigate the situation, pleased when they had a resolution. Clicking off the phone, she trailed up the stairs to Mark's room.

Gently pushing open the door, she found the bedroom empty and strained to hear the sound of the running shower in the adjoining bathroom. Stepping closer, she edged the door open, sucking in a breath at the sight before her.

Mark stood under the spray, naked as his palm rested flat against the tile under the showerhead. He held his cock in his other hand, slowly stroking as he groaned. Clearing her throat, she watched him turn his head, those striking eyes latching onto hers.

"Did you start without me?" she teased. The sight of his hand jerking his thick cock was so erotic, she rubbed her thighs together.

"I just got caught up thinking about you downstairs, knowing you were going to come up here and I would finally get to hold you." The muscles of his forearm strained as it undulated back and forth. "Figured I'd warm him up since it takes a while sometimes. Being forty isn't for the weary."

Laughing, she bit her lip. "You're still hot," she whispered, grasping the hem of her shirt and pulling it over her head before tossing it to the floor. "I'm never going to be able to rid my mind of the image of you doing that."

"Good," he gritted, the word strained. "I want you to think about me half as much as I think about you, Teresa. God, I think about you all the time, hon."

Kicking off her sandals, she unbuttoned her jeans and removed the rest of her clothes. Lowering to her knees on the soft rug, she cupped her breasts in her hands.

"Show me," she commanded softly.

Sliding open the clear shower door, he trailed toward her, dripping and wet, his stiff cock jutting from the dark hair between his thighs. Sliding his fingers under her chin, he tilted her head. "What do you want, sweetheart?"

Gliding her hands over the prickly hairs on his thighs, she cupped his balls while encircling his shaft with the other hand. "I want to suck you until you come all over me."

Spearing his fingers into her curls, he clenched tight. "Fuck, that's sexy. Here?" he asked, gently trailing his fingertips over her collarbone.

"Yes," she said, her voice raspy. "Come on my chest and my breasts. You can wash it off afterward." She chucked her brows.

"Holy shit," he breathed, running his thumb over her lower lip before inserting it inside her mouth. "I didn't realize you were this kinky, Dr. Roe."

Closing her lips around his thumb, she sucked, reveling in the desire that laced his features. "I'm not always but I feel so comfortable with you, Mark. So damn free." Squeezing the base of his cock, she began to work him in her hand. "Now be a good fake fiancé and put your cock in my mouth."

His joy-filled laughter surrounded them as he lifted his hands to her hair, clutching tightly. Inching forward, he touched the head of his cock to her lips. Purring, she extended her tongue and licked the sensitive skin. He undulated his hips, silently asking for more, and Teresa opened wide. Moaning, he inserted himself inside her wet mouth, closing his eyes when she enveloped him.

Fingers entwined in her hair, he began to jut back and forth, lifting his lids to gaze down at her. Red flushes stained his cheeks as he groaned her name. Teresa mewled around him, understanding she held all control even though he loomed above her. God, it was thrilling. Realizing she'd never been so open with a sexual partner, she embraced the feeling, thrilled she'd found Mark even if their time was temporary.

Tilting her head back, she opened her throat, welcoming him deep inside, wanting so badly to please him. Deep groans surrounded her, each one sending shivers of desire through her quivering body. Feeling his fingers fist tighter in her hair, he gazed into her eyes as the head of his cock jutted against the back of her throat.

"Yeah, baby," he murmured, pushing himself deep before pulling back. "You feel so good around me. You're so fucking beautiful."

Purring, she accepted his broad length, maintaining steady breaths in between the movements. They were locked in tandem, so in tune with each other, and tears stung her eyes as she reveled in their connection.

"You okay?" he whispered above her. "I can pull back..."

She slid her hand around to grip his buttock, showing him she wanted more...she wanted *everything*. Groaning, he pushed deeper, muscles straining as he reached the edge.

"I'm going to come on those pretty breasts, honey...oh, god..."

Dragging himself from her mouth, he pumped his cock in his hand, his breaths labored as he began to come. Thick jets pulsed from the throbbing head onto her skin as he marked her, claiming her as his. It was primal, watching his teeth clench as he sprayed his essence onto her chest. Lost in the sensual moment, she moaned, thrilled she could offer him such pleasure.

Expelling a deep breath, he placed his fingers over her collarbone, sliding them through the milky release. Spreading it lower, he used both hands to cover her nipples with the wetness and Teresa almost collapsed from the eroticism of the gesture. The pert buds tightened as he manipulated them, twisting and pulling them as he spread the evidence of their loving over the sensitive skin.

"I've never seen anything as remotely sexy as seeing your tight little nipples covered with my come, honey," he said, his tone so low it barely registered. "Holy shit."

Bending his knees, he slid his hands under her arms and lifted her as she squealed. Striding over to the counter, he placed her on top.

"Cold," she said, shivering atop the marble although steam was rapidly filling the bathroom.

Heading back toward the rug, he slid it over and lowered to his knees, balancing on the soft fabric. "Open up those legs, honey," he said, palming her inner thighs and pushing them apart. "Let me warm you up."

Teresa slid her legs over his shoulders, baring herself to him, trusting him to take care of her. Gently pulling apart her folds, he blew on them, causing her to shudder.

"Mark..." she whispered.

Gaze cemented to hers, he placed small kisses along her wet folds, up to her mound, before trailing back down. Opening her wide, he placed his tongue against her core and slowly licked her.

"Oh, god," she whimpered. "So good."

Extending his tongue, he flicked her opening, tasting her honey before dragging it higher. Widening her folds, he exposed her clit and searched for it with the tip of his tongue.

Her legs tightened around his neck as he flicked her sensitive bud, the ministrations sending shards of desire through every cell in her body. Holding onto his hair for dear life, she pushed into his face.

"Mmm..." he groaned, lids closing as he sucked the nub into his mouth. Alternating spikes of pleasure hummed in her veins as he sucked her clit between his lips while he stimulated it with his tongue.

When he lifted his lids, lust blazed in his eyes as he slid two fingers inside her, gyrating back and forth as his mouth worked magic up above. Undulating her hips, she tossed her head back, succumbing to the sensation of being so open in his embrace.

"I can't wait to see you come," he murmured against her core, hooking his fingers against the spot deep within that drove her insane. "I love being buried in your pussy, hon. Fuck, it's so good."

The dirty words sent her straight to the edge, so close to falling. Giving in to the pleasure, she cried his name, unable to control the shuddering of her frame atop the cool marble. Back arching, she dove off the cliff, succumbing to the orgasm.

Stars exploded behind her eyes as he mumbled soft, sweet words into her deepest place. Tightening her legs around his head, she silently indicated she could take no more. Mark read her signal, as he always read her so well, and lazily licked her as she strove to control the trembling.

Eventually, she released a ragged breath and lifted her head to smile down at him. Giving her a satisfied grin, he glided his tongue over her folds once more for good measure.

"I think you like licking me there," she said, her voice sultry.

"Every fucking drop, honey. I could stay here all day."

Snickering, she touched her chest. "As fun as that sounds, I'm kind of sticky here. Maybe we should finally shower."

Resting his hands on the counter, he rose and slid his hand into hers. Leading her to the shower, he urged her inside before stepping in behind. Closing the clear door, he picked up the shampoo bottle.

"Can I wash you?"

"Sure," she said, stepping under the spray to wet her hair. "You can try to wash my hair, but it's a thick mess when it's wet."

"I like a challenge," he teased, dispensing a dollop of shampoo into his palm. Turning her to face the spray, he began washing her hair. His broad hands massaged her scalp and she leaned back against him, his sated shaft resting between her buttocks. Sighing with pleasure, she closed her eyes and enjoyed the ministrations.

Eventually, he rotated her and washed his release from her chest. His palms cupped her breasts, sliding the suds over them and bringing them to turgid points once again.

"Your cheeks flush when I play with your nipples," he said, alternating between tugging and lightly pinching them. "It's so pretty."

Reaching for his shaft, she encircled it and began to slowly tug. "Keep saying sweet things like that and I might let you have your way with me again, Mr. D.A."

Lowering to kiss her, he drew them both under the spray, hastily rinsing them off before turning off the shower.

"Well, I guess we're done," Teresa said chuckling. Stepping onto the rug, she reached for one of the towels on the rack and began to dry herself.

"You're goddamn right we are," he growled, stepping out of the shower and pulling the towel from her hand. Crouching down, he slid his arm behind her knees and lifted her. Yelping, she encircled his neck and held tight as he carried her to the bed.

"We're wet," she said, scrunching her nose as he crawled above her.

"Exactly." Chucking his brows, he pushed her thigh with his knee, opening her. Gripping the base of his cock, he guided himself to her center. Staring into her eyes, he gritted, "I'm going to fuck you hard."

"Yes," she cried, sucking in a breath when he plunged deep inside, filling her with every inch of his thick cock. Spearing her nails into his shoulder, she pleaded, "More!"

Mark began to fuck her, fast and raw, his hips moving in a furious pace as he gazed at her with simmering eyes.

"Like that, hon?" The sounds of their wet flesh slapping together reverberated off the walls. "Do you like taking me deep inside that sweet pussy?"

"God, yes! You always hit the spot. How do you always hit the spot?"

He barked a desire-laden laugh above her. "I don't know, baby. All I know is that you feel so damn perfect. *Oh, god...*"

Lowering onto his forearms, he aligned their bodies, the angle drawing him even deeper inside. Teresa splayed her legs as far as they would go, craving every inch of his cock inside her quivering core. His firmness dragged against the walls of her tight channel, the feeling so intense, her muscles lost all semblance of consistency. Surrendering to the magnificent connection with her sexy lover, she closed her eyes and gave up every shred of control.

"Never been so deep..." he grunted into her neck, sprawled over her as his body gyrated with lustful frenzy. "Are you close?"

"Yes," she moaned, hoping the word formed on her lips, unable to focus on things like talking and thinking. She was only capable of *feeling* as he jutted inside her arousal-ravaged body. Suddenly, her spine snapped and she began to come, the walls of her core clenching him in a taut vise as he groaned her name.

He grunted as he began to come, the spurts of his release coating her deepest place. Teresa wrapped herself around him, unable to suppress the deeply embedded wish she could conceive his child. Pushing the thought away, she rode the wave, wrapped up in him as he whispered unintelligible words into the wet skin of her neck.

Short, labored breaths eventually slowed to longer ones as their bodies cooled atop the sheets. Teresa stroked his hair as he relaxed against her, his sated cock still firmly lodged inside her. The moment was poignant and she reminded herself to enjoy it. Life was filled with so few perfect moments, but this was certainly one she would cherish for eternity.

Mark's chest expanded and he slowly lifted his head. Pressing his lips to hers, he drew her into a lazy kiss, their tongues twining together as they played with each other. Drawing back, he leaned on his hand, tracing slow patterns over her collarbone.

"It's never been like this, Teresa," he said softly. "*Ever.*"

"For me either," she said, dragging her fingernails over his scalp. "I thought sex like this only existed in the smutty novels we exchange at our brunches."

"It seems the ladies entrepreneurs' club has a lot going on beneath the surface," he said, arching a brow.

"Oh, buddy, you have no idea. We might all be secret sex goddesses. You never know."

"Kinky," he teased, waggling his brows. Gliding his fingers up to her face, he caressed the curve of her jaw. "Sleep here with me tonight."

How could she say 'no' when he was pleading with those gorgeous eyes? Sighing, she nodded. "Okay, but the sheets are wet."

Chuckling, he glanced around at the disheveled sheets. "That they are. I'll put on new ones before we prep for bed. Deal?"

"Deal."

They helped each other out of bed so they could perform the mundane tasks of brushing their teeth and changing the sheets. Teresa ran a comb through her wet curls, thankful they were only slightly tangled. Entering his room, she slid into bed, curling herself around his body as she rested her head on his chest.

"Night, hon," he murmured, stroking her hair.

"I love it when you do that," she mumbled into the warm skin of his chest.

"I love it too," he whispered. "I love holding you, sweetheart."

Her heart thumped as she embraced the emotion coursing through her sated frame. It had been so long since she'd been in love. Would it end in heartache? Most likely. Did she give a damn? Lying there, wrapped in his arms, the answer flitted through her mind.

No fucking way.

She would enjoy each and every moment spent with the man she loved. And, when it was over, she would lift her head high and remain grateful for the moments they'd shared. Content, she sighed against his chest and tumbled into sleep.

Chapter 23

♥

T he week before Justine's trial sped along at a breakneck pace, and Mark struggled to keep up. He was now sheltering a fake fiancée and a child in his home, trying to exonerate his sister of attempted murder charges, and running an exhaustive public campaign.

On Tuesday, he drove Avery to the courthouse so she could meet with her court-appointed psychologist and give her statement. Of course, to a five-year-old, it was a fun trip where she got to meet new people and see new things. Mark was taken with her wide-eyed curiosity as she observed the tall columns of the courthouse.

"Ready to meet Dr. Singleton?" he asked, holding Avery's hand as they stood in front of the steps.

She nodded and they trailed up the wide stairs, locating the official room where she would speak with the psychologist.

"Well, hello," a smiling Black woman with shoulder-length curls said to Avery, bending down and resting her hands on her knees. "You must be Avery Rodgers. I'm Dr. Singleton. It's very nice to meet you."

Avery tentatively shook her hand as the woman's eyes sparkled.

"And you must be Mark," she said, extending her hand. "Teresa has told me great things."

"She said you two were close from the Sunday brunches," he said, shaking her hand. "I get the feeling these brunches are where it's at. I'm starting to feel left out."

Throwing her head back, she gave a hearty laugh. "The wine and gossip flow, that's for sure. Teresa's a good friend and an exceptional therapist." Glancing at Avery, she said, "Well, I think it's time we talked. Did Mark tell you why you're here today?"

Avery nodded, clutching Carrot. "I have to tell you about the night Mommy and Daddy fought and what I saw."

"Exactly. I'm going to record what you say and the most important thing is that you tell the truth about everything you remember. There's no wrong answer, okay?"

"Okay."

Footsteps sounded on the marble as James Chisolm approached. "Hello, Mark," he said, sparing a caustic glare at Avery. "Isn't this a fun family gathering? How much coaching did you give her to spread lies about her father?"

Mark smoothed Avery's hair as she burrowed into his side, obviously terrified of the man. "You're scaring her, Chisolm. You know neither you nor I can be in the room when she speaks to Dr. Singleton. I suggest you leave before I file a harassment claim and secure a restraining order. Don't think I won't do it."

Chisolm arched a brow and shot Avery one last dismissive look. "Won't matter anyway. Dean is prepared to tell the *actual* truth. Remember if you lie you'll be in big trouble, young lady."

Mark lifted his phone from his pocket. "I'm calling 911—"

"Forget it," Chisolm said, holding up a hand. "The little brat won't derail my case."

"I will be detailing this conversation in my report, Mr. Chisolm," Dr. Singleton said. "By all means, continue. I surmise it's only hurting your client."

Eyes narrowed, he shot them one last glare and walked away.

"He's mean," Avery said against Mark's thigh.

"You're telling me." Crouching down, he gripped her upper arms. "Go on into the room with Dr. Singleton and answer all her questions, okay? You're going to do great, munchkin." Kissing her on the forehead, he observed them walk inside before sitting on the nearby bench and opening his laptop.

An hour later, Avery exited, a huge smile on her face as she ran toward Mark. "We had fun, Uncle Mark!"

"Yeah?" he asked, grateful the experience had been seamless. "Dr. Singleton seems really nice. I'm glad to hear it."

"I got everything I needed," Dr. Singleton said as Mark stood. "I can't officially comment and don't want to put anything in jeopardy, but I'll say that Avery did a great job and told the truth, which I'll include in my report and testimony on Monday."

"Thank you," Mark said, relieved. "My sister is an amazing mom and a good person, Dr. Singleton. She just had the misfortune of falling in love with the wrong man."

"A misfortune that befalls many," she said, tilting her head. "The court has my cell if you need to call me for any follow-up. In the meantime, it was a pleasure to meet you, Avery."

"Nice to meet you!"

Hand in hand, Mark led his niece from the courthouse, hopeful things were turning around and his sister would soon be free.

Mark's demanding schedule meant he barely saw Teresa, which put a severe damper on his happiness. Yes, somewhere along the way, spending time with her had become the zenith of joy in his life, and he wished for the day they could just hang together without any other commitments or encumbrances.

Although he truly enjoyed having Avery nearby twenty-four-seven, finding the opportunity to have sexy-times in a two-bedroom townhome with a little girl was hard...especially when you were sleeping on your own damn couch. It was just one more reason to exonerate Justine and reunite her with Avery. After that, he could spend some time with Teresa, at least for the next few months until the election.

And after the election? Well, he honestly had no idea. They hadn't spoken about making their arrangement more serious and Mark just couldn't contemplate something so encompassing during the campaign. After he won, he would sit down and decide whether or not he was ready to make a commitment.

Marriage was still a far-off concept and the most important commitment of all. Could he enter into a *real* engagement with Teresa during his first term as D.A. when he would be busier than he was now? It was hard to envision but certainly not impossible.

And what about children? Mark had always imagined having children traditionally with someone he could share all the poignant moments with: the positive test result, the nine-month preparation, being present beside his partner as their child was born. Settling down with Teresa wouldn't afford him that. It made him incredibly sad, only because it was something he would've loved to share with her. To smile into her gorgeous eyes as she held their newborn child in her arms at the hospital.

Mark decided he needed to assess the idea further over the next several months. It was a decision that shouldn't be made lightly, but he was thankful there were other options in their modern world. He would make a conscious effort to research adoption, surrogacy, fostering, and other methods so he was educated about the possible future choices he could make. Firm in that vow, he forged ahead with the multitude of things he needed to accomplish in the present moment.

First and foremost, he needed to exonerate his sister. After strategizing with Evan, they decided Mark should have a press conference directly after the verdict from Justine's case was announced. As they sat in the diner the Sunday before the hearing, Evan expressed his concern.

"I love your confidence, Mark, but if you lose, the press conference could devolve quickly. It will most likely be the end of your campaign since Chisolm will be seen as the winner in the case."

"That's why I hired you, Evan," Mark said, stirring his coffee as he arched a brow. "I need someone to give me the gloom and doom scenarios since I'm pretty optimistic."

"It's not a joke," Evan said, his tone gruff. "There's still a possibility you could lose this case. Dean is on record that Justine assaulted him and Chisolm will certainly attack her credibility."

"Of course, he will," Mark sighed. "He's not going to win. I still believe that justice prevails in this cynical world. It's the entire reason I ran in the first place."

Sitting back, Evan laced his fingers behind his head. "All right, buddy. I'll set up the press conference. I hope you're right."

Monday arrived, along with the slight twinge of nerves in Mark's gut he always felt before a big case. Teresa approached him in the kitchen, the early-morning sky still dark, and slid her arms around his waist, aligning her front with his back.

"Good luck today, Mr. D.A.," she said in that silken voice, placing a tender kiss on his neck. "I can't wait for you to decimate that bastard."

Turning in her embrace, he smiled as he cupped her cheek. "You have a lot more faith in me than Evan has."

Chuckling, she shrugged. "I know you're going to win. There's not a doubt in my mind. I believe in you, Mark."

Emotion swirled in her multi-colored eyes, and he understood she was now dangling on the same precipice as he. Somewhere along the way, feelings and emotions had surfaced, and they were both in deep.

"Thank you," he whispered, placing a soft kiss on her lips. "If I win, we'll have the house back to ourselves."

"Then you'd better win," she said, chucking her brows. "I'm ready to act out more of my smutty book fantasies."

Expelling a breath, he caressed her face. "God, I want you—"

"Uncle Mark," Avery's voice interrupted as she padded into the kitchen. "Can I have Fruit Loops for breakfast?"

Giving Teresa a playful eye roll, he pulled away and nodded. "Sure can, munchkin. Remember that Grandma and Grandpa are going to watch you today while I help Mommy. You guys will have a good time."

"Can Mommy come home after you help her?"

Stroking her hair, his lips curved. "I hope so. I'm going to do my best."

"I know you'll do really good," was her beaming reply.

"Well, with this cheerleading squad, how can I go wrong?"

"So true," Teresa said, waving as she exited the kitchen. "Off to shower. Good luck!"

Chapter 24

♥

When Mark arrived at the courtroom, the nerves were all but gone, most likely thanks to the two ladies who'd given him such encouragement earlier. Justine was escorted in, wearing the suit he'd brought her on Saturday, and he gave her a reassuring smile.

"You're going home today, Jus. I feel it."

"I feel it too," she said wistfully. "I miss my baby, Mark."

"I know," he said, rubbing her arm. "Stay strong. We've got this."

The hearing was functional as the judge heard testimony from Dean, now sporting no less than five bandages and a crutch in an Oscar-worthy performance as he limped to the stand.

"Bastard," Justine murmured. "He's putting this on for the judge."

"Judge Reinhold is firm but fair," Mark said. "Don't give Dean the reaction he wants. I've got this."

After Dean's testimony, Justine testified, explaining what happened that fateful night.

"I swear," she said, wet eyes focused on the judge. "I was just trying to protect my child. I was so afraid for her."

Once her testimony was over, Mark noted the compassion on Judge Reinhold's features. Dr. Singleton took the stand next and reported the details of her session with Avery.

"Avery was extremely clear that Mr. Rodgers assaulted Mrs. Rodgers and then assaulted Avery when she tried to intervene to help her mother. I assess that Mrs. Rodgers acted in self-defense and in the interest of protecting her child. I would recommend all charges against Mrs. Rodgers be dismissed and implore the court to investigate Mr. Rodgers for domestic and child abuse."

"Lying bitch!" Dean screamed, lurching to his feet beside Chisolm at the prosecutor's table. "She attacked me." He pointed at Justine across the room.

"Sit down!" Chisolm said, rising and pushing Dean back into the chair.

"I will have order in this courtroom!" the judge scolded Chisolm.

"Understood. I'm sorry, Your Honor."

After all testimony was heard, the judge rendered his verdict.

"After hearing the facts of this case, I firmly believe this was a domestic violence situation in which Mrs. Rodgers was the victim. Any injuries inflicted on Mr. Rodgers were done in self-defense, and I hereby dismiss all charges against Mrs. Rodgers. Young lady, I wish you and your daughter the best and hope this will be the last incident of violence you encounter. Furthermore, Mrs. Rodgers will regain custody of Avery Rodgers, effective immediately."

Banging his gavel, Judge Reinhold stood as the bailiff called, "All rise!", and exited the courtroom.

"Oh, my god," Justine said, leaping from her seat and pulling Mark to his feet before giving him a smothering hug. "We did it! Well, *you* did it, but...yay!"

"We definitely did," he said, thrilled at the outcome as he smiled into her hair. "I knew justice would prevail."

Drawing back, she palmed his face. "My justice-warrior sibling wins again. You're going to make such a great D.A."

Chisolm and Dean ruined the moment by approaching them with scowls on their faces.

"You just freed a woman who violently stabbed her husband," Chisolm said, his tone nasty. "I'll paste that fact on every ad moving forward. You lost your campaign today, Lancaster."

"I'm not even honoring that with a response," Mark said, tamping down his fury. "You lost. It's over, Chisolm."

"You're a goddamn liar, Justine!" Dean said behind Chisolm, angrily jutting his finger in the air. "You're going to pay for this!"

Mark called the bailiff over, wanting to get Justine as far away as possible from their toxicity. "Sir, we'll be filing a restraining order against Mr. Rodgers shortly," he said to the uniformed bailiff. "Could you please ensure he doesn't harass my client?"

"Absolutely," the man said, gesturing to Dean. "Sir, it's time to exit the courtroom."

"This isn't over!" Dean called as Chisolm urged him toward the exit. "I'm suing for custody of Avery."

Justine watched them leave, absently chewing her lip. "Can he win custody of her, Mark? God, this is just the beginning of the nightmare, isn't it?"

"Hey," he said, cupping her shoulders. "This is the beginning of the end of your life with that jerk. I'm going to help you file for divorce and a restraining order, and ensure you retain custody of Avery."

"Okay," she said, wiping a stray tear that trailed down her cheek. "I'm ready. Can we file today? I want him out of my life for good."

"Thank god," Mark said, pulling her into an embrace. "Yes. Let me do the press conference and we'll file everything today."

Pulling back, she grinned. "I think I owe you, like, a million dollars in legal fees."

"You get a freebie because you're my sister. But I definitely expect you to canvass for your favorite District Attorney candidate."

Laughing, she nodded. "I'll visit every damn house in Ardor Creek and get their commitment to vote for you. Best brother ever. I love you so much, Mark. Thank you."

Kissing her forehead, he gave her one last squeeze before leading her outside. "Love you too, Jus."

Mark headed to the front steps of the courthouse where Evan was waiting with the podium ready.

"Great job, man," he said, shaking his hand. "You're pretty good at this attorney thing. The reporters are ready whenever you are."

Stepping to the podium, Mark addressed the crowd under the warm summer sun.

"Justice was served here today, reaffirming our system is designed to protect and preserve righteousness. My sister and niece, like so many other women and children, were victims of domestic abuse and we must fight for each and every one of them. As stated on my website, one of my main platforms will be to reform sentences imposed upon women imprisoned for defending themselves against their attackers. There is no place in this county, or this world, for violence against women and children, and I vow to implement laws that will protect rather than endanger."

Murmurs ran through the crowd as he assessed the throng of reporters.

"James Chisolm wants to run a dirty campaign because he has no platform. His entire strategy is to attack me and drag me through the mud, no matter who he harms along the way—my five-year-old niece, my sister, or my fiancée. That's his choice, but I'm choosing to run a different campaign. One where I speak about the policies I plan to implement and how I can help the citizens of Lackawanna County. I hope you all will join me on this journey and give air time to the optimism of my campaign versus the negativity of Chisolm's. Call upon your inner journalistic integrity and let's talk about issues, not personal smears."

Clenching the podium, he gave an assertive nod.

"With that, I'll take your questions."

After twenty minutes of intense questioning, Mark filed the remaining paperwork to secure Justine's release. Afterward, they headed back to the Ardor Creek police station so Justine could file the restraining order against Dean. Eventually, Mark returned to his office and began preparing the documents for her divorce. Thrilled she was finally ready to take the leap, he knew it signaled a new chapter in both her and Avery's lives. Hopefully, one where they would thrive and find true happiness.

That evening, he and Justine ate dinner at their parents' before Mark drove Justine and Avery home. Thanks to the restraining order, Dean had been removed from Justine's home earlier that day by a jubilant Gary Lincoln, who had threatened him with arrest if he fought the order. Dean complied and announced he was going to stay with his parents in Battle Falls. Mark hoped he never returned to Ardor Creek.

After making sure Justine and Avery were settled, Mark approached the police cruiser parked across the street from their home.

"You on duty this evening?" he asked, grinning down at Gary as he sat behind the wheel.

"Nope. Shift ended at five."

The corner of Mark's lips twitched. "You're going to stay here all night, aren't you?"

"Someone's got to keep an eye on 'em, Mark. Just in case that bastard tries to come back."

Nodding, Mark assessed his friend. "Are you ever going to tell her how you feel?"

Sighing, Gary shook his head. "Probably not. She's got enough to deal with. Don't want to complicate things."

"I get that. Maybe later, once things calm down..."

"Maybe," Gary said, lifting a shoulder. "For now, I'm fine with keeping them safe, which I can't do if you're breathing down my neck. Go on home to your pretty fake fiancée and leave me alone."

Laughing, Mark gave a salute. "Ten-four. Thanks for taking care of them, Gary."

"Sure thing. See ya around, Mark."

"See ya."

Heading to his car, Mark sat behind the wheel, already anticipating holding Teresa when he finally returned home after one of the longest days of his life.

When Mark entered the darkened townhome, the scent of Teresa's perfume surrounded him, causing him to smile. Trailing to the kitchen, he found her sitting at the table drinking a glass of red wine.

"Hey," he said, assessing her as he stood in the doorway. "I wasn't sure you'd be up."

Setting the glass down, she rose and sauntered toward him. Gliding her arms around his neck, she lifted to her toes and placed a tender kiss on his lips.

"I had to wait up for my fake fiancé," she said, tongue darting out to bathe her lips as his body grew hard. "I'm so damn proud of him and I wanted to show him. Think he has enough energy left for me to reward him for securing justice?" Arching a brow, she slid her hand down his body and cupped his rapidly-swelling cock.

"Oh, yeah," he murmured, lowering and gripping the gorgeous swells of her ass through the sweatpants she wore. "He definitely has enough energy." Lifting her, she giggled as her legs encircled his waist. Mark all but ran upstairs and collapsed with her on the bed, joy surging through his frame as he captured her lips.

"Oh, my, Mr. D.A.," she said, slipping her hand underneath his waistband. "You're certainly tense after your long day—"

Gripping her hair, he tilted her head back, his nose grazing hers. "Teresa," he growled.

"Yes..." She squeezed his cock beneath his pants.

"Stop talking so I can fuck you."

Slowly beginning to tug back and forth, the sexy temptress extended her tongue, running them over his lips as he shuddered.

"Make me—" she dared, squealing when he covered her mouth with his.

Inhaling her words, Mark reveled in her sexy legs wrapped around his body as he tasted the woman he'd anticipated holding throughout the long, exhausting day. And then, all talking ceased as Mark tore away their clothes and took them both to heaven.

Chapter 25

♥

Once the trial was over, life regained a semblance of normalcy, although Teresa wondered what could truly be considered "normal" when you were living in your fake fiancé's home during a grueling campaign. June bled into July and the summer chugged along with all the trappings that entailed: trips to the lake with Peter and Carrie, cookouts with the gang at Scott and Ashlyn's, dinners every so often with Mark's parents.

Teresa didn't want to impose, and certainly didn't want Mark's parents to assume their relationship was more serious than they claimed, so she only accepted the invite every third time or so. Still, she'd grown close to Avery during the weeks they'd lived together and she reveled in the opportunities to see her.

Justine's relationship with Brenda and Joseph seemed to be improving, as far as Teresa could tell with her super-Spidey therapy skills, and she was glad to see the family unit growing closer. As the summer dragged on, she knew each day brought her closer to inevitable heartbreak, but she forged ahead anyway, understanding her love for Mark healed something inside her broken soul. He made her feel cherished and beautiful and...worthy. Even though she was barren, he still desired her. It was a welcome reminder that she was still whole, despite the doubts that festered in the back of her mind.

August arrived, along with her forty-seventh birthday, threatening to shatter her normally unshakable confidence. But Mark greeted her in the comfy guest bed that morning, hazelnut coffee in hand, and thrust it toward her, armed with his adorable smile.

"Okay, birthday girl, here's your coffee. I'm making omelets too. We're still on for dinner tonight, right?"

"Yes," she said, sitting up against the pillows, thankful it was Friday and the week was almost over. "It will be a good opportunity for the reporters to snag some pictures of us."

"Are we even pretending that's why I want to take you to dinner anymore?" he asked.

Sipping the coffee, she shrugged. "I'm not sure."

Chuckling, he kissed her forehead and stood. "Come downstairs when you're ready. I hope you're as hungry as I am."

Once downstairs, she sat at the kitchen table, marveling at his broad shoulders as he prepared the birthday breakfast. Approaching the table, he set a plate with a steaming hot omelet in front of her and grabbed his own before sitting down.

"I guess it's good for the campaign if reporters snap some pictures of us, but I'd take you to dinner for your birthday regardless, Teresa," he said, taking a bite of his omelet. "You deserve to be wined and dined."

"That sounds very much like a formal date," she said, arching an eyebrow. "Quite serious for this casual fake engagement we're embroiled in."

He studied her as he chewed, those brown eyes swirling with thoughts she couldn't quite discern. "Less than three months 'til the election. Then you can extricate yourself from my scandal-ridden presence."

Laughing, she sipped her coffee. "Yes, it's been terrible. I'm having fantastic sex with a man who's introduced me to his adorable niece, family and friends. I can't wait to return to real life."

Swallowing, his throat bobbed as he seemed to contemplate. "Do you ever think of making it more permanent? This thing between us?"

Teresa ingested a bite of omelet, stalling so she could give the appropriate answer. "Do you? There's so much we'd need to discuss."

"Yeah," he said, sitting back in his chair. "If I win, I'm going to be swamped as I transition into the office. It's a difficult time to cultivate a relationship."

That was certainly one issue, although they didn't voice the elephant in the room. Bringing up her inability to have children would lead down a rabbit hole she just didn't feel like chasing. Deciding to change the subject, she lifted her mug.

"I like the way things are going, Mark," she said, shrugging before taking another sip. "I'm enjoying the whole 'live in the moment', 'no-strings-attached' thing we have going on. Maybe we could just leave it this way until November. After that, we can discuss our future or lack thereof."

He ran a hand over his face. "If you're sure. I just...you're important to me, Teresa. I need you to know that."

"Well, I kind of figured when you offered to take me to Al Fresco's tonight," she said, referencing the fancy restaurant in Battle Falls. "I didn't realize you were listening when I mentioned it was my favorite."

"I was listening," he said, winking. "Be ready at seven-thirty and wear something sexy I can drag off you with my teeth."

Laughing, she nodded. "Done."

Eventually, she showered and headed to work, anticipating the date-that-wasn't-a-date as she sat with her clients. She also finished a consultation report for a client of Mark's as part of her loan repayment. After emailing it to him, she stopped by the mall and decided to treat herself to a new dress for her birthday.

The skin-tight dress was red and hugged her curves in all the right places. That evening, as she prepared in the bathroom, she thought of Mark showering only several feet away. If she wasn't so excited about dinner, she would head over and seduce him, as she'd now done a few times during their cohabitation. But, alas, she was craving the fancy wine and short rib pappardelle, so sexy times would have to wait.

In the foyer, she was transferring some items from her purse to her clutch when Mark trailed down the stairs. Whistling, he shook his head as he stopped only inches away.

"Wow. I think you're the most beautiful woman I've ever seen. Look at that dress." Gently placing his hands on her waist, he ran them over the curves of her hips. "Your body is so damn gorgeous, Teresa."

Tears stung her eyes as told herself not to cry like a damn baby. "That's really encouraging to this...forty-seven-year-old. Uggh. I almost choked on the words."

"You look fantastic, honey," he said, running a finger over her cheek. "I hope they take a thousand pictures of us tonight, if only so everyone can see you."

The words were so romantic her knees almost buckled, and she turned away from his desire-laden gaze to finish packing her clutch.

Once they arrived at dinner, she noticed a few photographers who snapped their picture. Facing them head-on, she let them, now used to the small amount of media attention she garnered as Mark's fiancée. After the election, it would all die down and she'd go back to her boring life. Why not enjoy the excitement?

Dinner was amazing, filled with luscious wine, excellent food, and never-ending conversation with her handsome date. Their discussions always flowed so easily, reminding Teresa of how well they connected. It wasn't something one found every day and she was thankful she'd found Mark on a hook-up app she'd almost been too hesitant to try. Thank goodness she'd forged ahead.

When they returned home, he led her upstairs, as he often did on the few nights each week they were able to carve out time to love each other. Teresa snickered as he bit the fabric across her shoulder, tugging it from her skin with his teeth as he'd promised to do.

"I love the idea, but removing this dress with your teeth will take all night. It's really tight."

"Oh, I know," he said, kissing a path over her collarbone before pushing the backs of her legs against the bed. Resting his lips against hers, he murmured, "I've been hard since I walked down the stairs. I'm pretty sure my brain stopped processing rational thought as soon as I saw you in this dress."

Sliding his hands across her back, he gripped the zipper and tugged it down. "Okay, you win. I'll use my hands." Gripping the fabric, he pulled it lower, baring her skin inch by inch, the air cool on the exposed flesh. Once it was pooled on the floor, he unhooked her strapless bra before hooking his fingers in her thong and dragging it off her body.

"I think we both win," she said, naked and throbbing as she encircled his neck. "Except you still have your clothes on." Her lips formed a pout.

"I'm about to rip them off," he growled, nuzzling her nose. "I want to fuck you hard from behind. Is that okay?"

Pulling away, she crawled onto the bed, resting on her hands and knees, and looked at him over her shoulder. "Like this?"

He sprang into action, all but tearing off his clothes, spurring her to laugh at his eagerness. Climbing onto the bed, he shimmied against her body, the front of his thighs aligned with the backs of hers.

"Stop laughing at me, woman," he teased, lowering over her as he touched the head of his cock to her dripping opening. "I'm dying for you. Take pity on me."

Grinning over her shoulder, she gave him her sultriest look. "Grab my hair and use it to anchor me while you're inside. I love it when you grab my hair."

Entwining his fingers in her curls, he rested his lips against the shell of her ear. "Tell me if it's too much."

"Don't hold back—" the words ended with her breathy moan as he surged inside, claiming her in one thick thrust. Drawing back, his shaft dragged against her sensitive folds before impaling her once again.

"Right here," he said raggedly, his hips undulating against her as he loved her. "This is where I've wanted to be all night."

"I thought you were at least enjoying our dinner conversation," she teased, pushing against the bed with her palms to gain leverage. "But if you only want my body..."

"I want everything," he breathed, pressing the side of his face against hers as the intensity of his thrusts increased. "Every part of you, honey. Don't you know that?"

Burying her face in the mattress, she moaned, unable to reply to the tender words...incapable of discerning whether they were true or only spoken in the throes of desire. Giving in to the magnificent pleasure of being claimed by her sexy lover, she pushed her body into his, opening herself to the relentless rhythm of his hips.

The prickly hairs of his chest tickled her back as he held her close, their sweat-soaked bodies intertwined as he claimed her. Gliding her hand to her center, her fingers found her clit, stimulating the tiny bud as the head of his cock hit the spot deep within that drove her wild. That, combined with the dirty and sometimes unintelligible words he droned in her ear, sent her over the edge as she began to come.

"Mark!"

"You're so tight, honey," he groaned in her ear. "Oh, god…I feel you coming around me…" With one last moan, he snapped, his cock pulsing as he began to shoot jets of release inside her wet core.

Teresa whimpered, loving how his body collapsed onto hers while he buried his face in her neck. Squirming against him, she squeezed her inner muscles, accepting everything he pulsed inside her.

"Good god…" he breathed, cuddling her close as he shuddered against her cooling skin. Sighing into her neck, he nuzzled the sensitive spot. "I'm never moving again. Sorry. It's over for me."

Giving a sated chuckle, she nodded limply against the comforter. "Fine with me," she mumbled against the fabric. "I'm comfortable as hell."

"This position shouldn't be this comfortable for two forty-some-things. We might be sex superheroes who don't age."

"Okay," she murmured, lifting a lazy arm to sift her fingers through his hair. "Whatever you say, old man."

His contented laugh reverberated through the room as their breathing slowed. Eventually, he shifted atop her. "As much as I like being contorted against your body, I know my back will pay the price tomorrow." Sliding off, he trailed to the bathroom, returning with a warm cloth. Gently turning her over, he wiped away the evidence of their loving before tossing the cloth in the nearby hamper. Extending his hand, he pulled her to stand and turned down the covers.

"I can go to my room," she said, twisting her lip between her teeth. "I've been sleeping in here a lot after we have sex. If you want your space, that's fine."

His expression fell, causing him to look adorable in the moon-light. "I don't want space from you, honey." Extending his hand, he shook it. "Please stay here tonight."

Teresa hesitated, understanding they were breaking all sorts of barriers for their proclaimed casual relationship. "Remember the whole 'messy' conversation?"

He slowly nodded.

"It's getting messy for me," she almost whispered. "I want to be honest with you about that."

"Sweetheart," he said, stepping forward and placing his fingers under her chin, tilting her face to his. "It got messy for me the first night you slept in this bed. Might as well keep the streak alive."

Breathing a laugh, she studied him. "What are we doing, Mark?"

Cupping her cheeks, he rested his forehead against hers. "I'm pretty sure we're falling in love, Teresa."

Swallowing thickly, she tried not to collapse from the intense slamming of her heart inside her chest. "I'm not sure that's a good idea."

Lifting his shoulders, his lips formed a slight grin. "Probably not. Let's ride it out for the next few months. We'll discuss after the election, remember?"

Ragged breaths escaped her lungs as she strove to cling to reality. "We want different things. I can't give you—"

"Not right now," he interrupted, covering her lips with his fingers. "I'm not ready, honey. It's a discussion we need to have but, right now, I just want to hold you. Give me a few more months. Please."

Persuaded by his pleading, she nodded. "Okay."

Gliding his hands down her arms, he encircled her wrists and tugged her toward the bed. Teresa slid in beside him and rested her cheek over his heart, counting the steady beats beneath. Sleep was a far-off notion as he drifted below her. Instead, she spent several hours pondering how difficult it would be to leave him when that day ultimately came.

Chapter 26

September arrived, along with cooler weather and more intensity in the campaign. Mark was so consumed with appearances, fundraisers, and other functions that he barely saw Teresa unless Evan scheduled her to appear with him. Most nights, he would get home late since he was juggling clients and the campaign, and she would already be asleep.

Mark wondered if she was intentionally pulling back due to the somewhat awkward discussion they'd pushed aside the night of her birthday. With the whirlwind that comprised his life, he just wasn't ready to contemplate what moving forward with her would entail. If he decided to make their relationship more serious, it was most likely the end of the family he'd envisioned during his single years when the future had seemed so far away.

If he married Teresa, he wouldn't experience the pregnancy phase Justine and his friends had experienced with their children. He would skip the ultrasounds and doctor visits, helping his partner as her pregnancy grew, and the excitement of creating a child together. Incredibly saddened at the thought, he lamented at the unfairness of life.

On the other hand, he was extremely lucky to have found her. Someone so incredible who truly understood him. Never in his life had he connected with a woman the way he connected with Teresa. Mark wasn't sure he'd ever truly been in love before. The kind of deep-seated, heart-wrenching love one felt for the person they wanted to spend the rest of their life with.

But he felt it for Teresa. Lying to himself would be futile. He was consumed by her. Was that love enough to build a life together despite the obstacles? Mark just wasn't sure. He'd promised himself he would research adoption, surrogacy, and other options, but with the intensity of the campaign, he just hadn't found the time. Until he was able to sit down and truly process the situation, he didn't feel comfortable making such a huge decision.

His predicament was magnified when Carrie announced at Scott and Ashlyn's Labor Day cookout that she was pregnant. Peter was over the moon with excitement, and Mark felt a slight twinge of sadness he would never announce such news with Teresa.

She'd accompanied him to the cookout, after some mild pleading on his part, and he observed her as she reacted to the news.

"Carrie, I'm so thrilled for you," Teresa exclaimed, hugging her as she beamed. "Do you know if it's a boy or a girl yet?"

"Nope," Carrie said, grinning up at Peter who stood beside her. "I'm three months so we'll find out in October, but Peter swears it's a girl."

"A perfect little girl who I'm committed to keeping away from any teenage boy remotely resembling her father," Peter teased.

"Oh, no," Teresa said, lifting her brows. "Were you that bad?"

"My dad sure seemed to think so," Carrie muttered.

"But you still loved me anyway," he said, leaning down and trying to kiss her. "Come on, honey, tell everyone how crazy you were about me."

"If I remember correctly, *you* were the one always attempting to sneak a hand under my skirt."

"Because you were so cute," he said, sliding his arm around her waist and pulling her close. "You were the second hottest girl in school besides Heather Combs."

"Well, we're officially getting divorced," she teased, pulling away. "We almost made it a year. Better than I anticipated."

Peter grabbed her wrist and lowered to one knee. "I take it back. You know you're the most gorgeous woman I've ever seen." Resting his lips against her stomach, he murmured, "Help me out here, kid. I'm blowing this."

"For god's sake, stand up." Dragging him to his feet, she gave an exasperated sigh. "You're ridiculous."

"But you love me anyway." He waggled his brows.

Sighing, she leaned in and gave him a wet kiss. "But I love you anyway."

Mark watched the revelry, overjoyed at the news. Sliding his arm across Teresa's shoulders, he smiled at her as she burrowed into his side.

"They're adorable," she said as Mark noticed the sheen of tears in her eyes. "What a happy day."

"It really is." He placed a soft kiss on her forehead, understanding they each had unspoken emotions whirling inside. They stood firm in each other's embrace, observing the well-wishes, as Mark realized it was time he began to make some decisions.

That evening, when they returned home, they were quiet and the air was thick between them. Mark encircled her wrist and led her to his room, slowly undressing her as he memorized every birthmark and freckle. It was possible their time together would soon be over, if they decided their visions of the future were too different. Overcome with sadness, he gently urged her to lay on the sheets and slid over her.

Their lovemaking was poignant and slow, so different from the times they'd lost themselves to blazing passion. Moving deep inside her, Mark threaded his fingers through her hair atop the pillow.

"Teresa," he whispered, gazing into her eyes as they sparkled in the moonlight.

"I know," she said softly, hips lifting to meet his gentle thrusts.

Lost in her, he captured her lips, rendering them both speechless so they wouldn't have to say words that were too meaningful or profound. Afterward, she lazed in his arms before standing and gathering her clothes.

"Where are you going?" he asked, watching her from the bed.

"I have to get up early tomorrow," she said, slipping her shirt over her head. "I'm volunteering at the local hospital's mental health fair. Remember?"

"Yeah," he said, already missing her sweet warmth wrapped around him. "You can still sleep in here."

"Tomorrow's a holiday and it might be the only day you get to sleep in before the election. Take advantage of it. I have some errands to do after the health fair, so I'll be home late. Don't wait up." Leaning down, she kissed his forehead before exiting the room.

Rubbing his chest, Mark inhaled as he contemplated. She was certainly pulling away but he didn't blame her. They'd crossed so many lines that a return to casual was impossible. But a future together wasn't certain either. At this point, they were stuck in a sort of limbo fraught with uncertainty. Of course, she would protect her heart.

As his hand moved atop his chest, Mark wondered how in the hell he was going to protect his own.

Chapter 27

♥

The final two months of the campaign were grueling, and Teresa saw Mark less and less. Realizing that was probably for the best, she cherished the nights they were able to spend together, along with the functions she attended as his fiancée.

During one fundraiser in mid-October, Evan approached her, two champagne glasses in hand.

"To the woman who saved my candidate's campaign," he said, handing her a glass. "I don't know how to repay you."

Taking the glass, she clinked it with his. "While I appreciate the praise, your candidate is exceptional. I think he did it on his own."

"You both are pretty amazing," Evan said, sipping. "I guess now that we're a few weeks away from the election, we can begin discussing the exit strategy for your fake engagement."

"Exit strategy?"

"It will seem strange if you all break up right after the election on November 3rd, so I was hoping you'd agree to carry on the charade for a few more weeks. Mark always has Thanksgiving dinner with his friends and we were hoping you'd attend. He says you get along well with everyone and he can take some pictures of you with the group. It will be the last official function, I swear. After that, I think it's safe for you to fade into the sunset. The holidays will create a distraction and the new year will cement his new position. He won't need you to pretend anymore."

Clearing her throat, she nodded. "You've discussed this plan with him?"

"I have. He informed me your family isn't local so I was hoping you wouldn't mind spending Thanksgiving with him and his friends. Of course, it's up to you."

Teresa took a moment to acknowledge the staggering pain that welled inside at the knowledge that Mark had discussed the last encounter in their fake relationship as if it were just another campaign appearance. Telling herself to get a grip, she tried to process it. Perhaps he was just more pragmatic about the inevitable end of their arrangement. Still, it hurt so vehemently that her fingers clenched the glass, causing her to wonder how it didn't shatter.

"Teresa?"

"I'd love to spend Thanksgiving with Mark and his friends," she said, lifting her chin and telling herself to be strong. Hell, she'd faced unassuageable heartache more than once in her life. She could certainly face it now. "Sounds like the perfect plan."

"Wonderful. I'll let him know. In the meantime, enjoy this fabulous champagne the rich donor insisted on donating. We won't get this stuff after the election, that's for sure."

He trailed toward his wife and Teresa downed the rest of the champagne, hoping it would calm her nerves.

"Hey there, Betty Ford," Mark teased, sliding up beside her. "Are you chugging champagne without me?"

"Yep," she said, only able to form the barest hint of a smile. "I'd love another glass."

His eyes roved over her face, discerning her mood before he nodded. "Okay, let's make that happen. Come on."

Teresa slogged through the rest of the evening, the mindless conversations running together as she counted down the hours until she could rip off the dress and be alone with her thoughts. On the way home, she studied Mark as he drove.

"Evan told me about the Thanksgiving dinner plan. Sounds like a perfect way to wrap up things."

Mark scowled. "He was supposed to let me bring it up to you. It doesn't have to be our last encounter, Teresa, or some big goodbye. He was just worried you would stop making appearances the day after the election and I brought up Thanksgiving dinner to calm him down."

Reaching over, he slid his palm over hers, lacing their fingers. "Honestly, it was my idiotic way of ensuring you'd come to Thanksgiving dinner with me. I've always gone solo but want you to come as my plus one. If you want to."

Although she was still racked with pain from the inevitably of the end, there was no way she could say 'no' when he gave her that hopeful smile.

Squeezing his hand, she nodded. "I'd love to come."

"Thank you," he said, beaming as if he'd won the lottery, causing a small ember of hope to well in her chest. Dousing it, she reminded herself not to travel back to la-la land. What they had was nearing the end and he probably just wanted to make her feel comfortable.

That night, she stayed with him, even though he didn't ask. Wrapped in his arms, Teresa decided to enjoy their last moments together. Running her fingers over the tiny hairs on his chest, she committed the feel of them to memory, along with his sandalwood scent and the cadence of his breathing.

Chapter 28

Mark won the election in a landslide and quickly made his acceptance speech thanking Teresa, Evan, his family and friends, and everyone else who had ensured his victory. James Chisolm was finally out and Mark could finally do some good for the residents of Lackawanna County.

The Saturday after the election, his parents threw a huge party, and Mark joked that they'd invited the entire town of Ardor Creek. He wasn't far off. By seven p.m., the house was full to the brim with people having a fantastic time. All his friends were there, including Gary who every so often gazed at Justine with such longing, Mark had the urge to tell her about his feelings. But who was he to get involved? He was certainly no expert, judging by the situation with Teresa.

She spoke of the finality of their relationship more and more often, and now that the election was over, he was pretty sure she was ready to move on. Although she'd indicated the night of her birthday she was developing feelings, their interactions had been strained in recent weeks. Add in the fact that he'd almost strangled Evan for bringing up the Thanksgiving plan, and Mark was pretty sure he'd blown it.

And, in his heart of hearts, he wasn't sure he wanted to salvage it. Although he was certain he was in love with her, he still hadn't sat down and evaluated building a future with her. Why? What was he waiting for?

"If you think someone else is going to come along like her, you're a fucking idiot, man," he muttered to himself from the corner of the living room. Teresa was sitting on the couch, Avery on her lap, as she talked with Justine and Carrie. She fit with his family and friends as if she'd known them forever. So why in the hell was he stalling?

"You talking to yourself over here, buddy?" Scott asked, appearing at his side.

"Yeah." Rubbing the back of his neck, he sighed. "This fake engagement really upended everything. I'm not sure what to do."

Scott's eyebrows arched above his glasses. "Well, do you love her?"

Narrowing his eyes, Mark nodded.

Breaking into a huge smile, Scott patted him on the back. "That's awesome, man. She's amazing. Like, way better than you deserve."

Scoffing, Mark rolled his eyes. "Thanks."

"Seriously, though, I sense hesitation. Is it because of the kids thing? Teresa told Carrie, and Carrie told Ashlyn and, well, it is Ardor Creek. I'm pretty sure everyone knows at this point."

Mark took a sip of his drink. "Yeah, that's definitely one issue. I don't know why I'm procrastinating. I told myself I'd sit down and evaluate the idea of not having biological children. I don't think it's a dealbreaker, but it's something I really need to think about."

"You could have biological kids with a surrogate."

"Yes, that's one of the options I need to research. I've pushed it off too long."

"Is it possible you're just not ready to commit? You were the last happy bachelor I knew. I mean, Chad's a man-whore, but he's always got a girlfriend. You seemed to enjoy tackling life solo. It's a sacrifice to give up your independence. Maybe that's got you spooked."

"There's definitely some hesitancy. I was never any good at relationships, Scott. I'm a workaholic who enjoys my space. I like having sex and working, but I don't enjoy working on a relationship. Does that make sense?"

"Uh, yeah," Scott said, his lips thinning. "Relationships are hard. Sometimes, I revert into Surly-Scott-mode and say something super insensitive to Ashlyn. She makes me grovel for days afterward, although I think she secretly digs my whole surly vibe."

Mark chuckled. "I have heard her mention a few times how much she likes Grumpy Scott. Seems like you've figured it out."

"I think when it's right, you're able to figure it out. Maybe your relationships in the past didn't work because they weren't the right fit. I'm not the most observant person in the world, but when I see you with Teresa, you guys seem to get each other. Maybe she's the one you'll finally figure it out with."

"Maybe." Patting his shoulder, Mark grinned. "When did you become an expert in relationships, anyway?"

"Ask my wife when she's not mad at me. Apparently, I put the cake she made in the wrong container and it collapsed on the way over. I'm going to be paying for that for several hours, at least."

"And into tomorrow, buddy," Ashlyn said, breezing past them. "How hard is it to tell the difference between a cake container and a metal pan? Seriously, it's embarrassing."

"You said it was the container beside the sink, hon," he called to her back. "How was I supposed to know?"

"Tell it to someone who cares," she exclaimed, dismissively waving as she walked away.

Facing him, Scott had a goofy look on his face. "I love it when she's pissed. We have awesome make-up sex."

"TMI, but good for you," Mark muttered. "I need another beer. Thanks for the advice, Scott. I hope I can figure it out."

"You will. These things take time. You'll get there. In the meantime, let's celebrate your win."

The party stretched late into the evening, and before Mark knew it, it was midnight. Helping Teresa shrug on her coat in the foyer, he said goodbye to his mom as she approached.

"I know you're spending Thanksgiving with the crew since that's Mark's tradition, but he always spends Christmas Eve here. I hope you'll join us too, Teresa. We'd love to have you over. Mark said you don't travel to see your family over the holidays."

"No," she said, shaking her head. "We all meet up in Spain for a week in February. It's easier for everyone to travel then. And thank you for the lovely invitation. I'll certainly discuss it with Mark. This was a fantastic party, Brenda. I really enjoyed it."

"Thank you, dear." His mother pulled her into a warm embrace, the gesture causing something to shift inside Mark's solar plexus. It seemed his mother was as enamored with his fake fiancée as he was.

"Ready, hon?"

"Ready," Teresa said, her grin wide as they headed out the door.

"I'm going to start looking for a house," she said, head resting against the seat as she gazed at him while he drove. "I know you're not a real estate attorney, but I was hoping you could recommend someone."

"I can," he said, thinking of his friend Bill Pascal who was an excellent attorney. "And he owes me one, so he'll only charge you to cover his fees."

"Oh, no, you should save the favor for yourself. I'm happy to pay him, Mark."

"Please," he said, clutching her hand as he felt something dying inside. How had they reached this point? Months ago, it had seemed so far away. Now, she was ready to buy a home and move on, while he...well, he wasn't sure what the hell he wanted.

"Let me do this for you, Teresa. You've done so much."

"I still have tons of billable hours left to pay off your loan too," she said, lifting a finger. "Don't go easy on me."

"Never. But let me call in my favor with Bill."

Sighing, she relented. "Okay. One last big gesture. You're pretty great at them. You're definitely the Edward to my Vivian. He was an expert at big gestures."

"I'm honored to be your Edward." Lifting her hand, he kissed her knuckles. "You know that, right?"

"Well, I'm honored to be your Vivian. It's been a fun ride, Mr. D.A. One of the best experiences of my life was getting to know you and Avery and your friends and family. Thank you. It meant so much."

"We'll still see each other, right? I mean, you're not moving to Spain, are you? Because I'm not sure I'm down with that. I've gotten pretty used to seeing that pretty smile, hon."

Something flitted across her face, unintelligible in the moonlight, and she nodded.

"Of course, we'll see each other. We're friends. I'm honored to call you that."

"Me too, sweetheart."

They fell into silence as he drove, Mark pondering the entire way how he'd gotten to this indecipherable and confusing place with the only woman who'd ever claimed his heart.

Chapter 29

Teresa glanced at her watch, noting it was time to head to Scott and Ashlyn's. Although she wasn't supposed to be working on Thanksgiving Day, this project couldn't wait and the man on the other end of the phone had an important update.

"I can't believe Cassandra didn't take the job," Dr. Nathan Silverman said over the phone. "This is the first partnership that's opened up in our practice in almost ten years. We had over a thousand applicants from all over the country. But her loss is your gain, my friend."

"While I'm a bit pissed I was only second in line, I'll take solace in the fact you all want me over the other thousand candidates," she teased.

"Honestly, you were first in most of the partners' minds, Teresa. You know Cassie's father went to school with David," he said, referencing the senior partner. "Otherwise, you would've been first hands-down."

"It will be nice to get back to the city, and I do love the idea of working for an established therapy practice with a plethora of clients and the ability to do pro bono social work in the greater Philly area. It checks all my boxes, Nate."

"We're thrilled to have you although I was worried you wouldn't want to leave Central Pennsylvania. When you left Philly years ago, you seemed adamant you wanted a slower pace."

"I did and I've really enjoyed it, but I want to buy a home and put down some roots. While buying a home in small-town America as a single woman is perfectly fine, I think I'll thrive better in the city.

I had different dreams when I moved here and I need to embrace setting new goals for this next phase of my life."

"You were always the best at following your own advice, Teresa. The poster child of a well-adjusted therapist."

"It's all smoke and mirrors, my friend," she said, eyebrows lifting at how true the statement rang. "Inside, I'm a mess sometimes."

"Well, it's good to know you're mortal like the rest of us. All right, go on and enjoy your dinner. Call me tomorrow and we'll discuss the next steps."

"Will do. Thanks, Nate."

Clicking off the phone, Teresa expelled a breath of finality and turned back to her laptop to finish the electronic chart so she could head to Scott and Ashlyn's. She'd applied for the job the day after the election, although she hadn't told Mark. It seemed like something serious you would tell your partner, and they certainly weren't at that phase, especially now that the election was over.

Throwing on her jacket, she resolved to enjoy the day with her friends and cherish their time together. When she moved to Philly, she would miss them terribly and was excited to create a few lasting memories. Hopping in her car, she drove to Ardor Creek, pushing away the gloom and embracing the joy of her last encounter with Mark's friends.

When she arrived, Ashlyn stuffed a glass of cabernet in her hand and Mark leaned down to place a sweet kiss on her lips. "Did you finish the charts?"

"Every last one. I'm ready to relax and have some fun."

Running his fingers over her cheek, he said softly, "I'm so glad you're here."

"Me too."

The day was filled with wine, food, and lots of laughter, especially at Peter who was his usual gregarious self. After they were all stuffed to the brim, they headed outside to enjoy the semi-warm weather and watch the kids play soccer before the sun set.

Teresa sat with Ashlyn, discussing The Bachelorette, as she surreptitiously observed Mark speaking with Carrie while they watched the boys play. They had the easy comradery of old friends and, at one point, he turned and placed his hand atop her slightly distended abdomen, grinning down at her as she beamed up at him.

It was all Teresa needed to see—the love shining from his handsome face as he spoke to his pregnant friend. Mark deserved to experience that with his own wife and child, and she wouldn't deny him that. They'd been stuck in a strange sort of purgatory since the election which neither of them seemed strong enough to end. Vowing to make the choice they both knew was inevitable, Teresa stood and refilled her wine from the open bottle on the table. Turning to face the yard, she cleared her throat.

"I have an announcement to make if you all will humor me." Lifting her cup high, she waited for everyone to gather around although the boys still played across the yard.

"First of all, I would like to thank you all for accepting me into your group. It's been such an honor to meet all of you and I hope we can stay in touch once I move to Philly."

Mouths fell open as Teresa briefly locked gazes with everyone, eventually landing on Mark as he stared at her in confusion.

"I didn't want to let the cat out of the bag until it was official, but I've been offered a partner position at one of the most respected psychology firms in Philly. It allows me to expand my practice and still perform social work for children who need it. I was chosen from over a thousand other candidates and am thrilled at the opportunity."

"Wow," Ashlyn said, approaching her with arms extended. "I didn't realize you were looking to leave the area, but congratulations."

Hugging her, Teresa briefly closed her eyes, reminding herself of her vow not to cry. After all, this was good news and she was determined to remain jubilant during the announcement.

"Thank you, Ashlyn. I hope you'll let me come visit, and you have to come see me in Philly. Grant would love it."

"For sure," she said, drawing back. "We'll make it happen, Teresa."

"Congrats, honey," Carrie said, hugging her. "Sounds like a great opportunity. I hope it gives you the clarity you need."

"Thank you, Carrie," she almost whispered. "Please don't make me cry."

Pulling back, she shook her head before leaning closer. "I won't, but I don't think it's over yet. That's all I'll say." Winking, she stepped aside so Peter and Scott could hug her.

"Wow, man," Scott said, arm around Teresa's shoulders as he addressed a stunned Mark, who hadn't moved since she'd made the announcement. "A few months with you and she hightails it back to Philly. I might never forgive you."

"Actually, my months with Mark were some of the best of my life," she said reverently, still unable to discern his expression. "I'll miss him, and all of you, terribly. Please don't be strangers."

"Well, let's have a toast to Teresa's fancy new job," Ashlyn said, jogging up the stairs. "I have the perfect bottle of bubbly. Be right back."

Mark finally moved from his spot on the grass and approached her, encircling her arm and pulling her toward the corner of the house where they could speak privately.

"Philly?" he asked, confusion swirling with what appeared to be anger in his eyes. "Just like that?"

Shrugging, she kept her tone light, attempting to ease the situation. "I actually applied the day after the election. I didn't tell you because I wasn't sure they'd even consider me. Surprise," she said, lifting her hands.

"Wow," he said, expelling a breath. "So that was the weird look you gave me in the car ride home after my parents' party. You were already planning this. I guess our whole 'honesty' thing is out the window."

Bristling, her eyebrows drew together. "Um, if I remember correctly, you had an entire conversation with Evan and determined the details of our breakup without me, so I'm pretty sure you're not the one to lecture me on honesty and transparency."

"I explained that to you," he said, slicing his hand through the air. "It was my clumsy attempt to ensure you'd spend Thanksgiving with me, although I didn't realize you'd decimate me in the process."

"Decimate you? That's a bit dramatic, Mark. Today was the end anyway. It's the perfect day to announce my new job."

He studied her in silence, a thousand emotions lacing his features as she stood defiant, unwilling to let him blame her for choosing the inevitable.

"We said we'd remain friends—"

"And we will. Philly is only a few hours' drive from here. I'm not moving to China."

"You might as well be," he said, his lips forming the cute pout she'd come to love. "I'm never going to see you."

"That was our deal, Mark. It always has been. Let's not make it harder than it has to be. I want to end things on a positive note."

"Is it because you can't have kids?" he asked, stepping closer. "Because that's something we should discuss further, Teresa. I should've dedicated time to analyzing it and now I'm kicking myself that I didn't. You deserve better. I'm sorry."

The image of his hand upon Carrie's stomach flashed through her mind, reminding her of what she had to do.

"I miss the city, Mark," she lied. In truth, she loved Battle Falls and Ardor Creek to the depths of her soul but knew remaining there would remind her of things she could never have. "This is a great opportunity for me and I miss the hustle and bustle. It's time for me to start a new chapter."

Sighing, he rubbed the back of his neck, seeming to struggle with what to say. "I don't want to hold you back but...I mean, are we really finished here? I'm not sure we are."

"Like you said, we'll always be friends and I'm so grateful for that." Rising to her toes, she kissed his cheek. "Now, if you'll give your fake fiancée this one last honor, I think our host just popped some very expensive champagne I'd like to drink." Stepping back, she held out her hand and waggled her fingers. "Come on."

Sliding his palm over hers, he smiled although the sentiment didn't reach his eyes.

"Okay, hon," he said, squeezing her hand. "I'm really proud of you, by the way. They're very lucky to have you."

"Thank you," she whispered, grateful the sun was low so he couldn't see the tears that welled in her eyes.

Heading back to their friends, Teresa drank the magnificent champagne while silently congratulating herself she hadn't allowed a single tear to fall.

Mark trudged through the rest of the Thanksgiving celebration although his heart wasn't in it. How could Teresa just move away and leave everything behind? Leave *him* behind? Didn't their relationship mean more to her?

Unable to process the huge change, he didn't realize she'd stepped inside to shrug on her coat until Carrie waved her hand in front of his face.

"Uh, Teresa's leaving. Do you want to say goodbye?"

"Huh?" Mark asked, interrupting Peter as he detailed last night's basketball game.

"Ashlyn packed her some leftovers and she's heading out. Says she has an early morning tomorrow."

"Go on, buddy," Peter said. "Don't fuck this up worse."

Glaring at him, Mark jogged up the steps and found her in the foyer, pulling her curls from her leather jacket.

"Hey," he said, approaching. "Do you want to ride home with me?"

Shaking her head, those hazel eyes met his, full of resolve. "I have my car so I'm just going to head to my apartment. No use in keeping up the charade anymore, right? Plus, Ashlyn gave me leftovers and I'm probably going to devour them while I watch the multitude of trashy TV piled up on my DVR." Lifting the container, she spared a cheeky grin. "I'll stop by sometime this week to grab my things and leave your spare key under the front doormat."

Mark assessed her, analyzing the emotions swirling within. Sadness. Finality. Anger. God, he was angry. How could she dismiss him so easily?

"Why are you trying to push me away? I feel like you're punishing me. It fucking hurts, Teresa."

Her throat bobbed and he saw the sheen of tears in her eyes, spurring hope she was at least partially as devastated at the loss of their relationship as he was.

"Mark," she rasped, covering his heart with her hand. "I'm so sorry you're hurting. I am too. This situation sucks. I wish I had a solution but I don't. We're not kids here. We don't have time to waste. There are things you want and things I want, and I don't want to deny you."

"I thought we had so much time," he whispered, stepping closer and palming her cheek. "How did we run out of time?"

"We lived in the moment and it was so beautiful. One of the best years of my life." A tear skated down her cheek and she swiped it away. "Damn it. I was so proud of myself for not crying."

"I was worried because you *weren't* crying," he teased, tucking her hair behind her ear. "I wasn't sure you cared it was over."

"Of course, I care. I always will. When you care about someone, you make really hard decisions sometimes." Drawing back, she disengaged from his touch and inhaled a deep breath. "Please be happy, Mark. I want that for you and you truly deserve it." Securing her purse on her shoulder, she backed away. "I have to go and you need to let me. Goodbye. Thank you for...well, thank you. Don't be a stranger."

Opening the door, she breezed through, closing it behind her. Mark stood still...speechless...as the click of the latch rang in his ears. Rubbing his forehead with his fingers, he debated going after her. To do what? Beg her to reconsider? That wouldn't change their circumstances. Unsure what to do, he headed back outside to join his friends and reconcile the day's heavy events.

Chapter 30

M ark resumed his solo life, repeating the mantra that he'd lived that way for forty years—well, now *forty-one* years—and it had served him just fine. He'd gotten used to Teresa's presence, which was completely acceptable, and the sentiment would fade as real life resumed.

Since he would be sworn in on January 2nd, Mark took the month of December to transition his clients and cases to other attorneys in the county. He would still consult but wanted to focus on the plethora of cases that needed to be addressed by the District Attorney. The weather turned bitter, mimicking his mood, as Justine noted during one of their Sunday lunches at her house.

"Soooo, I don't want to poke the bear, but you look like you've just spent a thousand hours watching those commercials with the animals where they play Sarah McLachlan music in the background. It's kind of pathetic."

Scowling, Mark took a bite of pizza before answering. "Thanks. Now I understand why you weren't a cheerleader in high school."

Laughing, she rested her chin on her hand. "Come on, Mark. You obviously miss her. Why are you doing this to yourself? Just go to her house, tell her you love her, and beg her not to move to Philly. It's what Edward would do for Vivian."

Mark almost dropped his pizza. "How do you know about that?"

"Teresa's awesome. Avery formed a bond with her and she stops by every so often to see her. She brings her little trinkets—like the glittery stickers on the back of her tablet case—and even sewed Carrot's ear back on."

Mark looked at Avery, who was munching pizza to his right. "She did?"

Nodding, Avery sprang from the table and ran back, holding Carrot high. "She sews really good and said she'd teach me one day."

"Wow," he said, wiping his hands and sitting back in the chair. "I had no idea she stopped by to visit. That's really cool."

"*She's* really cool. What the heck is wrong with you? Oh, and she mentioned the Pretty Woman reference during one of her visits. I'm obsessed with that movie."

Pursing his lips, Mark considered his words. "I don't know what I'm doing. I think I'm caught up in the gravity of the choices I need to make if we build a future together."

"Okay, let's go through these huge choices," she said, lifting a finger. "Number one, she can't have kids. It certainly sucks, because you guys would make gorgeous babies, but life sucks sometimes. Are you dead set on having biological kids with the woman you marry? I mean, you're forty-one, bro. That's putting a lot of stock in meeting someone who wants your old ass."

Mark squinted. "Why did I fight to get you released from jail?"

"Funny." Rolling her eyes, she continued. "If it's truly a dealbreaker, you can hire a surrogate. That will at least give you biological kids, even if they're not technically Teresa's."

"Honestly, I don't know if it is a dealbreaker. It's something I promised myself I'd consider and I just didn't."

"Ah, okay. That leads us to point number two." She held up two fingers. "You're kind of a commitment-phobe."

"I'm not sure if it's that drastic, but I do worry a relationship will require work I don't have time for and loss of independence. You remember some of the women I've dated. Remember how Jennifer would guilt text me if I didn't make a point to see her at least every three days? It drove me nuts."

"But Teresa's not like that. You two lived together for months. Did she give you space?"

"Yeah," he said, rubbing the back of his neck. "Actually, I was usually the one who begged her to hang out with my friends and asked her to stay with me after"—glancing at Avery, he lifted his brows— "well, you know."

Justine snickered, furthering his annoyance.

"I fail to see what's so funny."

"*You* were the Jennifer with her. Maybe she got tired of *you!*"

Although the situation wasn't funny, Mark found himself laughing at his sister's obvious mirth. "Holy crap, you're right. I was the Jennifer. What if she thinks I'm going to smother her? No wonder she ran away after Thanksgiving dinner."

"I have a theory on why she ran away but what do I know?"

"Okay, let's hear it."

"She stopped by the other day to drop off this cute little locket for Avery and looked as terrible as you. It's obvious she's crazy about you, Mark. I think she ended it because she doesn't want you to sacrifice anything for her."

Mark's brows drew together as he contemplated.

"I really need to think about this kid thing." Standing, he carried his plate to the sink and washed his hands. "Do you mind if I bow out early? I know we were going to watch a movie, but I don't want to put this off any longer."

"Go for it," she said, smiling at Avery. "You okay with that, baby?"

Avery nodded, smiling with red teeth from the pizza sauce. "I want you to marry Teresa, Uncle Mark."

Laughing, Mark gave a nod. "Well, I'll take that into consideration." Leaning down, he kissed both of their foreheads and headed home. Once in his office, he opened his laptop, the smell of Teresa's perfume surrounding him with its sweet scent. She'd used the office quite often and the smell lingered, spurring a deep yearning in his heart. Opening the browser, he got to work.

Mark researched surrogacy, adoption, fostering, and everything else he could find about having kids with non-traditional methods. After several hours, he'd taken a multitude of notes on the yellow notepad beside the laptop. Flipping through the pages, he digested everything before relaxing in the chair and considering.

Honestly, he had no idea there were so many ways to form a family. He was lucky to live in a modern world where a wealth of options existed. Knowing everything he did now, how could he choose to let Teresa go? If she was willing to choose him back, they could find a way to have a family down the road, couldn't they?

Mulling everything over, he began forming a plan, hoping like hell she'd be open to listening.

Chapter 31

Teresa hooked the tiny ornament on the two-foot-tall fake tree that sat atop the table in her living room. It was pathetic, but so was her life, so it pretty much fit the bill. Shaking her head, she scolded herself for the negative inner dialogue. It reared its head quite often lately, ever since she'd ended things with Mark, and her inner therapist knew it wasn't healthy.

As for the inner broken-hearted woman? Well, she was rather bitchy and clutched onto the negative thoughts quite vehemently. Chuckling, Teresa admitted the inner dialogue was pretty entertaining so at least there was that.

She'd video chatted with her brother's family and her parents in Spain earlier, and her brother had commented that her sad little tree was too sparse. She'd promptly told him to stuff it and then headed to the local drug store where she bought some extra ornaments.

"There," she said, placing the last one on the tree. "Sparse my ass. It's perfect."

The branch fell under the weight of the ornament and she snickered. "Even your tree is sad, Teresa. Good lord. What a mess."

Deciding she needed some rocky road and Real Housewives drama stat, she headed toward the kitchen to grab the ice cream.

A knock sounded on her door and she wondered if it was the mailman. Did they deliver mail on Christmas Eve? Pulling it open, she was stunned to find a beaming Mark Lancaster on her stoop, Avery in his arms as she held Carrot.

"Uh...hi. What are you doing here?"

Glancing at Avery, Mark murmured, "Not the greeting I was looking for."

Avery giggled and Teresa ushered them inside. "Sorry, it's freezing out there. I just...well, I'm surprised to see you."

"Merry Christmas, Teresa," Avery said.

"Merry Christmas, sweetheart," she said, taking their coats as they brushed off the snow. "I was about to devour some ice cream. You want some?"

She nodded and Teresa urged them to sit on the couch while she prepared everything. "Do you want some too?"

"Sure," Mark said. "One scoop, though. We're having dinner in an hour at my parents.'"

"Got it. Be right back."

She returned with three bowls and sat beside Mark on the couch as Avery plopped in front of the TV. "I love the parade," she said, staring at the screen.

"Oh, here," Teresa said, turning up the volume. "I had it on in the background."

Finishing her scoop, she collected the bowls and placed them in the sink, noticing her hands were shaking. Although she was thrilled to see Mark and Avery, she wondered why they'd showed up on her doorstep on Christmas Eve.

"Need help?"

"Oh, no," she said, smiling as Mark entered. "Just going to load them in the dishwasher." After placing the bowls inside, she faced him, rubbing her wet palms over her sweat pant-covered thighs. "If I'd known you guys were coming, I would've dressed a bit nicer."

Stepping closer, his eyes roved over her. "You look beautiful. You always do."

Gulp. Needing to feel something solid beneath her, she trailed to the small kitchen table and sat, pulling out the chair next to her. "Want to sit?"

"Sure." Walking over, he sat and she glanced toward the living room. "Think she'll be okay in there watching the parade?"

He nodded. "She's enthralled, which is good because there are some things I need to say to you privately."

Breathing a laugh, she asked, "Why did you bring her? I mean, I'm happy to see her, but aren't you guys celebrating Christmas Eve at your parents?'"

"It was getting a bit crazy over there. Mom and Dad were debating how long to cook the turkey and Justine is exhausted from a late gallery showing last night. I figured I'd give everyone a break, and Avery and I needed some fresh air." Reaching over, he clutched her hand. "Also, I wasn't sure if you'd let me inside if I didn't bring her."

Teresa squeezed his hand. "Of course, I would let you inside. Don't be silly."

Studying her, he seemed...sure...resolved somehow, and Teresa's heart began to pound.

"Justine told me about your visits to see Avery. That's really awesome. Thanks for checking in on them. She's enamored with you."

"I love her too, Mark. She's such a sweet little girl and I really like Justine."

His thumb trailed over the skin of her hand, slow and steady as she struggled to breathe.

"When are you moving to Philly?"

"I...um, well, about that." Sighing, she ran a hand through her hair. "I decided not to take the job. I began the process of transitioning my local clients to other therapists and realized how much I enjoyed running my practice in Lackawanna County. Being part of a large practice offers some great benefits, but owning my own practice is a better fit for me. I'm an entrepreneur at heart and love the autonomy."

Expelling a breath, he closed his eyes. "Thank god."

Her brows lifted. "You're glad I'm staying?"

"So damn glad." Leaning forward, he slid his free hand to cup the back of her neck. "It affords me the opportunity to win you back."

Teresa bit her lip to contain her grin. "Did you lose me somehow?"

"Yes, because I'm a fucking idiot." Shaking his head, he ran the pad of his thumb over her cheek. "Justine and Carrie both gleefully informed me that men are huge idiots. Not sure I *completely* agree, but I certainly was with you."

"We entered into an honest relationship and knew the terms. There's nothing idiotic about that."

"Yes, but we kind of messed up the honesty at the end. I think it was because we were both scared of navigating something new. I was, at least."

"I was too," she whispered.

"Do you really miss the city?" he asked, stroking her cheek. "Because I could consider living there but it's pretty tough since I'm going to be sworn in as county D.A. in a week."

Laughing, she shook her head. "I love it here, Mark. I just said that because I thought it would help you accept the inevitable."

"Ah, yes, our inevitable break up," he teased, playfully rolling his eyes. "Well, I'd like to discuss that with you."

"Okay." Her voice was raspy as blood pounded through her veins.

"I finally took the time to research having kids by nontraditional methods. Surrogacy, adoption, fostering—there are so many options out there, Teresa."

Shaking her head, she felt the tears form. "You shouldn't have to sacrifice—"

"Please don't say that," he interrupted, emotion in his eyes. "Choosing to be with you is not a sacrifice, Teresa. *Loving* you is not a sacrifice. It's a gift and a privilege I almost threw away because I wasn't ready to step up. But I'm stepping up now. I don't want to live one more day without you, honey. I love you."

Teresa buried her face in her hand, overcome with tears. "Mark…" she warbled.

Tugging her hand, he drew her to sit on his lap. Palming her cheeks, he tilted her face. "Please don't cry. Unless they're happy tears. Are they happy tears?" he asked, swiping one from her face.

Laughing, she nodded. "They're happy tears."

"But?"

"But you'd be giving up so much to be with me," she said, covering his lips when he opened his mouth to argue. "Let me just say this, okay?"

Nodding, he smiled against her fingers.

"I truly appreciate you looking into other options and being open, but I see this all the time in my therapy practice. People make life-altering decisions because they're in love and, years later, they resent their partner and the relationship crumbles. I don't want you to resent me. I'd rather let you go than tie you to someone who can't give you what you ultimately want."

Remaining silent, he reverently stroked her face as he gazed at her.

"Mark?"

"You're so selfless," he murmured. "I've never met anyone like you, Teresa."

"It's better to make choices that ensure the people you love will be happy, even if it hurts. I want you to find happiness, Mark."

His eyes darted between hers. "Are you open to adoption or surrogacy?"

"Yes. But I don't want you to be limited to that. Don't you want the entire traditional experience of having children?"

"Honestly, I don't. I want whatever experience I can have with you. Whatever that looks like and whatever form it takes, that's what I want."

"It's not fair for me to ask you to choose that."

"You're not," he said, lifting his shoulders. "I'm offering. Mostly because I think my family and friends are going to cut ties with me if I continue living without you. Turns out, I'm a terror to be around if I'm not with you. Go figure."

"You seem fine to me," she said, winking.

"Seriously, hon, we made this so much harder than it had to be. I love you, and I think you love me, and that's all we really need, isn't it? We can figure the other stuff out."

Inhaling a breath, she stroked his face. "I do love you. So much, Mark."

Breathing a sigh of relief, he rested his forehead against hers. "Thank goodness. I was sure I ruined everything."

"No way. And I really messed up too. I never should've lied to you about missing the city. I just thought it would help push you toward something I couldn't give you."

"I hope you'll stop that destructive talk because it's bullshit, Teresa. You give me so much. I don't give a damn you can't have biological kids. When we're ready, we'll build a family on our own terms and it will be perfect. Got it?"

"Got it. That's some really great advice. You would've been an awesome therapist."

"There's always time," he said, waggling his brows.

"Uh, yeah. I think you have your hands full, Mr. D.A. Speaking of that, we can finally tell the world we're actually together. It took us a while but we got there."

"Evan will be thrilled. He's already planning my reelection campaign," he said, grimacing.

Teresa's brows lifted. "Never too early to plan, I guess."

Avery jogged into the room, excitement on her face. "Are you guys getting married?"

Laughing, Teresa stood and smoothed her hair. "One step at a time. But I'm happy to report I love your Uncle Mark very much. What do you think about that?"

"He loves you too," she said, grinning.

"I sure do. And, if you're up to it, Avery and I would like to formally invite you to Christmas dinner at my parents'. It will be loud and crazy, which I secretly enjoy more than I let on."

Throwing back her head, Teresa laughed. "Well, how can I pass up that invite? I need to take a quick shower though. Should I just head over afterward?"

"Sure," he said, leaning down to pick up Avery. "We'll wait to eat until you get there. Just come on in. The front door will be unlocked."

Rising to her toes, she kissed him. "I love you," she whispered, wiping her chapstick from his lips.

"Love you too, hon," he said, tucking a curl behind her ear. "See you soon. Come on, munchkin. Let's go." They headed down the hallway and Teresa closed the door behind them, locking it before jogging toward the bedroom. With an excited squeal, she pulled off her comfy clothes and hopped in the shower.

An hour later, Teresa arrived at Brenda and Joseph's, tentatively pushing the door open.

"Hello?"

Voices sounded from the kitchen and she closed the door behind her before hanging her coat on the hook. Trailing down the hallway, she found Brenda leaning over the oven, door open, as Joseph shook his head.

"It needs fifteen more minutes, Brenda. You know I like it well done."

"You like it *too* well done," Justine said from the nearby island. "If we had it Dad's way, the turkey could double for a hammer. Can we leave a little moisture so it doesn't taste like sandpaper?" She held her thumb and forefinger an inch apart.

"Welcome to insanity," Mark said softly, nestling behind her as his lips rested on the shell of her ear. "At least I warned you."

"It's awesome," she said, smiling up at him. "I'm so happy to see everyone. Thank you for inviting me."

"The first of many holidays together, honey," he said, squeezing her hand. "Can't wait."

"Oh, Teresa's here," Brenda said, rushing over to hug her. "We're so glad you're spending Christmas Eve with us, dear. I was sure Mark ruined everything. I told him he'd never meet another lovely young lady like you. So pretty and a *doctor*? Well, I'm glad he didn't blow it."

"Okay, okay," Mark said, pulling Teresa from Brenda's embrace. "Leave your favorite son alone."

"He's her only son," Joseph teased, a sparkle in his eye.

Teresa laughed at the revelry, so thrilled to be included in the celebration. Eventually, they sat down for dinner at the long dining room table, and Teresa complimented Brenda on the turkey. "It's absolutely perfect. I'm not sure what Joseph recommended, but you two make a darn good turkey."

"See?" Joseph asked, arching a brow. "I always know when it needs a few more minutes."

"Oh, you hush. Back seat driver is what you are. Or back seat cook, should I say? Here, eat this so you won't say something else ridiculous." Brenda scooped another helping of turkey on his plate.

After dinner, they retired to the living room where a gorgeous tree sparkled with lights and ornaments. Teresa sipped wine as Mark sat beside her on the couch, arm over her shoulders as he drank a beer. Snuggling into his side, she was overcome with the realization she had a new family. It was poignant and her eyes welled as gratefulness washed over her.

"Oh, no, she's crying," Mark teased, smiling down at her. "Dad will get tired and go to bed soon. I promise."

Teresa laughed at his chiding.

"That's probably true," Brenda said, "so you should get on with it, Mark."

"Ah, yes. I guess I should."

Teresa's eyes darted around the room, wondering what they were referring to. Standing, Mark set his bottle on the side table before taking her wine and doing the same. Grasping her hand, he pulled her to her feet and led her to stand in front of the tree.

"I have no idea what's going on," she said, lifting her brows.

Reaching into the pocket of his slacks, he removed something before lowering to one knee. Opening the box, he smiled up at her, so handsome as his grandmother's ring sparkled inside.

"Several months ago, I showed you this ring. I told you I imagined getting married and having kids one day, and I wanted to give this ring to the woman on the other end of that vision. You're the only woman who's ever been on the other end of that vision, Teresa. I think I already knew that deep inside when I tried to give it to you the first time."

Swiping away an errant tear, she laughed. "That's so sweet, Mark. I was honored that you wanted me to wear it, even back then when it wasn't real."

"It's been real since the first night I met you, honey. I can't even lie to myself about that anymore. I would be incredibly honored if you would choose to wear this ring and be my wife. I love you with all my heart, Teresa. Will you marry me?"

"Yes!" she cried, pulling him to his feet and throwing her arms around him. "I love you so much."

He slipped the ring on her shaking hand before drawing her in for a passionate kiss. His family cheered as Avery ran to their sides.

"Grandma said I can be the flower girl!"

Chuckling, Teresa nodded. "I think you'll make the perfect flower girl. Can't wait."

"Okay, I'm breaking out the whiskey," Joseph called, heading to the adjoining room before returning with a bottle filled with brown liquid. "We had whiskey the night Brenda and I got engaged, and the night Justine got engaged, and we're going to have it tonight too."

"Not sure my engagement was one to celebrate, but okay," Justine muttered.

"I'll get the glasses," Brenda said, gesturing to Justine. "Come help me, dear."

Teresa waited for them to return and smiled up at Mark. "I hope Justine finds love again one day. She deserves it."

"Well," he said, arching a brow. "She might be closer than you think."

"Meaning?"

"My buddy Gary's in love with her."

"Gary the cop?"

He nodded.

"Does she know?"

"Nope. I decided not to say anything because I was in the middle of making a mess of my own love life."

"Wow," Teresa said, eyes wide. "He's such a nice man. They'd be really cute together."

"We'll see. For now, let's drink Dad's Macallan. It's good stuff. You're going to love it."

Encircling his neck with her arms, she lifted her lips to meet his tender kiss.

"Thank you, Mark. This is so romantic."

"Better than Edward and Vivian?"

Laughing, she bit her lip. "So much better. It's my very own happy ending. I love you so much."

"Love you too, sweetheart. Just remember that if I pass out from too much Macallan tonight. I promise, once I sleep it off, we're totally going to have fantastic sex. And you're definitely sleeping in my bed. Forever. Thank goodness I don't have to beg you anymore."

"Did you beg me? I always found it so cute when you asked me to sleep with you."

"I definitely begged."

Chuckling, she saw Brenda and Justine return with the glasses. "Well, your begging days are over. I'm waking up in your bed whether you like it or not."

"I like it," he growled in her ear. "I'll show you how much when we get home."

Shooting him a sultry glare, she took the glass Joseph poured and tasted the whiskey, the liquid smooth and warm on her tongue. Settling back on the couch with Mark, she sank into his side, reveling in the joy of spending time with her newfound family.

Epilogue

One year later...

Teresa struggled to catch her breath, unable to see since her hair covered the majority of her face.

"Holy shit," Mark panted in her ear. "We're supposed to be walking out the door right now."

"*Mmm...*" she moaned into the pillow, unable to contemplate moving for the foreseeable future. "We'll make it to the wedding. Don't worry."

"I heard Carrie and Peter's car start somewhere in between our transition from missionary to corkscrew."

Snickering, she waved a lazy arm. "I should probably be worried you know all the names for our weird sexual positions, but I don't have the energy. And Carrie and Peter are always early even though they have three kids. They're overachievers."

"Think we'll be overachievers when we have a kid? The call from the adoption agency could come any day."

"I think we'll do just fine. If life gets messy, we'll have each other. We're pretty great together when things are messy."

"We are," he said, kissing her temple.

"I'm almost ready. Just need to recover for a minute..."

"Guess I'm ready too if we count my pants being half-on and my shirt missing two buttons. Nice job, by the way, Superwoman."

"I tried to rip it off but I only got halfway. Oops."

"I swear, I was going to wait to make love to you until we were home, but you look so damn good in that dress, Teresa."

"I'm glad you like it. I bought it with Ashlyn last week when we went shopping. She's feeling super-pregnant and wanted to find something pretty for Chad's wedding."

Nuzzling her neck, he sighed. "As much as I want to stay like this, I think we have to go."

Nodding, she wiggled and turned to gaze up at him. "Is my makeup smeared?"

"No, but your hair is...uh...everywhere."

Laughing, she sat up and attempted to smooth it. "You know what? Screw it. I just had amazing sex with my husband and I don't care if I look like a hussy. I mean, we *did* meet on Pure after all. What do they expect?"

Rising, he walked to the closet and picked out a new shirt. Sliding it over his torso, he smiled as he buttoned it. "You're the sexiest hussy I've ever seen."

"Why, thank you. You're a very hot man-whore yourself."

His deep-throated laugh reverberated off the walls. Teresa slipped on her heels before trailing over to straighten his tie. Once he'd donned his suit coat, they assessed each other.

"I think we look fine."

"Me too," he said, extending his hand. "Should we try again?"

With a nod, she took his hand. "We might actually make it this time."

Following him down the stairs of the new home they'd purchased beside Carrie and Peter's, she slung her purse over her arm.

"Take two."

Slipping her arm through his, her gorgeous husband led her to the car.

It was time for yet another wedding in Ardor Creek.

Before You Go

Well, Dear Reader, our fearless lovers got their happy ending. *Sigh*. I guess it's time to find out how serial dater and Ardor Creek mayor, Chad Hanson, finally falls in love. Check out his book, **Resolutions Embraced**, right now! Oh, and don't worry—Justine and Gary *will* be getting their own book! For now, thanks so much for spending some time in Ardor Creek with me.

Please consider leaving a review on your retailer's site, Book-Bub, and/or Goodreads. Your reviews help spread the word for indie authors so we can keep writing smokin' hot books for you to devour. Thanks so much for reading!

About the Author

Ayla Asher is the pen name for a USA Today bestselling author who writes steamy fantasy romance under a different pseudonym. However, she loves a spicy, fast-paced contemporary romance too! Therefore, she's decided to share some of her contemporary stories, hoping to spread a little joy one HEA at a time. She would love to connect with you on social media, where she enjoys making dorky TikToks, FB/IG posts and fun book trailers!

ALSO BY AYLA ASHER

Manhattan Holiday Loves Trilogy
Book 1: His Holiday Pact
Book 2: Her Valentine Surprise
Book 3: Her Patriotic Prince

Ardor Creek Series
Book 1: Hearts Reclaimed
Book 2: Illusions Unveiled
Book 3: Desires Uncovered
Book 4: Resolutions Embraced
Book 5: Passions Fulfilled
Book 6: Futures Entwined